Anne Mallory

The Bride Price

AVON

An Imprint of HarperCollinsPublishers

This is a work of fiction. Names, characters, places, and incidents are drawn from the author's imagination or are used fictitiously and are not to be construed as real. Any resemblance to actual events, locales, organizations or persons, living or dead, is entirely coincidental.

AVON BOOKS
An Imprint of HarperCollins*Publishers*
10 East 53rd Street
New York, New York 10022-5299

Copyright © 2008 by Anne Hearn
ISBN 978-0-06-157913-4
www.avonromance.com

First Avon Books paperback printing: November 2008

To N&P, with hugs and love

Acknowledgments

Thanks to the three M's—Mom, Matt, and May Chen for your direct contributions to this book. There aren't enough thanks for that. Thanks to Dad for always giving me a grin during my writing days. And thanks to the Starbucks writing crew—Bella Andre, Jami Alden, Barbara Freethy and Jacqueline You—for endless fun times clicking and gabbing away.

Special thanks to Tracy Grant and Candice Hern for their brilliant historical prowess and help!

Author's Note

There was never a recorded competition like the one described within these pages. I'd like to think, though, that if there had been one, this is the way it might have unraveled . . .

Chapter 1

The Times of London, June 1822—*Scritches on parchment. Secret conversations in the shadows. Devilish deeds in dark chambers. Dear Reader, something of magnitude is happening under the cover of darkness in the highest strata of the land. Time will tell what it is . . .*

The flip of a card decided the match.

A round of swearing coursed through the thick smoke and dull chatter in the gilt and leathered men's club.

"A round to you again, Deville." Eyes deep with suspicion held his. "That makes it, what, four thousand this night?"

Sebastien raked his winnings with a negligent hand. "Good of you to keep track, Compton."

"I keep track of far more than that," Compton said, his gaunt frame pitching forward in order to curl skeletal fingers around a brandy snifter.

"I can't believe your bloody luck. Unnatural," the man to his left spit, and tossed his moppish brown hair with an unsteady hand. He'd lost heavily. As usual.

"Before you curse the spirits, Benedict, perhaps you should examine your absence of skill." Sebastien kept his voice lazy, but stayed aware of the crowd in his periphery. Surrounded by the cream of London society—unfortunately the male half of it—he was an island of disrepute. On paper he was at a distinct social disadvantage in his present position, but that had never stopped him from tempting fate—or making it obey his will.

"Don't take that tone with me, Deville. I can have *you* removed from here in the flick of a finger."

You and your tainted blood.

"Of course, Benny. Your *grace* alone is my reason for existing."

Lord Benedict Alvarest's color darkened at the wording, and his dull brown eyes flashed with something approaching animation. Unfortunately, intelligence and imagination were infrequent visitors to Benedict. Such a disappointment in an enemy.

The fourth man in the game tapped a perfectly manicured, lily-white finger against the parquet table. "Enough. Are we rubbering up? I, for one, wish to win my money back."

"Little good it will do you, Everly. Deville obviously has a trick up his sleeve," Benedict said.

Sebastien flicked his cuffs and reached for his drink. "Or two even, the way you lose. Seem determined to lose everything."

His drawl produced a shiver of rage in the man, just as he'd hoped.

"At least I have something to lose, Deville."

The crowd hushed, leaning in on tipped feet.

Sharks scenting for blood, vultures seeking carnage, speaking of him in harsh, delighted whispers, and then inviting him to gatherings in order to provoke more.

"How tired you've become, *Lord* Benedict." Benedict's color turned puce. "Such a *disappointment*." Sebastien leaned back languidly and tipped his glass, the smooth edge of the brandy sliding down his throat, temporarily warming his cold stomach—a constant pit of ice these days. "Being merely a third son, it seems so removed to use the title 'lord' when referencing you."

Too enraged to retaliate immediately, Benedict's hand shook around his clutched cards. Sebastien caught a sliver of movement behind the greedy crowd. An older, mirrored image of himself beckoned imperiously. The echo of Benedict's rage, though quieter and cooler in nature, slid through Sebastien's gut at the motion, but he turned back to Benedict and gave a sly smirk to the brother he'd never know outside of their taunts and envy. "Pardon me, gentlemen; it seems you will have to win your money back another day."

He gathered his winnings among protests and groans and threw a note on the table. Benedict's eyes were dark with loathing, as he saw both the man beckoning and the direction of Sebastien's gaze. Sebastien ignored him and walked away from the crowd. Ten steps closer to the hangman's noose.

"Sebastien. Sit." The man indicated the heavy mahogany chair across from him with a casual wave of his bejeweled hand. "I see you've done well at the tables tonight."

Would that he could believe in the false pride and slippery words of the man across from him—a vision of what he would look like at fifty—rich brown hair edged with silver. Eyes a shade of bluish-green—*aquamarine*, he'd heard the ladies sigh.

Of course, they might sigh and blush, but looks and character hardly mattered in a game where the winners possessed the best titles, the most power, the greatest wealth. Anyone else was merely a diversion. Someone to giggle over as they pushed the boundaries imposed by their guardians. Allowed to look and flirt, but never touch. No, someone like him *just wouldn't do* for society's precious charges.

"I saw you with the Plumley chit."

"Is that censure I see in your eyes, Your Grace?" Your Grace, not Father. Never Father.

"I know better by now, Sebastien, than to think my regard will sway you in any way."

If only the words were true and the reality false. The man across from him knew exactly how Sebastien had groveled for each kind word from him years ago. The memories made him nauseated. He lit a cheroot, then banished the ghosts with the smoke he exhaled.

"Then what have you to say, Your Grace? Will they revoke my social card for dancing with a debutante?"

"You were very nearly caught on the balcony. You should know by now that there would be no quick marriage. No heiress in your pocket. Plumley would hush it up by marrying her to someone like Compton." He waved a hand toward the gaming table where the decrepit man sat. "Then remarry her after the man breathes his last."

"The Plumley chit is hardly a prize. Why would you think I'd even want her?"

"Is it not your wish to spoil them all? Come now, Sebastien, it is not as if we haven't had this conversation before." The duke's eyes were dark, but there was a glaze there. Pride in his dark son. After all, the duke's philandering ways bore proof to how Sebastien's own twice-damned life had come about.

"How little there is to spoil these days. Not a diamond left in the bunch." He tapped his cheroot, and the duke's disapproving gaze followed the ash to the expensive Aubusson rug below. "And their guardians grow ever warier, not that I happen to see the twits that often. Little angels wrapped in gossamer bundles only attending the very best parties, of which I am hardly a part."

Narrowed eyes surveyed him. "Then Browett's girl—what was that?"

"Merely a game. One in which I won. I always do." He smiled and breathed in another smoky breath.

He so loved his little games. If *he* wasn't good enough, then neither were they. And having them gagging for his every word—when denied other, deeper pleasures—was far too enjoyable a game to play.

"She married Baron Tewks's youngest son this Saturday last," the duke said. "The banns hadn't stopped ringing before the deed was done."

Sebastien shrugged. "Good match for the *ton*. I daresay no one is disappointed." He watched the smoke curl from the tip with each movement of his hand as he pulled the cheroot back and forth, just enough to annoy the man across from him.

"Not even you?"

"Come now, Your Grace. I am long past the stage for disappointment." Now he was simply apathetic.

The duke's disregard had shattered him with disappointment too many years ago to count. Then Harrow had beaten it right out of him. He wasn't the only bastard to matriculate through her hallowed halls, but she tended to be unpleasant to boys like him—anyone who was the slightest bit different or lacked sponsorship. But he'd carved his niche. A scathing tongue, clever mind, and bottomless pit of vengeance made for a deadly enemy.

He'd learned to be a right little bastard, and had grown into a much larger one. He smiled. "I hear that Valpage's youngest darling will be out next year. Should prove entertaining."

"Valpage will rend you limb from limb."

Sebastien tipped his head back and blew a tight ring of smoke toward the gilded ceiling. "Then I will have to be very circumspect, won't I?"

"Sebastien—"

"Come now." His head tipped forward on a cocked brow. "You didn't come here to talk about the young flowers. Not with your dear son Benedict glaring holes through us both."

"No." The duke's eyes gleamed as they caught the light from a sconce. "I come to offer a proposition."

"Oh? Suddenly realize Lord Grint isn't up to snuff? And that Benny isn't worth the clothes he wears so poorly?"

The duke's eyes narrowed. "Be careful, Sebastien. That is my heir and a spare you mock."

"And yet I do it so effortlessly." Sebastien watched the duke's mouth clench and took another careless drag from the rolled cloves between his lips.

"I can limit your monies."

"That should prove entertaining, Your Grace. Haven't you realized that I've been off your bankroll for years now?"

A perfect eyebrow lifted. "Oh? Then the monthly income that I transfer is useless, is it? It should be stopped?"

The part of Sebastien that used to count his coppers and scrutinize bank statements cringed, but the larger part of him, his pride, tattered edges of cloth coating steel, smiled in satisfaction. "Do as you wish, Your Grace. I have no need of your money." He flourished a hand above his winnings. "As you can see."

"Gaming? The cards turn on a man. The dice tumble from the table. The horses buck and fall."

"Something you should spend a little time preaching to your son, Your Grace." Your *real* son. The duke's lips pinched together in a satisfying manner. "Much of this is, or should I say, *was*, his." He swept his cheroot over the bundle again, a line of smoke blessing the top and then floating upward.

"But then money isn't what you desire, is it,

Sebastien?" Sharp, glittering eyes surveyed him. Predatory mirrors of his own.

"I daresay I desire money as keenly as the next gentleman, Your Grace."

"Are you considered a gentleman, Sebastien?"

His shoulder muscles tightened. He took another drag and forced the tension out with his breath. He stared at the duke, unwilling to answer and cede anything. No answer would make him the winner.

"The crux, is it not, Sebastien? You could have been like that namby ponce of Dullesfield's loins. Obsequious and accommodating. Gaining more invitations and a step higher in standing due to his willingness to splay himself before the field." The duke snapped his fingers for a drink. "Yet you chose to take the other path. To make yourself less of a catch. A reputation blackened and disagreeable—and every penny of it earned."

"Why, Your Grace, do you even care? I've long since known that you do not. I've long since ceased to cry in my buttercups." He purposefully tapped ash onto the rug again.

"If you had been born on the right side, I might. As it is, you still bear a reflection upon me." A nearly exact reflection, if one needed a looking glass. "I have seen that you are taken care of, after a fashion."

Yes, school, clothing, entrance to certain levels of society, he had. Nothing would remove the taint though. Nothing would remove the betrayal. And nothing would replace the cold emptiness in his chest.

"You made quite the gentleman of me."

The duke's drink appeared before him, a waiter slipping away almost before he was noticed. "A gentleman wouldn't have had the Plumley chit splayed on the balcony, ready to spread her legs to the heavens."

The Plumley twit could only wish. "I merely follow your flawless lead, Your Grace."

The duke's long fingers tightened around the bowl of the brandy glass. "You are a trial to talk to, Sebastien."

Sebastien smiled mockingly and stubbed his cheroot before dropping it into his half-empty glass. It gave a hiss before sinking to the bottom. "Why thank you, Your Grace."

"One of these days you will impregnate some chit, and then what will you do, Sebastien? Knowing you have a little bastard running about?"

If the duke knew him as well as he pretended to, he would know that such was highly unlikely. Debauched the debutantes? Yes. Titillated and teased them? Yes. Introduced them to pleasure? Yes. Caused them to nearly defy their guardians and run away with him? Yes. Deflowered them? No. If he needed to indulge, he went to women who knew how to take care of such things and prevent untoward occurrences.

"Sob into my sherry like you did perhaps." The duke was the one responsible for his appearance in the club tonight, and he welcomed the largesse from the toads who thought they knew how to play cards, but he suddenly didn't care that he was jeopardizing his chance to wring another fortune into his pockets. He had reached his threshold. "After all, you know me *so* well, Your Grace."

The duke's eyes narrowed. "I do know you, Sebastien. Better than you think. I know what you long for." He took a drink, one edge of his mouth pulling into a smirk as the glass left his lips.

"Do you?"

"Power. Respect. A title."

Sebastien drummed his fingers on the chair's arm in a bored manner. "Don't all of us who do not have them? Hardly a deduction."

"I can give you all three."

He examined the duke's face to determine his level of drink. "Last I knew, a title was something not even you could grant me, Your Grace. Such pesky laws concerning entailment, articles of succession. And bastards." He flashed even, straight teeth, another gift from the duke that hadn't been passed on to his *real* sons.

"No, but the King can."

The cold, swirling emptiness in his chest froze for a second, before regaining its aimless movements. "And why would the King grant me anything, least of all a title? I'm not a war hero, a politician, a scientist, or a favored child of England."

He picked at the edge of the leather chair, the action twofold. It gave his aimless fingers purpose, and he prided himself on leaving unnoticed destruction in his wake whenever possible. He was a guest at the club, not a member. Never a member.

"To get a title, you have to earn it."

Rage walked a tightrope up his spine. "Or be

born to it—little enough earning there. If that is all, I believe it is time to retire." He rose. "I grow weary of the company."

He'd head down to the gaming hells in the east. Places where the men in this club would never go or be welcome. Dens of iniquity just for men like him.

"Sit. Down."

The duke's steely voice was low, but punctuated each word. For a man who valued emotional control, it was out of character. Sebastien narrowed his eyes and slowly sank back into his chair.

"The season ends next week. Everyone will be leaving London soon. Two weeks from today a tournament will begin that will progress through the summer. Ten tasks. Each with a monetary reward. Competitors will vie for the ultimate prize that includes a viscountcy and a fortune."

Sebastien tried to relax into the chair, but his back remained stiff.

The duke continued, still agitated. "The King has sanctioned this tournament. The winner will have the backing of all involved. Entry into all events for one year. Membership to all the right clubs. A seat. The rest of the tide is up to the winner to sway."

Sebastien had no idea what showed on his face, but he desperately hoped it was as little as possible.

The duke took a deep breath, and a well-rehearsed calm returned to his features. "A title, money, a wellborn bride, a platform to start. All ingredients that can launch a determined man to success." The duke drank his brandy, but his eyes never left Sebastien's.

Sebastien said nothing, shocked, his insides charged with anger and something wild. Power. The offer was inherently one of power.

But his mocking, destructive nature was never silent. "I have money. What use have I of a title, a seat, a wife, and some land?" Besides power and temptation . . .

"What about your mother's land?"

The emptiness froze again. "What about it?"

"I'm giving it away. To the winner of the tournament."

Loathing, fierce and deep, ran through him. Worse than before. Steaming and coiling in his gut, searching for an outlet.

Iron pride clashed with longing. Roseford Grange was the only thing for which he had ever begged. The duke had purchased it from the lien holder when Sebastien was sixteen just for that reason.

A taunt, a way to keep his bastard son in line.

It hadn't worked yet. But then the duke had never gone so far.

Sebastien took a deep breath, shoving the anger and hatred below an icy barrier in his mind. He tapped his fingers on the chair's arms, thinking, coldly plotting. The duke smiled in a satisfied manner, telling Sebastien that he was not successfully hiding his emotions.

He examined the man across from him, looking for weakness. "A wellborn bride? Some poor chit coerced into being the prize for a bunch of bastards or third-born sons?" The shifting of the light on the duke's eyes confirmed his guess on the participants. "Who is the girl? Why even include her? Better to have the choice once the winner hits the bosom of the *ton*."

"Lady Sarah Pims."

Ah. The girl was passably attractive, if you could separate her from the wallpaper, and an heiress, but possessed of a temperament that made the sconces on the walls seem interesting. He wasn't quite sure he had ever heard her string two words together, no less two sentences. No worthy suitors, at least to Lord Cheevers's exacting standards, had lasted long this past year, her first out after her mourning period, and her father, the earl, was said to be at wit's end. Too, he was a crony of the duke's.

"The Tipping Seven, is it? Or have you finally increased your number to ten?"

The duke's stare hardened. "Yes, it is mostly our crowd."

The Tipping Seven formed a formidable faction despite their blackened past. They could do exactly as promised—open society to whomever they willed. And with the King involved . . .

Sebastien rubbed his lips against each other. Sponsorship was everything. His own state in society proved that.

Roseford Grange . . .

The duke would refuse any offers to buy the property, even at twice the price. He had refused every time Sebastien had asked. It was a sign of weakness now to even bring it up. A show of his hand, even though his cards were in plain view.

The duke must desperately want Sebastien in

the competition if he was offering his trump. That alone was nearly enough to get Sebastien to refuse.

But the prize . . . what it entailed . . . what he could do with it . . . the revenge he could take . . .

"A title with papers? Full sponsorship? And deeds to all lands up front and awaiting turn-over?" He wanted a solid lock on the deed to Rose-ford, one that the duke couldn't pull away from.

"And an heiress. All or nothing. Consider the winnings the bride price."

He couldn't care less about some twit of a girl that Cheevers couldn't get rid of another way. She was a means to an end. He shrugged.

"I want to review the documents."

The duke's lips curled. Triumph shone in his eyes. Sebastien was a game to his sire, and he'd known it since his disillusionment had begun. "I knew you would. Come."

The duke abandoned his half-drunk brandy and signaled to a man at the front of the club. Sebastien rose and followed him from the room, but not before he smirked at the rage in his half brother's eyes as he watched them leave together. Harrow had been a hell for both of them, forced together at school, so close in age.

If those papers promised what the duke im-plied . . . not only would he finally gain his moth-er's land, but also a title and the inherent power associated. He brushed the sleeve of his coat. A past taunt rang through his ears—*That expensive material can't hide the lack of quality beneath, Deville.*

He smiled darkly and stepped through the door.

Chapter 2

⌒◦◦⌒

Lady Sarah Pims, the only daughter of Earl Cheevers, is reported to be off the mart. Though, Dear Reader, we don't know to whom she has been paper bound. As she is a meek, biddable girl, one doesn't as much interact with her in the ballrooms as pass her by for the more interesting potted plants in attendance . . .

"**P**roject? Is this how you define the sale of your daughter?"

"Watch yourself, Mrs. Martin." Lord Cheevers tapped an authoritative finger on his desk. "I'm doing what every parent should. I'm securing her a husband. A strong one."

The oppressive feel of the Brown Room closed around Caroline Martin. The muted golds and dark earthy woods of the earl's study all combined to create a sort of world-weary and high kingdom that she could never breach. Caroline walked to the edge of the heavy mahogany desk, a barrier titanic in size and nature. "A strong one? You have no idea who will even win this competition."

"I dislike your tone."

She was a tenant on the land. A mere nobody, but for the fact that their families were distantly related—and more recently favor bound. It allowed for more familiarity, but she still trod dangerous ground.

She took a deep breath, ran a hand over her tight blond bun, and asked more calmly, "What if the man who wins is the lowest sort of blackguard?"

"Oh, that is unlikely to happen. The winner is likely to be one of four men." He made another notation in the ledger in front of him. "Three out of the four are good choices."

"Three out of—" Her voice strangled. "And the fourth?"

He waved a hand. "An outside chance. Besides" —his eyes stayed on his ledger—"whoever the winner, the prize will be immense enough that he will become a prize himself, whatever his previous faults or station. Sarah will finally make a worthy match."

"She could make a worthy match if you but give her time."

He threw down his pen. "Worthy? She showed me what type of match she'd make during the season. Likely run off with the first fortune hunter who gave her notice. I daresay your disastrous marriage would look a picnic, and you barely qualify as gentry. A similar mistake in the *ton* would be beyond embarrassing for the family."

She bared her teeth, forcing her wince away. "You do her no credit."

"She does herself no credit. How I could have raised such a spineless weakling—"

"She is not spineless!"

"—it was obviously her mother's fault."

Caroline narrowed her eyes. "Stop this tournament. There is still time to do so."

He flicked back sandy blond hair streaked lightly with silver. Gray eyes narrowed in irritation. "I will not. And even if I wanted to, it is far too late now. The King has given his blessing. The London papers have started reporting."

"You could have the King rescind it."

The crackle of paper sounded as his grip tightened. "You overstep yourself, Mrs. Martin. I thought you had become a better model of behavior."

A drumbeat of fear thumped in her belly, but she drew herself up. "You will not dissuade me from this way of thinking. You can still have the tournament. But if you nullify Sarah's role, perhaps she will find a suitor on her own while the games are in progress."

"Absolutely not. This is to her benefit. And to mine. You don't think the men participating would be clamoring for her hand otherwise, do you?"

"You were hardly encouraging her to seek third and fourth sons and *bastards* during the season." She pinned him with the most ferocious stare she could muster. "Her first season out of mourning, if I need remind you. She was quiet for a purpose. Besides, many a smart woman waits to see the new crop of suitors."

"The new crop will be much like the old, and Sarah will still be too lackluster to take advantage.

Their eyes slip right past her." Caroline heard a gasp and saw a brown head duck away from the door. Turning back to the earl, she saw that he had noticed it too, and she gripped her fingers tighter.

"Girl, come in here."

Lady Sarah Pims slowly emerged from behind the half-closed door, brown head tilted down; if she weren't a lady her shoulders would be drooping and her feet dragging.

"Should have known you were lurking about behind Mrs. Martin's skirts."

"Yes, Father."

He walked over to her and lifted her chin. "You will make the best match of the decade. Celebrated, with a husband powerful enough to move the world. My daughter. A gem. A father's fondest wish."

The look of longing on Sarah's face was almost enough to make Caroline weep.

"You will participate in this tournament with nary a word of defiance, won't you? Be the good daughter of which every father dreams?"

Her friend's throat worked. "Yes, Father," she whispered.

"Good. Mind Lady Tevon. She is here to help. Now go outside and close the door."

As soon as the lock clicked into place, he turned abruptly and stalked back to his desk. "Being biddable is a good trait in a wife. Where she got her meekness from . . ."

He shook his head, and she bit her lip to keep from unwisely responding with exactly where that meekness stemmed.

"The only way she will make a good match is if I choose one for her." He sifted through the papers on his desk, mind already made. "As the prize of this tournament, she will be the gem of her age group."

"But the winner . . . what if . . ." The memory of Sarah's downturned eyes and distressed brown hair spurred her on. "Give her another opportunity to make a brilliant match on her own. Next season. Let me accompany her. All she needs is a boost in her confidence."

The earl's cynically amused eyes met hers. "You can't possibly believe that I will sponsor *you* for society? Someone who ran off with a stable hand because she was in *love*? *Mrs.* Martin." He snorted. "Someone who acted against the express wishes of her parents? Someone barely related to this family?"

She molded her fingers into fists, not allowing his words to cut more deeply than they already had. There was nothing she could do about the past. She could only look forward. And that meant helping Sarah. "No. But I can remain in the background assisting Lady Sarah—a silent chaperone. I do not seek a season, nor the attention of society."

He looked her over, a snide perusal. "And you think that by standing at Sarah's side the beaus will flock to her? Even with your severe hairstyles and unflattering dresses? More likely that every widow hunter and rake will flock to you instead, looking for exactly the challenge you present. And we will be back to the beginning, except with a year wasted, and in an even worse position."

The color drained from her face. The last thing Caroline wanted was to be in society's eye playing the widow-and-rake game, but the image of Sarah . . . "Let Sarah have a *choice* in whom she weds. She is your daughter. I won't ask anything of you ever again. You owe it to us, my lord."

"Owe you?" He raised a brow.

She touched the locket around her neck and looked him straight in the eye. "Owe Papa, at the least."

Every line around his eyes creased in anger. "No, Mrs. Martin. I fulfilled any debt when I covered for you after that debacle of your own making."

He thumped a hand on top of a stack of books. "Sarah will do her duty. And you are not to interfere, do you understand?" He observed her silence for a moment, and the steel he was noted for reflected silver in his gaze. "Furthermore, you will assist in making this tournament a success and do anything I require."

When she didn't respond, his eyes narrowed. "I will ship you off to another estate, if I need to. I'd rather you stayed here and kept Sarah in line. She has always been best with you for whatever godforsaken reason. But if you put one toe out of line, I may just decide to take away everything. The village celebrations, your house, your monies, your access to Sarah. *Everything*. Do I make myself clear?"

She could hear her own breathing. "Perfectly."

"Good. I have need of you at Roseford Grange tomorrow. Be by in the morning. You are dismissed."

The earl bent back over his figures, his plans,

his empire building. The earl's heir was on the continent, fulfilling his last bits of education. Not that George would have gone against his father, but she could have used some help.

Caroline marched from the room, her own plans forming. She gathered the shrunken form of her companion outside the door and continued toward the east wing. "There's nothing for it, Sarah. We will have to work from within the tournament."

"Caro." The nineteen-year-old girl gripped her arm. "You shouldn't have argued with Father."

"Your father needs to be challenged every once in a while. Sometimes I think that is the only reason he allows me such liberties." But she had to be careful of going too far. She had read the threat in his eyes. The seriousness there. He might indulge her due to their entwined pasts, but that would last only so long.

"But—"

"Not here." The servants watched them, bowing to Lady Sarah as they moved toward Sarah's rooms.

As soon as they were safely ensconced inside with a pot of tea, Caroline tucked a blanket around her friend's legs. Six years' difference in age had firmly established their hierarchy of need, no matter the distance in social standing or family connection.

"We will need to look closely at each participant. Determine who is worthy and who is not."

"Does it matter?" Sarah leaned her head back against the chair.

"Of course it does! They can't all be bad, right?" She tried not to inject the uncertainty she felt.

Sarah shook her head.

"We will just have to cull the Anthonys from the list."

Her friend forced a smile.

"I never liked him from your letters," Caroline said loyally, disliking the man she had never met. "He is the one lacking, not you."

"He was a lovely poet." Her friend's eyes sought the window. "He particularly liked to compare my skin to all manners of attractive things. Roses, lilies, dahlias. Once he even used a turnip to describe my lips."

Caroline set out a cup of milk and a few lumps of sugar, trying to hide a smile at Sarah's attempt at a jest. "Artists are a strange lot. And poets—always trying to find something to rhyme with rutabaga. It would have driven you mad."

Sarah's smile curved into something more genuine. "Yes, well, I won't have to worry about rogue rutabagas anymore."

Caroline returned her smile and tried to keep things upbeat. She could always hope that Anthony, the unreliable fortune hunter, showed up to the estate for the games. She had all manner of nice surprises for a guest of his ilk. "You can plant rutabagas on your new properties. Roseford Grange is part of the prize, and I hear it is a lovely piece of land. Perfect as the country seat for the winner, and not overly far from here, so you can visit on a regular basis."

"Oh?"

"Yes, the Duke of Grandien is including the estate as part of the prize. The earl wants me to visit it tomorrow and sketch the manor. Will you come?"

Sarah smiled, the edges of her eyes still taut with stress. "Yes, if I can part from Lady Tevon, my new chaperone, I most definitely would like to do that. I need to keep a positive perspective."

Caroline fiddled with her cup. "Do you think we could petition the King?"

The lines around Sarah's eyes grew. "No. The King sees the whole competition as an incentive to make sure one of his godchildren is married well."

She took a deep breath before continuing. "I saw him a few days past. He has signed a document promising the winner a viscountcy. After the competition ends, he'll have the letters-patent drawn up and—" She waved a hand in a fatalistic manner. "I tried to beg him to revoke his blessings, but you know how I freeze up so terribly. He just patted me on the head and said the games were designed to weed out the unworthy. Only a true gentleman could win."

"A true gentleman."

"Yes." Sarah tugged at the bow on her dress, mangling it further.

A man who was good at shooting, boxing, gaming, and wenching could easily fulfill the terms of a "true gentleman." Not the type of man who was generous and understanding, courteous and patient. A man like Sarah needed. Someone who could bring out her gentle spirit and appreciate her kindness.

"This competition will bring the winner a fortune, not just from me. That's part of the reason the King agreed to it, outside of his ties to the group. The monetary rewards are a joint offering from all the men sponsoring the tournament, and it 'promotes good English stock and fun.' The winner will be"—Sarah waved her hand again, then dropped it to her lap—"celebrated and titled. *Prestigious.* A connection Father covets, like every other man of the *ton*."

"Yes, but—"

"Father is so *pleased*," she whispered.

"Well, that is hardly—"

"It's so hard, Caro." Fingers wrung the blanket. "Your parents loved you unconditionally, even when you went against them. But it's so hard to please Father. And the diamonds fairly sparkled this year before they were snatched up. There were so many on the mart at the beginning of the season. I thought myself a fairly decent catch before I left, especially with your confidence behind me. But the competition . . . I was just lost in the shuffle. And without you—"

Sarah's voice lowered. "You know there is no way for me to make a powerful marriage otherwise. I need Father's help. I'm just not—"

Caroline tipped her chin up. "You are a wonderful woman, Sarah. The right man will see that. *You* need to see it."

Sarah bit her lip, tears shimmering in her eyes.

Caroline steepled her fingers on the table, anger at the *ton* and at the earl battling with the need to comfort Cheevers's daughter. "We'll just have to run away, nothing for it."

She grabbed a pen and a piece of paper from a neatly stacked pile. "Find some handsome prince for you. Perhaps a solid businessman for me."

Sarah choked.

"Shall we go to France?" She tapped the table. "No, too continental. India?" She wrote it down. "Plenty of tea, but too dangerous." She crossed it out. "Spain?" She pretended to think on it. "Too hot."

Sarah cracked a smile and resumed sipping her tea.

Caroline leaned back in her chair. "America? Too colonial, I think."

Some of the tension left Sarah's shoulders.

She picked up the teapot again, not giving away the fact that she was only half joking. Sarah was her sister in everything but the eyes of the world. If the competition turned out to be disastrous, despite the ill-suited nature they both possessed for running away, and their limited funds, Caroline would attempt to smuggle her out of the country.

"Well, until we can come up with the perfect destination, let's see what we can do about this competition. Illegitimate children and latter-born sons, hmmm . . ."

"Hungry, to the last."

"Do you know any of them?"

"A few. But they are mostly rogues and rakes and men not interested in wallflowers. There are fifteen of them." She rattled off a few names that Caroline recognized from notes, the London sheets, and the earl, but few that she could identify by face, never having had a season herself.

"In a few days most of them will be here to look over the documents." Sarah's voice grew weary. "Lady Tevon has been trying to drum excitement into me. She would be overjoyed to share all she knows—I know Father has told her everything. She sleeps in his room, though they think I don't know." Caroline blinked, momentarily side-tracked by Sarah's glib announcement of the earl's new mistress. "I can have you over for tea, and you can ask during the visit."

"Excellent."

She kept up a steady chatter designed to keep Sarah laughing, all the while plotting which part of the competition she planned to destroy first.

Chapter 3

❧ ∞ ❧

Dear Reader, shadowy appeals from every corner are turning into intriguing tidbits. Our sources tell us that many of society's sons—the favorite and the notorious—are set to compete in a tournament. Among them are Marcus Sloane, the natural son of the Marquess of Sloanestone, and Sebastien Deville, the natural son of the Duke of Grandien. As you are undoubtedly aware from the social on-dits, Deville is best known for his unpredictability and his exploits with the women in Town . . .

Caroline tiredly dropped her papers onto a curved stone bench in the front garden of the vacant, but charming, Roseford Grange. She'd completed a pencil sketch of the grounds and now needed to illustrate the house proper on the page.

The words of the earl and Sarah's new chaperone played through her mind. She had exhausted most of her ire during the carriage ride, but the product remained.

Lady Sarah's marriage to the tournament winner

*will be the event of the season. Married to the new
viscount. A man demonstrating strength in all areas
and supported by the most powerful men in England.
Think of your father's pride, Lady Sarah!*

With great difficulty Caroline had restrained
herself from giving Lady Tevon a box on the ears
for dangling the earl's regard before Sarah like
a carrot on a stick. Repeated over and over, the
effect had been brutal.

"Your father wants to see you married well. His
affection for you would be untold. The sheer amount
of *pride* he would have in you—unfathomable."
Caroline mimicked the speech, the authoritarian
power that Lady Tevon dripped with every new
word. Her anger with the earl grew ever larger.

She gave a vicious little tug of her black chalk
over the paper. Undoubtedly the winner of this
redoubtable tournament would make a powerful
match—Lady Tevon was correct.

That didn't mean that the contestants themselves
would be wonderful. Men in power, or seeking it,
rarely were. And several of the men were widely
known as out-and-out rakes. Men who seduced
women into believing they were special. Men who
moved on as soon as the next beautiful or powerful
thing crossed their paths. Men like—

She scratched out another line along with the
thought, making sure the placement of the line
was perfect, with no excess marks or flavor.

She critically examined the Grange, focusing
on her task instead of memories best left forgotten. The main house was a lovely structure with
brown peaks and sloping roofs. Large windows

and thoughtful architecture. Warm and inviting, yet wild and free. Long-stemmed flowers and curling ivy twined around it, encompassing it in long green arms and colorful fingers.

If she were an artist, it would be a heavenly sight to paint. A sight in and of itself that would perhaps encourage one to become an artist. This was the type of home in which she'd like to see Sarah reside. She had always thought her friend more at ease in her own wild cottage garden than in the confines of the strict manor with its rigid layout and oppressive stones.

The last thing Sarah needed was a domineering or roguish man to inhabit it with her.

"You are trespassing on private property," a deep, smooth voice stated. "If you would kindly be on your way."

She whipped around to see a well-dressed, *very* handsome man leaning casually against a garden pillar no more than five paces away. But for the look in his eyes, a jaded prince.

The hum of a befuddled cricket echoed her feelings. "Trespassing?" she asked, unnerved by his presence.

He cocked a brow. "The act of walking onto property that is forbidden to you."

"No, I mean, I believe you are mistaken, sir. I'm not trespassing—"

"Oh? Just marking the time in the shade then?"

Irritated, she turned more fully toward him. "No. I'm not a trespasser. I have permission to be on the property."

"Permission from the duke?" He looked down a perfectly formed nose. "Consider him a trespasser as well."

"The duke?" Did he mean the Duke of Grandien? An owner could hardly trespass on his own estate. Momentarily confused, she examined the man more fully. He wasn't just fashionably dressed, he was a model of fashion, but for the languid way he stood in his clothes. The strange feeling that he would mock her were she to comment on his clothing, as if he was having a laugh at someone else's expense by wearing it so well, settled upon her.

"The highest rank of nobility," he said unhelpfully.

She bristled. "I know what a duke is."

His brow rose again and his gaze washed over her. "Do you?"

She couldn't restrain the flush. She was hardly dressed in her best outfit, not having expected to run into anyone but skeleton staff on the temporarily abandoned estate, and she automatically knew that even her best wouldn't be on par with this man's worst. "Yes, even scullery maids know what a duke is."

"Is that how the doddering old man is dressing his scullers these days?" He whistled. "A sad state of affairs."

"What a horrible—" She stopped and took a breath. "I don't even know how to begin responding to your rude comments. I'm here on the orders of the earl. I won't be but an hour, then you will be well rid of me." She added under her breath, "And I will be happy for it now."

"The earl?" His eyes narrowed.

"Earl Cheevers."

He gave a short laugh, unpleasant in nature. "The earl holds no sway here. Meadowbrook is an hour's ride that way." He pointed. "Now scurry off; I'm sure there is work to be done in the earl's *magnificent* kitchens."

What a horrible man. Any male beauty was dwarfed by his unpleasant nature. "I'm sorry for whatever the earl has done to rile you so, but I will just be an hour more."

"No. Whatever the earl wants with Roseford"— he made a striking motion with his hand, a sinister smile on his face—"I will take great pleasure in thwarting."

"He but needs a drawing for a tournament that is . . ." She trailed off at the look of utter rage that passed over the man's face before his features settled back into cold lines.

"I know what the damn drawing is for."

"Oh." She didn't know what else to say. Part of her thought she should commit the building and grounds to memory right now and run back to the safety of the carriage and driver. The other part was screaming for her not to turn her back on the man in front of her. He didn't exactly seem the model of stability.

She had heard somewhere that the most beautiful members of society, of which his clothes and face clearly claimed him a part, were some of the most unstable. Too much inbreeding.

"Pardon me?" The look on the man's face hinted he was two steps from throttling her where she stood.

Oh dear. The last bit had slipped right out.

A dozen excuses and apologies jostled through her brain as death stared her in the face. She was trying to formulate an appropriate response when his forbidding look changed suddenly into one full of dark humor, making him even more attractive. Like a puckish cupid on an evil mission.

"No, no, that is delicious actually." His lips curved into an appealing smile that caused alarming warmth to curl in her belly. "Terrible inbreeding is exactly what is wrong with me. I believe you are too right in that assessment, Miss—?"

She didn't answer, still speechless.

"Shall I just call you Miss Sculler, then?" He pushed away from the pillar and approached her, dropping into the seat beside her and stretching long legs. If she were a small animal of prey she'd be in deep, deep trouble at the moment.

Rich brown hair hung slightly too long; a clump fell into shaded eyes, framing arrogant, sharp features. His body held the lithe type of grace found in the best predators as he leaned negligently against the back of the bench, exuding a feeling of danger mixed with ease.

"I blame the male side, of course. Do you think if we mated, the children would be better off?"

"No," she choked out.

"Pity. I'll have to find some other woman of solid stock to stop the flow of beauty and insanity." He put one hand to his chest and one to his head in a pose that would have made Kean envious. "My curse."

She could feel her mouth part, but there was

little to be done about her gawking. If she said what she was thinking, all those years of restraint would be for naught.

He turned and inspected her from the toes of her slippers to the tip of her bonnet. "Now that I fully see you, hidden underneath that hideous thing, I can see that our mating wouldn't have helped the curse anyway."

Before she could determine his meaning, he was stretching out, his body resting like velvet over the stone.

"The earl sent you all the way over here to sketch tiny Roseford Grange for his tournament." He tapped his fingers together. "There is so much irony in this whole scenario to appreciate."

She tried to edge away without his noticing, but he pinned her with an amused gaze.

"You seemed much more animated before, Miss Sculler. Come now, the sketch." He made a motion with his hand. "I'm anxious to see your work."

The man was daft. Completely and utterly daft. He used her inattention to lean over and peer at her paper.

"I don't know whether to be thrilled that you plan to serve this to Cheevers, or appalled at Roseford being so visually mauled." He looked up through long lashes, one lock of hair falling into his eye. "Would you rather draw the butterflies? Your mouth is so agape as to catch at least one."

A butterfly flitted between them, near enough for either to touch. He traced the air around it.

"Something that seems simply pretty to most, yet underneath shows a complicated bit of artistry." The butterfly landed, slowly flapped its wings twice, then lifted off. The man's head cocked to the side, watching her. "At least then your sketch would be adequately pretty to most, and would cover the damning coldness."

She couldn't resist the response that sprang to her lips. "I beg your pardon?"

"Excellent. Begging this early in our acquaintance." Another horribly appealing smile curved perfect lips as he leaned back once more, somehow closer to her than before. "You are pardoned."

Her grip on the paper slackened along with her jaw. "You terrible man." She wasn't sure she had ever met anyone so forward. Not even Patrick had been this silver-tongued.

He cocked a brow, surveying her with hot eyes, and relaxed further into his negligent pose.

Far from the maniac she had first assumed, *this* was the type of rake who carefully cultivated his projected image under a veneer of disrepute. The type of man who fulfilled every fantasy and then left women crying and broken in his wake.

Now that he wasn't using his forbidding-lord look on her, he practically *oozed* illicit desire and temptation, like a fresh summer strawberry coated in sugar and wickedness. Or a juicy pomegranate seed that would send a woman straight to Hades.

She was quite familiar with his type, both his types, though she'd never been quite so stunned by either of them before.

"You are quite beautiful up close, under that dreadful bonnet." His tone was musing as he tapped a finger against the stone of the bench.

"I wasn't expecting that. A pleasant surprise, of course, though you seem to be something of an ice princess in need of thawing, if that drawing is any indication. Then again, Cheevers likes his women stern and full-bodied."

His words blurred together in a sort of red film of outrage, as she watched the movements of his hands, his hair, his facial expressions.

She would not respond.

He smiled—lips curving in a manner that said he knew exactly what she was thinking.

She would not respond.

A rustle alerted her too late. She tried to grab for her paper as he snatched it. A second later he had balled it up and tossed it over his shoulder. It sailed into twining plants, which seemed to gulp and swallow as the ball disappeared into depths of green.

Ire returned to her tongue like an old friend. "That was thirty minutes' worth of work you destroyed, you inbred goat."

He raised an elegant brow. "Thirty minutes? For that? You should thank your inbred pasture animals then. Lifeless piece, it was."

"Thank you?" she sputtered. "I should thank you because I've lost thirty minutes of work that you deem *lifeless*?"

He cocked that same brow, the elegance of his bearing at odds with the look in his eyes—far too dark and savage for a face so young. He couldn't be more than thirty. "What are you afraid of?"

Everything in her bristled. "I'm afraid of doing permanent damage to the underside of a braying animal with horns," she said with a relish she hadn't enjoyed in years. Unease slithered through her at the depth of the feeling. She took a deep breath, pulling forth the calm facade she had forced herself to perfect. "What I meant to say—"

He moved forward and touched her face with expensively gloved fingers. Her mouth snapped shut at his sheer nerve and proximity as supple leather slid over her skin. Eyes the oddest shade of blue examined her critically. Bluish-green, like an exotic orchid. She shook her head to stop their mesmerizing effect and pulled her cheek from his touch.

"Classic beauty, fine features, but afraid of her own passion," he said, showing himself even more of an ass by talking to himself, cataloging her assets as if she were a broodmare. "How disappointing. And tantalizing, of course. I hadn't realized scullery maids could be so intriguing."

She didn't know which segment of his assessment insulted her more. She swallowed her immediate reply, refusing to play his game.

Full lips pulled across straight white teeth. "And here I was hoping that you'd beg me so prettily once again."

She pulled an escaped bit of hair back under her bonnet, and kept her lips pressed tightly together.

"Is that spirit you are vainly trying to suppress?" His eyes were heavy—lazy and satisfied. "I don't know whether to be pleased at the immediate progress or irritated that my new game has been cut short."

"I seriously doubt you can handle my unsuppressed spirit," she said, a little viciously, irritated and unnerved by the whole encounter. The hair escaped again with her head shake.

"I seriously doubt that," he mocked. His head cocked to the side, and one lock of rich brown hair slid farther over his eye—unlike hers, though, she was sure the gesture was calculated. Hair too long, brilliant eyes too full of shadows. "You are trying much too hard to be restrained. It's in your every line, from your severe hair knot tucked in that awful bonnet that cannot quite keep that one piece of hair in place, to the abbey-worthy scullery dress that barely fits you. And then there is your abominable drawing. The less said about that, the better."

Her chin jutted. "I dress the way I please. And why am I bothering to respond to you?"

"Because underneath all of that prim severity, there is passion tethered and waiting, and you want it released." Another slow, lazy smile. "I can see it in the pulse at your throat, in the flush on your cheeks."

She could feel her cheeks heat further even as she shook her head.

"No? Women are such contrary creatures at times. I'm simply reading your body's reaction." He leaned closer, and her heart skipped ahead three beats. He smiled in satisfaction. "Your reactions show promise. Your sketch does not."

"And what would you know of it?" She leaned away from him, looking him over from toe to tip with as much disdain as she could muster over a racing heart and burning cheeks.

"I need not be a master of the brush to recognize a shocking suffocation of emotion." His head rolled around his neck, as if he was casually rotating out the kinks. The motion stopped so that he was looking at her from under long lashes. "Though I can be your master, should you need that."

"I do *not*."

"It seems as if you need something to incite you."

"I'm perfectly capable of—of *inciting* myself—"

He smiled wickedly.

"—as well as being intelligently cautious." Why in all that was holy was she defending herself like a caught novice? She tried to ignore the answer wrapped in her body's thrum, the heavy beat of her heart.

"Cautious? You didn't know until I said something that you weren't alone. The groom who accompanied you is napping soundly on his perch. What's the use of caution if there is no one around to dupe? You could have been out here *inciting* yourself and no one would have known." He smiled lazily. "Except me, of course. And I do have to tell you that would be a sight for which I'd pay the ticket price."

Her jaw dropped.

He leaned closer, too near for comfort, looking at the next paper on her stack—an earlier version of the scene. "Maybe you should try something more ladylike, that you could wave off as simply pretty. A lovely accessory." He looked up at her with those eyes. "Many ladies get by on simply being one themselves."

Too near. Too near, her senses screamed.

She leaned away from him, swallowing, trying not to let too much of her skittishness show. "I'll have you know that sketching landscapes is perfectly ladylike. Have you never been to a parlor, sir?"

He was still so close that she could see the small creases in his brow as one lifted. "I try to stay away from activities so dreadfully boring."

"I daresay that you have a hard time being alone then."

"A dreadful time. Alas, I often must amuse myself."

He leaned back and stretched his legs, perfectly tailored trousers whispering across slate. "Let's see what you try for your next barely passable sketch."

"Sir, if you were a gentleman, you would hie on to parts unknown."

He bent one knee, a booted foot dislodging bits of gravel as it scraped up. "But who said I was a gentleman?"

She didn't even know his name, and at this point she was unlikely to ask. The answer to his question was obvious.

She decided to ignore him and began sketching again, using the previous outline she had drawn.

A rip of material, and her new effort joined its brother.

"No, put a little passion into it."

She had no idea what the man was talking about. Daft, hateful, motherless rat. She grabbed a new piece of paper and had barely finished a new outline of the house, before long fingers removed it from her lap. The sound of paper hitting leaves thudded in her ears.

She bit her lip to keep tears of frustration at bay over the wasted time, the wasted work, the wasted goodwill she would have received from the earl.

She rose. "You *and* the earl can go to the devil."

"Oh, come now, don't lump me in with Cheevers." He mock-shuddered, and she hated him for it.

"Little difference is there. Bullying those you see as inferior. Lording over those in your power. Being petty just because you can."

His eyes shuttered, but she didn't care. She turned and strode in the direction of the carriage. Three steps later a body was in front of her, a hand at her elbow.

"In my power, are you?"

"Is that what you absorbed from my speech? Pity that your brain seems little more than a snail's."

"In two hours it will be dusk," the too-handsome demon said, eyes still shuttered, body too large in front of her as he pressed forward, backing her up with his proximity. "The light will be gone and you will be without your sketch."

The backs of her legs hit the bench. She lifted her chin and met his eyes, refusing to be intimidated even as her heart thumped in her chest. "I suppose I will."

"The earl will be displeased."

"Most likely. But I don't let the earl's displeasure overrun my will, and neither will I let yours."

His eyes narrowed on hers. "You are lying.

The earl's displeasure is a keen thing to you." She pressed her lips together. "You will lose your position."

"Perhaps. If you recognize such, what will it take for you to leave me be? For you to let me sketch the house and leave?"

Something shifted in his expression. "Oh, I'm not sure you are willing to pay the price."

She focused on the falling sun, the heavy shadows. "Perhaps I'm not, but what is it?"

"What if I demand you naked here, splayed on your back, arching against me as I drive into you?" One edge of his mouth lifted in a hot smile that matched entirely with the look in his sarcastic eyes. Not the type of smile that gentlemen wore.

Her mouth dropped open. "N-no. I don't think that is at all what I had in mind."

"No? Perhaps a meeting for tea? A drive through the park? Surely a maid doesn't expect to be courted?"

She looked determinedly at the waning golden rays, unable to speak. It wasn't her station in life that sparked tears in her eyes. It wasn't the proof once more that men were fickle and free. It wasn't disappointment over the hand that the dealer of life had dealt her.

Soft leather gripped her chin, turning her face toward him. Aquamarine eyes surveyed hers. "Damn the duke to hell," he muttered.

He pushed her with just enough force to plop her rear on the stone seat.

"A sketch of Roseford." The demented man paced in front of her. "Just a sketch."

He looked at the house, then back at her, arguing internally with himself as she watched. "I'm a bastard, I know. Nothing will change that."

She wanted to agree with this assessment of his character, but decided that saying nothing was the wisest course of action now that the mercurial man had shifted his temperament once again.

"And I'm still going to charge you the price. I'll pull every bit from you. In every denomination."

Relief and anxiety vied. There was some money in the carriage. If monetary payment was all it took to get out of here, she'd pay. She just hoped it was enough. The man unnerved her in every way. He irritated and befuddled her. And the heat of him, the unmistakable pull of the most virile man she'd ever come across, snapped across the inches separating them, pushing against the slight madness that seemed to grip him whenever Roseford was mentioned.

"A kiss, I think, to start."

She jolted, the predatory look in his eyes spiking an answering call. "I beg your pardon?"

Legs pressed intimately between her knees. "Hopefully. We'll have to see."

Smooth lips descended upon hers, featherlight. Shock pulsed through her, and the lightness changed to a firmer pressure against her mouth. Strong and sweet. The feeling was like tasting a fine dessert, and she was too stunned to do anything but enjoy it. The garden smells wrapped around her senses as the last hanging rays of the sun pierced the trees.

His mouth lifted, and a smooth thumb drew

along her lips. "Yes, I think we'll make a game of it, Miss Sculler. Fresh as a country daisy with your milky skin and rosy cheeks." He sprawled onto the seat, eyelids half covering his eyes as he surveyed her. "You want that sketch, and I've decided I want you."

"Well, that is not going to happen." Reason returned, along with tight stirrings of desire that penetrated through her rigid control and demanded more. Alarmed, she pushed her materials together haphazardly. She hadn't felt this out of sorts in a long time. And the last time she had felt the stirrings of such overwhelming desire, she had gotten into a sea of trouble.

She started to shakily stand. A firm hand on her thigh held her in place.

His hand didn't move, but warnings and flares fired. She had maintained a tight leash on her desire—he had nailed that from the first look. And the evidence that she still possessed the emotion terrified her as much as it made her yearn to let it free.

Passion mistaken for love had led her astray once. Terribly astray. But there was no declaration of love here to fool her. There was no reason to be so troubled, yet something about the deranged man who kissed like a master threatened something within her.

His fingers trailed to the stack of papers. He lifted the top one, and she waited for it to be tossed with the rest.

"You keep making the same mistake."

Her mouth kicked back into battle, happy to

have something to distract her, trying to discount the double meaning of his words, and concentrating on the war. "All of the lines are perfect." She jabbed a finger at the sloped roof of one of the sections of the house that was under repair. "Representative of the structure."

"If you want a completely plain, boring representation."

She stared at him. "It's a building."

"No structure is *just* a building. Just like no man is *just* a man. There is an identity to everything. Look at the loneliness in the peak." He visually traced the real edges with his finger through the air. "The way it tips toward a lost support. Calling for that which is missing. Rubbish to call it just a structure."

She watched him, unnerved. He smiled lazily, all traces of seriousness disappearing behind a mask. "It is simple aesthetics."

The wisps of a brief window of something far deeper than any other trait he had shown dissipated. Her nerves increased, but for a different reason.

"Who are you?"

"A man who appreciates aesthetics. For instance, every aesthetic sense says that you are quite beautiful," he said, tossing the paper back to her, leaning back to prop himself with an elbow on the back of the sloping support.

Her previous irritation resumed. "Flattery," she deadpanned. "Empty and boring. A plain representation of a real conversation."

Something sparked in his eyes again, some sort of pleasure this time.

"Perhaps this conquest will truly be worth the cost. If I had known, I would have worn something more suitable."

"Conquest? You call charging someone to kiss you a conquest?"

"A kiss is merely the toll. The real conquest happens when you beg for more." A finger idly moved over his full lower lip. "Passion unleashed."

She knew firsthand that unleashed desire could easily revert to caged aggression. "Passion burns brightly, then fizzles away."

Expressions, mercurial and rapid, charged across his face.

He reached over so quickly that she was too late to move away. He swiped a thumb across the top of the drawn roof on her lap, depressing the papers into her thighs.

"But if you capture desire, if you hold it . . ." He pulled his expensively gloved thumb across the bottom of the pillar and leaned toward her, a hairbreadth from her lips. ". . . then that moment will burn indelibly."

His eyes held hers, his face so close that if they blinked in tandem, their eyelashes might brush together. Desire like none she had felt in years pulsed through her, fear following on its heels with stomping strides.

A dark, satisfied smile curved his lips. He leaned back against the stone and motioned with one hand. "Please, sketch while you can, Miss Sculler."

She looked down at her paper, at the smudges he had made, then at the roof—the solitary slope he had traced in the air, the one that on paper now leaned indelibly toward something. There was movement and a shard of emotion in the rough smudges. Unfinished, but evoking a shred of life.

Unnerving. The sight of something beneath the facade. But then Patrick had had many depths. They just hadn't all been good ones.

She concentrated on filling in the rest of the lines. Stagnant, clean lines without life. She peeked sideways to see him leaning with his head back against the stone armrest, legs sprawled out toward her, the edge of his boot touching her slipper, the edge of his left trouser caressing her dress.

She surreptitiously drew a bare finger along the chalk line, trying to imitate his actions. No, it just looked like a smudge. She frowned.

"Magnificent, isn't it?"

She jerked guiltily, but his eyes were still closed.

"One could lie here forever listening to the wind."

His eyes remained shut, so she watched him, trying to understand how someone wearing such expensive clothes would so willingly wrinkle and dirty them. None of the guests at Meadowbrook would dare sit on a bench that hadn't received a thorough scrubbing that morning, no less sit on one that had been left unattended beneath the glow of more than a few full moons.

He either possessed extreme wealth or was a spoiled son with a complete and total lack of responsibility.

She was inclined toward the latter.

And he was full of contradictions. His demeanor and actions, at odds with each other one moment, pulling her in the next, entangled her in knots. A consummate rake, a *master* of the breed—she'd bet every groat. His relaxation on the bench was a show, a patient waiting, of that she had no doubt. The problem was that a part of her was tensed in anticipation, not outrage.

And she'd thought Patrick had that indefinable quality that made women, *smart* women, beg. This man made him seem a silly boy. It made the rational, intellectual part of her uneasy, and the more wild side . . . Well, best not to think about that.

Damnable curiosity made her play her part for the moment. "The wind?"

"Do you not hear it? The melody and soft refrain? You should channel it into your sketch."

She cocked her head. She loved to sit outside her cottage and listen to the sounds, but she had never tried to channel them into anything else, always content to simply enjoy.

"The song of the trees swaying to the gentle rhythm of a conductor we cannot see. Listen to the music, Miss Sculler. Roseford follows nature. Only by opening yourself up can you capture it and break the lifeless chill."

She gave him a sharp glance, but he merely smiled and hid aquamarine eyes once again, his fingers tapping some rhythm against his chest.

Caroline watched the breeze shift the wildflowers and crazed leaves of the ivy as they curled around whatever surface they could find, wrapping the Grange in an embrace. Something shifted in her mind, and she touched the chalk once more to the page. Her lines grew less straight and more fluid as she sketched the grounds, leaving the house alone for the moment. Her motions took on a staccato in the bounce of a squirrel, a slur as a snake slithered through the grass, and a run as nuts and leaves fluttered down the chimney bricks.

Two cooing doves caused her to speculate on the curve of the garden, and she pulled a finger around the edge.

The chattering of the robins, crows, and finches grew louder as aviary territory was determined.

"I do not require battlements, but if they mount a force for war, we may be in trouble," she muttered.

One eye opened, and an amused indentation appeared in one cheek. "That we would." He looked up into the trees. "When I was a boy, I wished to transform into a bird and fly away."

"A vulture?" She settled in her seat, more relaxed now. While no one in her right mind would call the man harmless, there was something suddenly conspiratorial about him. She wondered if small prey were lulled into a false sense of security in the same way.

His mouth curved. "Nothing quite so vivid. I always admired the falcons, but a simple sparrow would have done."

She looked down at the page. "When I was a girl I wished to be a princess."

"A common dream, I'd think."

"For a common girl." She pulled a line across

the page that was more characteristic of how she'd been drawing at the start. A gloved finger trailed along the chalk path, and the heat of his body reached toward her as he rose and leaned closer.

"Perhaps not quite so common." Fingers lifted her chin, then slid across the sensitive line of her throat and into her hair, pulling her closer. "Perhaps not quite so common at all."

His fingers curled around her nape, a thumb touched her cheek, sliding across her skin. He pulled her toward him slowly, and when their lips connected this time, it was with a burst of fire. The gentle, slow slide of the first kiss giving way to a more overwhelming claim, his mouth parting hers, drawing her in with heat and tense hunger. She felt the pull of the spell, the insidious song teasing her to give in to that which she had so long denied.

When he finally released her, the look in his eyes promised a myriad of craven delights were she to give in. To give up the lonely world she had locked herself within.

"Are you going to finish the sketch of the house, or shall I continue kissing you?" He smiled slowly.

Calculated, assuredly. She concentrated on his raised brow instead of his heated eyes or curved lips. She couldn't forget and get lost in the danger of the spell. She lifted the chalk in a shaky grip and drew another line, then two, following his example. She imbued movement into each line, seeking something. Yearning. A peak in isolation that craved contact.

"Much better." His hand moved to her neck, rubbing and caressing, warmth springing beneath gloved fingers. The hum of the breeze charged, yet soothing. "What is it you see, lovely?"

She saw a house that was waiting. Slightly overgrown and wild, but a *home* nonetheless. A house in need of someone or something. She drew in the windows, glass peering outward like great eyes searching for their owner to return.

"Yes." Fingers undid the strings of her bonnet, tugging it back from her crown. She let him, eyes closing as the shield was removed, but too desirous of the magic to tell him to stop. She tried not to watch as he peeled his gloves from his hands. "Much, much better."

She pulled the stick over the outline of the gardens, suddenly drawing with more talent than she had any right to claim.

Bare fingers popped one pin from her hair, then two. Her hair fell in long chunks as it was freed. "A crime to hide this waterfall."

Fingertips gently drew her hair to the other side, and she shuddered as his lips touched her neck. "Keep drawing, dear Miss Sculler. But listen to yourself this time instead."

Wild lines formed as he did sinful things to the back and sides of her neck. Instead of taking her interest away, his lips and seeking fingers seemed to push the chalk faster and in the correct direction. Shapes formed; lines full of life and depth took hold.

Hands touched her nape, catching the valley and pressing, rubbing down the column of her back. She drew in the chimney spine as he traced hers.

The roof pulled into domed tips as he pressed against her back, hugging her to him, his palms running down the sides of her body, over her stomach and up to caress the sides of her breasts. His hands drew peaks over the tips.

"Sir?" Her breath caught, her head tilted back on his shoulder as a thumb slipped inside the bodice of her dress and his other hand touched her knee, pulling her skirt up, up, up, then slipping underneath. He pressed his palm against the inside of her right knee and pulled it away from her other one, her ladylike position turning into something open and wanton, on view for the entire Grange, if not for the waist-high bushes in front of them.

The edge of his thumb tweaked her nipple under the rigid edge of her corset, causing her to shudder. She moved into the touch instead of away, having never felt the overwhelming magic of this type of desire where she didn't have any inhibitions—just the touch of a man who was a master at his craft. She felt him smile against her throat. Skilled fingers investigated beneath her knees, her stockings, her garters, then moved farther up.

"I wonder what other things you are hiding?" he whispered into her ear. Fingertips curled around the heat at her base, as he successfully navigated the cloth of her drawers.

Overwhelming sensation filled her as she arched back against him. The paper fell from her hand; the chalk slipped from her grip. She gripped his thigh, and a finger curved into her, causing her to arch further, her breast pushing into his hand, which had slipped inside her bodice to palm her, his other thumb rubbing a spot nestled between her legs.

A dam broke that had too long been controlled. Lingering anger with the earl mixed with the earlier frustration at the man devouring her, and swirled with the irritation over the hand fate had dealt Sarah. Here was someone allowing her to release those emotions instead of swallowing them like a lump of coal. All the past years' turmoil—keeping herself in line and isolated—pushed out.

She could be anyone at the moment. Do anything. Here was someone she'd likely never see again. She was in fact not seeing him anyway, since he was sitting behind her, a phantom lover with skilled hands and a questing mouth who was mapping the planes of her neck more thoroughly than she'd mapped the estate grounds.

A second finger requested entry, and some semblance of sense returned at the thought that she'd never felt this vulnerable or out of control with Patrick. He'd never played her body with this sort of undeniable skill.

Her knees automatically pushed together. "I—"

He nipped her neck, and his palm hooked under her knee, pulling it over his thigh, opening her completely. Only this time, when she arched back, he easily slipped another finger in with the first, his thumb playing her like a mandolin player plucking at strings.

The sensations were vicious, delicious, and all-encompassing, reality and fantasy mingling. She moved rhythmically against his hand and violently arched back against him, whimpering for release.

He whispered words of encouragement as his fingers moved within her. Sharp waves of desire built into a crescendo for one, two, three beats of her heart before she convulsed wildly around his fingers, straining into him. He held her arched against him for a long minute, breathing heavily himself, before removing his hand and lowering her on the bench, one of her legs still draped over his lap, the other dangling uselessly on the grass.

He smoothed his hands down her flesh, down her dress, petting and soothing her as she gave a small shudder every few seconds, her breathing still heavy. His face was shuttered as if nothing monumental had occurred. He nonchalantly bent over her and lifted something from the ground. Her throat closed as she heard the crinkle of paper. She was in no position to stop him from destroying the sketch while lying on her back, her dress splayed about her, her body boneless. Betrayal and resignation washed through her as she watched him grip the paper's edge. She closed her eyes as his fingers moved away, waiting for the first rip, the first crumple.

The steady sound of chalk pulling along paper popped her eyes open. "No, please—" She struggled upward, thinking she could stop him from ruining the sketch.

One hand touched her breastbone and pushed

her back down, not unkindly. He cocked a brow, turning his attention back to her prized work. She closed her eyes again, listening to the scritches and swipes. Trying to keep her overwrought emotions in a tight grip.

He shifted over her, a hand wrapped around her nape, and pulled her to meet warm lips in a drugging caress. Her eyes opened as his lips left hers, and he lowered her head gently back to the bench. A slow smile pulled across his lips, and a piece of paper settled on her chest.

"Until the next time, dear Miss Sculler," he said in his deep, smooth voice. "Consider that a gift."

His bare fingers pulled along her jaw, then he sauntered away, disappearing into the gardens.

She hastily sat up to inspect the vandalized drawing in the waning light. Shock held her immobile as she took in the lines and curves. The drawing had been decent before, if she did say so, but now . . . it was as if the house was alive on the page. Anyone seeing this would have the urge to visit, to see if real experience matched the vision. Only a truly gifted artist with an emotional eye could capture the essence like this and put it to the page.

Or someone who had a stake in the subject drawn.

She looked up sharply, but the man was gone.

Chapter 4

Dear Reader, it has come to our attention that the men once known as the Tipping Seven, seven wastrels who became upstanding members of the ton, powerful men once shrouded in secrecy and darkness, are sponsoring a one-time competition to bestow riches on one of their progeny. King George the Fourth was an uncounted member in his days before he was Regent. Thus, it is little surprise that this tournament has the blessing of the King himself . . .

Tall, powerful oaks and maples lined the drive to Meadowbrook, Lord Cheevers's country estate. Perfect gardens, manicured lawns, the trappings of wealth spilling out into the rich soil. Sebastien couldn't care less about the landscaping, but what it represented, in the detail it was cared for, was power. And here where a tiny weed would be ruthlessly stamped out, where the curling ivy that some thought charming was killed at its root, the details were everything.

It was nothing like Roseford, where vegetation grew unchecked and free, twining vines that spoke of life and fragrant wildflowers that spoke of happiness.

The face of the woman spilled into his vision, her wavy blonde hair freed and flowing over the stones and greenery of the Grange, head extended back in ecstasy.

He had been so angry to see someone there, cataloging the property. *His* property. The only home he had ever known.

And he had treated her horribly. But she had been a sweet fruit, ripe and blossoming. Something in him had snapped to know that she was another soldier of the earl, of the duke, taunting and taking that which he wanted most.

The kisses, the seduction, her response had made the entire episode worth his frustration. How close he had come to taking her and exorcising his ghosts. It would have been a first for him with someone he hadn't fully investigated. There was something about the way she'd looked at him . . .

He wondered in what nook he'd find her here at Meadowbrook. Hopefully not in Cheevers's chambers. A messy business that would be, to steal her from under the earl's nose.

But on the other hand that would be very satisfying as well. He'd see where the cards fell.

He fully intended to have her again. She wasn't a giggling debutante or blushing virgin, to his satisfaction. She might even occupy his bed for more than a few days. Few had before, but there was something about her, in her eyes, in her verbal and physical reactions, that indicated she would be anything but boring. Something that proclaimed her a kindred spirit in her solitude. And there was so much potential there—wild and untamed.

The carriage slowed before the doors of the stately manor. One hundred rooms strong, situated on thousands of acres, it was a veritable trough of excess.

Sebastien stepped from the vehicle into the courtyard. A few carriages had arrived already, and he sent a cynical glance toward a man of his acquaintance who was nearly salivating as he surveyed the estate. His clothing was expensive, but his face held all the salacious slobbering of a scrawny fox. No breeding.

The man turned, and his eyes swept over Sebastien. "Deville." Jack Bateman, the by-blow of the Earl of Browett, didn't offer his hand. Sebastien didn't offer his either. "Probably think you have a chance here. But this isn't a card game, is it? I intend to win, Deville. Remember that."

"I'm more likely to remember you for other failings, Bateman." Sebastien continued forward without looking back.

Three other men near his age were standing beneath the towering portico. Two were friendly faces, if any of them could be considered friends for the next two months. The third was not unknown to him, but they'd never been introduced.

"Deville." Timothy Timtree held out his hand, his dark hooded eyes sarcastic and jaded above his hooked nose. "Come to join the pony show?"

"Indeed."

They shook hands, and Timtree gave him a

knowing look before introducing him to the third man. "John Parley, may I introduce Sebastien Deville?" He turned back to Sebastien with a smirk. "John is Basil Parley's *third* son."

"I've heard talk about you, Deville." John Parley was a prig, with his slick pomade and nose two inches too high.

"Likewise," he drawled, turning away from him.

Marcus Sloane, the remaining man, looked amused and extended his hand. "Deville."

Marcus Sloane was a golden child, for all his illegitimacy. He even fit the description, with his blond hair and light brown eyes. He was invited to the best events and traveled in the highest circles. The Marquess of Sloanestone had no legitimate children, and treated his bastard son better than most peers treated their legitimate firstborns. He'd even given him part of his name for the birth certificate.

Too bad he was a bastard. The entailed estates would pass him by and revert to a cousin when the marquess died.

"Deville is Grandien's bastard," Timtree said to Parley.

"That much is obvious, Timtree. You'd have to be blind not to notice," Sloane said wryly, as Parley sniffed his response.

Sebastien had long since learned to mask any feelings provoked by such comments. "Damn shame, as it prevents me from telling him what an ugly troll he is."

Timtree cackled. There was no love lost between himself and his father, Baron Tewks. He and Sebastien shared that trait, unlike Sloane.

A butler welcomed them inside, and along with Bateman, they followed the man into a great hall dripping with gold. Vast Corinthian columns and tall arches soared above.

"Capital," Timtree uttered, jaded eyes firmly in place.

Bateman scrutinized everything, his eyes chronicling the wealth. Parley was trying hard to portray the priggish man that he was, pretending a nonchalance that everything in his vicinity was beneath him. Sloane looked perfectly at ease, which made sense since he lived on the extensive Sloanestone properties. But there was something in his eyes as well. Desire. Or maybe hope.

Sebastien surveyed the surroundings through a narrowed view—the gilt knobs, the frescoes that showed scenes of conquering armies and ruling deities. He had been surrounded by gilt and glitter his entire life—never quite touching it, always out of his reach.

He had never been inside the duke's main country estate, his *sire's*, but he knew it rivaled this one. He stamped out any traces of extraneous emotion, and kept a dark smile on his face, a long history at the card tables making the expression natural and usually unnerving.

The butler led them to the grand library. Several gentlemen were standing by the long row of windows overlooking the sidegrounds. He saw the duke holding court in a chair near the back. Their eyes met and held, before Sebastien continued his perusal of the guests. The Tipping Seven were here in force, their bastards and spares present or trickling in behind him. As Timtree said, a pony show indeed.

His pride, the only thing he could call his, twitched.

"What's this? A bunch of bastards wearing their hopes on their sleeves?"

Sebastien kept his hand in motion, fiddling with the watch at his pocket, not allowing his muscles to stiffen any more than they already had. He slowly turned, rage forming and then sliding, shoved, beneath a simmering pool.

"Lord Benedict. How . . . lovely."

Benedict raised a brow. He might take after his mother in most physical aspects, but his brows were pure Grandien. A mirror of Sebastien's own. "Surprised, Deville?" He smirked. "I see my father forgot to mention to you that I would be joining the merriment. Sad that they felt the need to include *natural* sons. Heard it was Sloanestone's provision."

Timtree snorted. "I heard it was because the stock was so poor in the crop of thirds and fourthies that they wanted to bring in some real contenders."

Benedict inspected his cuffs. "Your father barely even rates on the social scale, Timtree. Do mind your manners."

Timtree simply laughed. "You know even less than I credited, and believe me, I hadn't credited you with much. Come, Deville, brighter pastures beckon."

"Yes, run away, Deville," Benedict whispered as Sebastien passed with Timtree. "Do it before you completely embarrass yourself."

Sebastien turned and walked backward for a few steps, saluting Benedict in a base manner. "Because I so often embarrass myself where you are concerned. Ta, Benny," he said, refusing to address him properly. "I look forward to the competition in a way I hadn't quite expected."

They passed the plinth in the center of the room, a mountain of documents meticulously stacked on top. Real. Sealed water-tight. The rewards of the games laid out and present. If he won he would gain a great deal. Power. Revenge. Satisfaction.

His mother's land. Benedict's humiliation. Revenge against his sire.

"Gentlemen, may I have your attention." Cheevers raised his hands imperiously. "Welcome to Meadowbrook. My distinguished friends and I are anxious to begin this unique and extraordinary competition. We will hold the majority of the games here on the estate, though we will be venturing to London for several games, since many in Town are privy to the competition and wish to observe some of the exploits. You are all aware of the prizes, but there are rules to review before we begin. If you agree to compete, you will sign the sworn statement to abide by the terms set forth. The terms are all or nothing. You don't make the rules, you follow them. Is that understood?"

No one spoke, but the charged air said that everyone was listening.

"Various games will be involved. Everything

from shooting to gambling to boxing to studies. We seek a well-rounded gentleman. A Renaissance man. You will be put to the test. You will be ridiculed. You will be celebrated. Every participant who makes it to the end will receive an award. Each winner of the various games will receive monetary compensation. But there can be only one true winner."

Sebastien knew that every man in that room expected that he or his progeny would be the victor.

"Points will be tallied from each game. If you dip below a minimum level in either the individual games or in the overall score, you *will* be ousted from the competition."

Murmurs swept the room.

"Furthermore—" Cheevers gave a swift shake to his head, blond hair settling above light eyes. "Cheating will be punished swiftly and severely. If you are caught cheating you will be immediately ejected, and any persons involved will be dealt with as well."

Sebastien watched the older men. The smirks that appeared told him everything he needed to know. Cheating was *expected*. Getting caught was not.

"There are fifteen participants. Winning an event is worth twenty-five points. Second place receives twenty, third equals fifteen, fourth receives twelve, and so on until the two last contenders receive zero. Once the third game begins, a competitor with less than five points will be eliminated. That level will be raised five points, and then ten, as we cycle through to the end, until only those with a score over one hundred will be eligible."

One man cleared his throat. "What if no one is above one hundred points, my lord?"

"Then you are all worthless."

The older men laughed. Few of the younger did—thirds and bastards alike.

"The winner has the chance to forge his own destiny—to carry on the family tradition in a new way and on his own. Winning should prove that man up to the task."

Silence.

"The terms are all here, if you haven't read the documents already."

Some of the men walked forward, Bateman among them. Sebastien watched his eyes shift back and forth over the words and was close enough to hear the conversation, hushed so as not to reach the older men on the edges of the room who had already started to place bets.

"Two thousand pounds a victory. Is that all?" Bateman groused.

"Forty thousand pounds to the ultimate winner and a producing property in Yorkshire, along with four other properties with moderate income. Enough to keep a man's pockets full."

"For one card game, perhaps. Especially for you, Petrie."

Vicious snickers ensued.

"What's this? A bride? Already selected?"

"What difference does it make? Any woman will do. Doesn't much matter."

"Ambitious of you," Timtree drawled, his voice carrying.

"Chew my boot, Timtree."

"It's a bit rough on the leather, man. I prefer shinier fare."

Someone whistled. "Look at this." The sketch of Roseford was in his hands. "Beauty of a place."

Benedict's face became a study in gleeful malice as he peered at the drawing. He smirked at Sebastien. "A bit small, but the property is adequate. I'll enjoy tearing down the house when I win."

Murderous impulses rushed through him. Only if he was crippled and on his deathbed would he let Benedict win.

Sebastien looked to the edges of the room as the participants began to squabble. He curled, then uncurled his fingers, unwilling to let Benedict draw him into a scuffle this early. There were more formidable enemies in the room.

The older men watched with avaricious eyes. The duke's stare was amused as he met Sebastien's, then shifted eyes to Benedict, who had strode over to speak with Thomas Everly, another third son. The bitter, hollow place expanded. Revenge. It was the only thing that filled the void. If he won, two years from now things would be different. He would make things *very* different.

"Deville, what the devil are you doing? Look over the terms, man," one of the illegitimate sons said. The contestants had started shifting, legitimate thirds and fourthies to one side, bastards to the other. Factions already in place, even in a competition that was completely every man for himself.

"I've already seen them," he answered indifferently, absently watching Lord Cheevers leave the room.

The terms were well laid out. Implacable for all parties concerned. The problem was that the terms never told the whole story.

"Good, you're here on time," the earl said to Caroline as he strode into the study. He cast a critical glance at her clothing. "And at least you have on a clean dress today. The other night you looked as if you'd bathed in charcoal."

She wiped surreptitiously at her pristine skirt. Thank God the earl hadn't peered too hard at the marks. *Fingers gripping her thighs, hands touching her everywhere.* The evidence of her failure to keep herself in line. Perhaps she was destined to repeat her mother's mistakes. Her *own* mistakes now.

"A mishap, as I told you."

"Borrow some of Sarah's dresses. Should have had you fitted for better garments. Puttering around with the villagers has turned you into one."

She lifted her chin; the initial taunting words of the man from Roseford ran through her head. "I have a few appropriate dresses. I didn't realize I was to be present for the events today until a footman delivered your orders."

"I told you to be prepared for everything. You refuse to listen. But you can stay in your cottage today after you report to Lady Tevon. She has some tasks for you. She'll tell you when you need to be here." His eyes narrowed on her before he rifled through some papers. "I expect you to follow her instructions."

"Of course." Lady Tevon was easily led if she thought a plan was her own idea.

"And I have need of your help in arranging the last two games of the tournament. There will be a large amount of work involved and the villagers will need to contribute."

"Of course I will help."

"I expect no less."

She continued to stand in her place. Something had switched inside her at Roseford when she'd let the dam free. She would not let bottled anger direct her actions, but instead use guile to convince Cheevers to her way of thinking.

The earl looked up and watched her. "You did a good job with the sketch, if I didn't tell you the other night," he said gruffly.

He hadn't, and it made her swallow to feel the absurd gratefulness well inside her. "Thank you."

He inclined his head and turned back to his papers. "Off with you," he said, but there was no edge. It was a start.

The gathering quickly grew tedious. The younger men postured. The older men postured. Sizing up the competition, as he did in every card or dice game, Sebastien quickly discarded most of the posturing males of the younger generation. The competitors that mattered were Sloane, Timtree, Everly, Benedict, Parley, and Bateman. Three bastards, three legitimate sons. With him included, there was a slight edge to the illegitimate side of the board. The other participants would be weeded in due course.

A tittering noise drew his attention to the hall, where a number of women were doing their own posturing. Impetuous companions and flashy widows. Women who had been invited to the estate before the games began and before the heiress and the more high-minded society guests joined them socially. Another sort of sport.

The women entered and began making the rounds of the room.

"Sebastien, dear. How good to see you," Harriet Noke cooed.

Sebastien looked over the saucy widow. She was always dressed in the latest fashions, the tilt of her head both inviting and demanding. "Harriet."

"I knew you'd be here." She placed a gloved hand on his arm, stroking the material gently beneath. "I expect you to win, of course. I have a hundred pounds on you to win the first game."

He regarded her, more than familiar with her tactics and flattery. "Money well placed."

"If you should need . . . advice." She tipped her head. "Do come see me." Her almond eyes were smoky.

He lifted her fingertips from his arm, stroking beneath them in a visually apparent way, watching Benedict's rage grow from the corner of his eye. "Of course."

She sashayed away, and he dealt with a repeat performance from three of the other women. Tiresome. The same faces. The same overtures. The same pat, tittering responses. No risk. No adventure. No challenge. Not even Benedict's jealousy could perk his mood.

While some flighty bird twittered about her new bonnet, he surveyed the room again, watching the women and men work their charms. Or lack thereof. Movement in the hall focused his attention as three women walked into view.

Lady Sarah Pims. The bride. Plain. Meek. She was likely to wither away under marriage to any of them. Not that he particularly cared about her feelings, but she wasn't a glorified debutante, sashaying her way through the parties and begging to be taken down a peg. He'd left her alone in London. He'd likely leave her alone in marriage as well.

Lady Tevon, Cheevers's mistress in London, was at her side. Good. The willowy siren from Roseford wouldn't be in Cheevers's bed then. Lady Tevon took Sarah's arm in a commanding manner and the girl's head dropped, like a horse broken too early to the saddle.

The third woman wore a plain blue dress, one at odds with the sumptuous materials on fervent female display, and stood at the edge of the door, just outside of full view. Ladies' maids rarely interested him—they made poor conquests. Then again, the woman from Roseford could have been a ladies' maid, or more likely a governess. She'd been too cultured to be a scullery maid, for all his taunting.

The blue-frocked woman stepped farther into the frame of the door, and a drum started to beat under his skin. A low hum vibrated in his blood. Her shoulders were firmly set and she was arguing with Lady Tevon, a feat that would have earned his attention alone.

But her familiar features, her carriage, the expression on her face . . .

Impassioned. Determined. High cheekbones, delicate jaw, straight nose. Classic lines. Blonde hair pinned to her crown in a coronet. A restrained young queen, but for the lock of wavy hair that threatened to break free with every decisive movement of her head. But for the common garb she wore. But for the fire that broke beneath the ice.

He knew that her eyes were a tumult of blue and gray. Entrancing.

She said something to the heiress and strode off. The meek girl perked up, showing real enthusiasm for once, and followed behind. Lady Tevon looked disgruntled as she trailed in their wake, both attendants to the blonde's tow.

He smiled slowly, ignoring the other women vying for his attention, picturing that one lock of wavy hair joined by a waterfall of more, pins falling at his feet. Freed from every confine like passion from a Puritan cage.

Yes, another sort of sport indeed.

Chapter 5

◁─◦○◦─▷

The first game begins today. Do not fret, Dear Reader, that we will not bring you the latest news and standings, for we are determined to do so, even if it requires a transformation into a lark or chickadee in order to accomplish the task. London is in an uproar over anything and everything to do with the tournament. One can only imagine the spectacle taking place at this very moment . . .

"What the devil is this? This isn't mine."

"Well, it isn't mine, you arse," someone answered Bateman in an equally strident voice.

"How poetic. Why they have allowed such riff-raff into civilized society, one will never know." Benedict's world-weary tones added to the unpleasantness of Sebastien's afternoon as he strode into the overflowing stable yard.

After putting his valet on the scent last night, he had been told that his lovely little blonde would be joining them for the day. He had thought the day was looking up until she had failed to show to the breakfast table. Then he'd seen the remnants of some type of substance in the bottom of his teacup, luckily before he'd had a taste. Two other men hadn't been as lucky. They were hugging chamber pots currently, and didn't seem to be in any hurry to separate from their newfound ceramic companions. The late risers had studiously avoided drinking anything after that.

And now this. Whatever *this* was.

Bateman's strident voice continued to yell, "What do you mean by putting this rubbish on Prancer? A navy blanket?"

He reached his own mount, Herakles, and saw what the commotion was about. There was a patterned blanket—garish in its mix of colors—on his horse's back, underneath an equally foreign saddle. Herakles threw him a look full of disgust and stepped irritably from side to side.

Sebastien stroked his nose, letting the horse nudge into the caress. "I think we've found Prancer's blanket, don't you?" he murmured. He called a stable hand over.

"Someone has switched them all," Timtree drawled as he joined him. "A prank. Probably Petrie, the puck."

Sebastien looked at Petrie, Valpage's third son, and wasn't so sure. He looked as irritated and baffled as the others, and he was the type of man who couldn't hide anything on his face—one of the reasons he was so terrible at gambling.

The grooms bustled about trying to figure out which tack went with which horse, obviously confused as to how such a thing could have happened. Whoever had done this had done it well.

As it turned out, more than just the tack had been swapped. Each blanket *and* each saddle had been exchanged. It took two grooms to negotiate each one. One to remove the saddle, one to grab the blanket. Then they had to find the correct horse and switch those with the correct tack. Repeating that process more than a dozen times took well past an hour. It was another half hour before each horse was cinched into the correct equipment, and each rider was satisfied.

Unlike straight cheating, this maneuver had affected everyone. He gazed around the yard wondering who had done such a thing, and whether it was going to be an isolated incident.

"An idiotic prank of yours, Deville?"

Benedict approached, and Sebastien wondered if the day was ever going to get better.

Dear God, dear God, dear God. The prayer was a litany in her head as she peered through the fronds and watched the demon from Roseford inspect the crowd.

A participant. In the games. All the information she had pieced together about him at Roseford—his conflicting actions and words—barreled together. She had thought him a spoiled and world-weary son, one who might be hiding depths that only required some careful uncovering. But this . . . his words and actions were explained in a much different manner. Spoiled became bitter, world-weary became jaded. Hidden depths became hunger. He was a man who believed himself above the rule of others.

He had utterly seduced her. She had *let* him.

Her nails dug into her palms. The overtly sensual man started speaking with a participant with a hooked nose, then a third man with brown hair and an entitled swagger joined them. She pulled back, closing her eyes.

Skilled hands and haunting words.

The man had given her plenty of clues to his involvement, if she had but listened. Nothing specifically stated, but he'd known that Roseford was a prize, he'd reacted to Cheevers's name and obviously had known the duke. She should have put it all together.

She peered through the fronds once more, watching the tableau and trying to keep her eyes away from *him*.

The rest of the men were milling and squeaking. Just as she'd thought. A bunch of men who hadn't a thought in their heads but to squawk like chickens. There were three or four that held themselves admirably, but that one man . . . the man from Roseford . . . He stood to the side with his beast of a horse, stroking the horse's nose, alternately arguing with the brown-haired man and watching the scene unfold.

A gambler. She'd bet her eyeteeth he was a gambler.

Rotten gamblers. Rotten luck. Rotten choices.

She worried her lip.

"Caro, what are you—" Sarah gave a squawk as Caroline yanked her into the bushes.

"Shhh! I'm examining your suitors," she whispered, trying to keep her heartbeat steady.

"Hardly my suitors," Sarah whispered back.

Caroline could hear the grimace in her voice, but she kept her eyes firmly on the spectacle. They kept straying to *him*, and she forced herself to focus on the others. She couldn't lose sight of her goal here, even if everything in her said to run far away.

Sarah scooted in and peered through the opening. "What are you doing? We can simply walk over—"

"We'd never be able to observe them in the same way." And there was no way she was going out there now that *he* was there. She tried to think of a way to leave the county instead.

"And why do we need to observe them?"

"I'm looking for weaknesses."

Sarah's brows shot straight into her hairline. "Weaknesses?"

The men started moving, the saddle situation having apparently been resolved. It had taken a solid hour though, much to Caroline's delight.

Caroline moved her head back and forth to get a better view. "So what can you tell me about them now that they are nearly all present and accounted for?"

Sarah pressed in next to her as the men mounted and queued up in line. "That is Marcus Sloane. The golden one there." She pointed to one of the men who held himself confidently. "The *ton* loves him. He has a fortune and could have married well four times over by now. It's the title that is driving him here—it has to be. He's the son of the Marquess of Sloanestone." She lowered her voice. "Illegitimate."

Caroline gave her an amused look. "From what I understand, at least half of them are. You can just say it Sarah. He's a bastard."

Sarah's eyes went round and her cheeks pinked. "Caroline!"

"What about that one?" She pointed to a decently fit man with an avaricious and intent expression. He was the type of man that made her hackles rise.

"Mr. Bateman. Browett's ba—" Sarah struggled for a second on the word. "Oh, drat it, the Earl of Browett's natural son."

Caroline smiled and continued to catalog each man in her mind, noting weaknesses as Sarah described them.

"Lord Benedict Alvarest and Sebastien Deville." Something in Sarah's voice made her turn toward her friend. There was a strange expression in Sarah's eyes.

Caroline was surprised. "Don't tell me you have a tendre for one of them?"

Sarah quickly shook her head. "No, no. But Sebastien Deville, he's . . . well, look at him. Looks just like the duke, and there never was a more sought-after man in the *ton* than the duke, I'm told."

The duke. Caroline reluctantly looked to where she was pointing, already heaving an inward sigh at who she knew it would be. Of course. Rumors and gossip swirled through her head. "He is minorly handsome, I suppose, in that rakish way some women enjoy," she said grudgingly.

It was Sarah's turn to look amused. "Really,

Caro. The man is deadly handsome. And dangerous." Her smile died. "He has ruined a good many of society's darlings. I'd be surprised if you hadn't heard of him. It's a wonder that he hasn't been ostracized from the *ton* completely. I'm sure the duke, his father, has something to do with that. Though there seems to be no love lost there. A peculiar situation, and all the more fascinating for society."

"I'm sure he revels in it." If she had seen him for the first time right now, with the easy, focused way he stood, she might not think so, but with the cutting way he had spoken of the duke, and his actions at the Grange with her . . .

His reputation preceded him. She had heard of him from the gossip sheets. Even Lady Tevon had spoken of Sebastien Deville in deliciously scandalized tones. Spinning tales and delivering secretive glances.

"And the other one?" Her voice was already weary. She was in deep, deep trouble.

"Lord Benedict Alvarest is the third son of the duke. Legitimate."

She watched the two men interact. "They don't seem to like each other much."

"An understatement. They loathe each other. Only a few months separated in age—you can imagine the gossip that caused. Lord Benedict is *entitled* to anything he wants. Deville *gets* everything he wants."

"Sounds like a pleasant pair. Not sure which one is worse, though if I had to place my bets, Deville seems like the more dangerous." Everything about him fairly screamed it, and the sum of her experience with him confirmed it. "The legitimate sons always have a chance at their fathers' titles if something happens to the heirs ahead of them. Lord Benedict is probably high on the earl's list, as a potential heir to a dukedom too."

Sarah didn't respond, and Caroline cursed herself for thinking aloud. Her words could be interpreted in a manner she hadn't meant. "I'm sorry, Sarah, that was thoughtless. What I meant by that—"

"No." She shook her head. "I know. But it *is* just what you said. Lord Benedict, Everly, Petrie, they are potential heirs and men about Town. Men that wouldn't be interested in me, under other circumstances."

"Don't say that. Of course they would. They will," she amended.

Sarah's chin lifted. "For a match with Father, maybe. For good breeding stock as a daughter of an earl, maybe. But not for *me*. I know it. You weren't there this season, Caroline. The matches I *could* make weren't good enough. The matches Father wanted me to pursue weren't remotely interested in me. The silent, mannerly girl my mother raised just isn't interesting to most men. Look at Father. How many mistresses has he had? I'm just surprised he doesn't have a bastard out there competing in this tournament." She smiled a thin smile. "Though that would remove me from the competition then."

Caroline swallowed. "And the earl thinks these men better than ones you could choose? Men like Deville and Bateman?"

"He was nice to me once."

Caroline couldn't credit that she could be talking about *him*. "Which one?"

"Deville."

A tiny bit of anger that felt an awful lot like a worse emotion threaded through her. "He was likely trying to worm his way past your skirts, Sarah," she said pragmatically, trying not to wince. It was obviously one of the man's traits.

"Caro!" she admonished. Her expression turned thoughtful. "No, I don't think so. I don't rate on his scale of regard. You should see him in action at a *ton* event, Caro. It's—" She shivered. "I can tell you that nearly every unmarried lady fancies him to some extent. Wishes that for just one night . . ."

Caroline grimaced, the notions striking too close for comfort. "Lovely."

A smile cracked Sarah's face. "Oh, of course you wouldn't be taken in, Caro. But he veritably prowls the rooms. And he is everything that the other men are not. It makes things so simple for him. I can't believe no one has eloped with him, though he seems as far from marriage-minded as a man could get."

"It sounds as if he has the *ton* firmly in his grasp." Irritation ran through her at the games he obviously played. At the one he'd played with her, not that she'd been an unwilling participant, but all of a sudden there was something personally stinging about it. "Little reason for him to participate here."

"No. It is the opposite. He is an outsider, only occasionally invited to the best parties, and only when someone is hoping for a scandal. The duke has never firmly sponsored him."

"But you said—"

"Don't ask, because I don't understand either. It is something none of us do. But being an outsider—it just adds to his allure, don't you see? The debutantes drop like flies. The older married women do as well. Scandal simply swirls around him."

Caroline muttered under her breath.

"As much as I can joke about all of the women wanting him in their beds—" Sarah's knowledge of the marriage state had Caroline silently cursing the earl and his steady stream of mistresses. "I—I can't—" She looked away. "I don't want a marriage like my parents. Mother was miserable."

Caroline remembered the pasty-faced woman the earl had married. The oldest daughter of a duke, she had been secured for power and property and then been disposed of at Meadowbrook.

"Sarah—"

"No." She took a deep breath. "I will do my duty. Forgive me my weakness?"

Caroline took her by the arms. "It's not weakness. I . . ."

If only she hadn't made the mistake with Patrick . . . she might have been able to help Sarah in London . . . to prevent this fiasco of a contest from occurring. She could have begged the earl to let her go as Sarah's companion. Could have . . .

She shoved the thoughts firmly away. She had a chance to make the right decision this time, to help Sarah, and she would.

Caroline slipped an arm around her. "Things will work out. I won't let them work out in any way other than the best for you."

She'd keep her away from the likes of Sebastien Deville. Make sure that he and his kind did not win.

"How?"

"With magic, if need be." She gave her a bright smile, which Sarah tentatively returned.

Sarah turned back to the spectacle. "Oh no. There's Lady Tevon." Lady Tevon searched the crowd, features furrowed.

Sarah tugged the sleeve of Caroline's dress. "We should join them. Or else she will bring Father's attention to my absence and he will be displeased with me."

Caroline opened her mouth to tell her to go ahead, but Sarah's pleading gaze stopped her. Reluctantly, she nodded. It was way too late for recriminations. Way too late to avoid her fate.

As soon as they emerged from the grove, Lady Tevon's face cleared and she beckoned them over. "Lady Sarah, where have you been?"

"I was walking with Caroline while the grooms readied the horses."

Lady Tevon shot her a look of disapproval. "Mrs. Martin, I thought we had come to a thorough understanding of how best to improve Sarah's chances."

Chances for unhappiness? she wanted to respond. "Yes, Lady Tevon," she said instead, her voice sounding thoroughly chastened, even if it was because of another event entirely.

"We were here before the game began," Sarah said in her quiet way.

"Fashionably walking in at just the right moment," Caroline added with as much spark and innocence as she could muster.

Lady Tevon frowned, nodded, then switched her gaze back to Sarah. "Well then, I suppose that is good. But be careful in the future. You don't want the competitors to think you are hiding from them, do you?"

Caroline had the distinct impression as they patted their horses, made ribald jokes, and eyed the available women that most of the competitors didn't even notice Sarah's presence, nor did they care—more fools they. Sarah was a prize far greater than these men deserved.

Her eyes collided with a whirlpool of aquamarine, and suddenly she could hear nothing above the hammering of her heart, the beat of her bell tolling, the promise of a painful death as she looked into Sebastien Deville's eyes. A slow smirk curved his mouth as one hand absently played with his horse's reins.

Sweat broke along her brow. She gathered every last reserve and purposefully turned away.

"Well, Lady Sarah, at least you show a little more spirit with Mrs. Martin around." Lady Tevon pinned Caroline with a glance. "See to it that she chats with the competitors. Nothing like adding a little incentive to the proceedings."

Lady Tevon tried to inject some excitement into the statements, but unfortunately, she didn't even look like she believed her own words.

Why no one could see the kind, beautiful girl beneath Sarah's calm demeanor, Caroline didn't know. It seemed obvious to her, but then people rarely looked beneath that which they wanted to see.

Caroline nodded to Lady Tevon, smoothing her hands over her dress in an effort to calm her body. "The party should prove a perfect venue to do so." Should she survive the week, *the day*, with her already spotty reputation intact, the party would be a perfect venue to see which competitors she would allow to continue, and which ones she would seek to crush. There was one man already firmly on the latter list.

"Quite so." Lady Tevon definitively agreed. "The men will be strutting after the game this afternoon."

"Line up," a voice shouted.

The fifteen riders trotted into place at the starting line. She tried to catalog each of their expressions, but her eyes continued to wander to Deville sitting on his horse, perfectly still, waiting.

A crack sounded and sixty hooves beat down on the earth. The riders galloped over the flat expanse, leaning forward, the best horseflesh and most skilled riders breaking away from the pack as they rode harder. Deville was in the front with three others—the golden Sloane, Lord Benedict, and the hook-nosed man Sarah had identified as Timothy Timtree. Deville's horse took a tight turn and he held out a gloved hand to a branch. He must have caught the ring, because a few of the riders behind veered off to the other side.

Caroline had walked the course earlier looking for opportunities—the circuits of the wide expanse were useless, but the forays through the forest paths had held promise. Rings were placed throughout, so that more than one participant could gather them. Two riders riding together could each grab one from a different side and break even. The men who had set the course would be baffled if they could see the rings now, however. Some were hanging in *slightly* different homes.

She had heard the excited stable hands talking about a complicated calculation between the time one finished the race and the number of rings collected. The calculations hadn't interested her, but the stable hands' undivided attention on one another, and *off* the stalls, had. Her helpmates had encountered no trouble completing their tasks.

"What are they doing?" Lady Tevon peered through a pair of opera glasses.

"I believe they are looking for their second rings. They seem to be encountering difficulty doing so." Caroline tried to rein in her self-satisfied smirk, she really did.

The men moved along the field, jockeying for position as they madly searched the area where the rings should have been prominently displayed.

Sarah gave her a questioning glance, then raised her own glasses. Caroline raised hers too.

It was a mad field. Horses everywhere, men shoving bushes hither and yon. A few clueless ones scratched their ill-used noggins and wandered aimlessly. This was a favor to them really.

As either an early weed-out, or good practice for the hunt that would be held in a few weeks.

She wasn't surprised when Deville reached up to grab something. Bateman shoved sideways, nearly unseating Deville. Deville's horse buckled beneath him, but at the last moment he leaned back, the horse righted itself, and they sped off. Sloane's hand also closed around something shiny, and he too raced forward to the next thicket.

The rest of the pack raced after them. Midway to the next grove, one of the men turned sharply and galloped down the course, following the untampered-with markings.

"What is Mr. Timtree doing?"

"Smart man," Caroline murmured. "He saw the trouble they were having and has decided to forgo the points collected from the rings."

"What do you mean?" Lady Tevon demanded.

"The winner's score is a combination of race time and the number of rings collected. If it takes the others too long to collect the rings, Mr. Timtree can win purely by crossing the finish line first."

Another few men caught on, including Benedict, who raced after Timtree, eager to emulate his strategy.

Caroline saw Deville's eyes follow Timtree and Benedict. Deville could follow. It had been a rather brilliant move on Timtree's part. It was even possibly in Deville's best interests as he appeared to be a better rider. And Deville had two rings, so he'd be ahead of Timtree, and all the others who had followed him, in the standings for sure.

Deville's type always settled for the easy way out.

He shifted in the direction of the finish line. "I knew it," she muttered. Then his horse's head swung toward the next thicket, and horse and rider flung themselves inside.

She stood shocked, her mouth parting. A gambler. Definitely a gambler.

"I told you."

Caroline kept her glasses up, ignoring Sarah's low-voiced whisper as she anxiously searched the trees for movement. A few of the other men, including Bateman, blindly followed Deville. Sloane chose his own path.

A few terse minutes later, Deville's horse burst into the open. Sloane and Bateman pounded after him, the others on their heels.

Eyes intent upon their prey. The race continued, up, down, and around the course. The lesser riders began to lag behind or decided to take the easy way out, cross the finish line, and put themselves in the middle of the standings. The risk takers pushed ahead. When they reached the last two patches, which were near the spectators' area, Caroline cursed herself for becoming too predictable in where she had placed the rings. Deville seemed to zero in on them faster every time. She tried switching her eyes away from him, but couldn't.

He smoothly bent down and plucked another ring, shooting one of the other contestants a smirk as he cut in front, leaving the man swearing in his kicked dirt. He charged toward the next flag. Every line of his body at Roseford had shouted that he was a predator. Every press of his body to hers had proclaimed him a rogue. Every movement now confirmed both.

He leaned out from his horse, one long arm thrust out, and gripped another ring. His head flipped up as he regained his seat, long strands of hair arcing and settling messily across his face. Something hot and wild raced down her spine. He leaned against his horse's neck, man and horse racing as one. A shake of his head in the wind whipped the strands back into place as he shot toward the finish.

He was the breed of man to which she was most susceptible. She swallowed heavily. That much was obvious.

Arrogant, dark, and dangerous. She needed to remove him from the competition and her life as quickly as possible.

Sebastien rounded the last corner.

Herakles's hooves beat at the dirt, spraying it to the sides. He leaned right and snatched the last ring from the branches. He'd missed one when Bateman had shoved him for the third time. Bateman would pay for those tactics later. Sebastien heard Sloane's mount at his side, but he didn't spare a glance as they raced to the finish line. Everly shot in from the right and Bateman cut across.

Bateman was too far outside to give chase. He'd be third at best, if Timtree hadn't beaten them all, clever bastard. And Benedict had taken obvious advantage of the strategy, knowing he wasn't the best rider. If Benedict beat him in the first game . . .

Sloane and he were neck and neck for the finish. A fine piece of horseflesh there.

They crossed.

Cheers went up through the crowd.

Sebastien let Herakles slow and pulled around in an arc. He tossed the rings on the ground—seven. And saw Sloane do the same. Seven. Sloane gave him a grin, which he couldn't stop himself from returning, fire still running through his veins. Riding was one of the few things that reminded him that he was alive.

The older men all huddled together, fishwives clacking over their daily profits. Tallying times, rings, and scores. Sebastien patted Herakles and dismounted, allowing one of the grooms to take the animal for a cooldown.

The Tipping Seven seemed to arrive at a decision, as Cheevers turned to the waiting crowd.

"The first game, and why not end in a tie," Cheevers shouted. "Split the first and second place prize money and points. Well done, lads."

He shook Sloane's hand. First place, even shared, was perfectly fine. He'd overtake Sloane on some of the later games, of that he had no doubt.

Timtree and the closest finisher behind him, Benedict, took third and fourth. The top three finishers were all bastards—making the unofficial tally heavy to one side. He exchanged smirks with Timtree.

Timtree had almost beaten them all with his strategy. If Sebastien hadn't discerned the pattern in the way the rings had been placed—the most inaccessible locations that could be had—Timtree would have won. He knew Sloane had figured out the arrangement too. The others hadn't been as lucky, it seemed, merely following behind, hoping to catch one.

Everly and Bateman had each collected two rings—moving ahead of them about halfway through the course, before being overtaken again during a further search. They placed fifth and sixth.

"The prankster responsible for the blankets, saddles, and the rings . . . yes, good show, good show, but I will remind everyone that tampering with the games is an offense punishable by expulsion." There was a bite of steel beneath the earl's words. "The same goes for the unfortunate events this morning."

Harriet Noke's hand wound around Sebastien's shoulder and down his arm. "Congratulations."

"Not going to offer your congratulations to Sloane?"

"Mmm. Maybe later. I've always been more interested in dark than light."

"Yes, I seem to recall."

"Good. I hope your memory is as *long* as I remember it to be."

Harriet was a consummate woman of the world—one who knew how to maximize pleasure while taking precautions. And Benedict had fancied her for years—so any dalliance with her served multiple purposes. So why then was he utterly uninterested?

A flit of blonde drew his attention. The beautiful woman from Roseford stood to the side, hands on her hips, tart and sweet like the deceptively sugary confection she was.

His blood still raced from the ride. From the hunt. Fueled by the promise of more hunting on a different playing field, it was small wonder why the woman hanging on his arm held such little of his interest.

Lady Sarah whispered something to the blonde.

"Darling, don't pay the little bride any mind. No need to woo anyone in that quarter." Harriet pulled a long nail down his coat.

He shot her a look, half in amusement, half in irritation. Another woman came over, sizing up the competition. The increasing feeling of apathy crept over his skin.

Then the blonde looked directly at him. Blue eyes piercing him, straight nose sniffing to the side as she looked away. Not making moon eyes at him, not simpering and clinging, instead challenging him to walk over there and wipe that supercilious expression from her face. To make her pant and moan again, beneath him this time instead.

The hunting instinct, deep, fierce, and predatory, overtook him. His apathy pushed aside—no room for it to remain.

Her identity tickled his skin. He scratched the back of his hand as the two women in front of him squabbled over something ridiculous.

There was little to satisfy these days. Revenge, satisfaction, power . . .

The hunt.

Yes, the delicious hunt.

Chapter 6

∽◦◦◦∽

The tournament is London's, nay England's, worst kept secret, and everyone who is anyone is trying to gain entrance to the show. Invitations to Meadowbrook, the Earl Cheevers's elegant estate just outside London proper, are the most coveted items of the year. We here at the Times *are of the opinion that if they had chosen to hold the competition during the season instead of in the summer, the ballrooms would have remained empty, the punch bowls dry, the marriage mart disbanded.*

Or perhaps the mart would have simply moved to the estate . . .

A dozen servants hurried along a path in front of Caroline and Sarah. They split ranks at the maze, half heading toward the stables, half heading toward the village. Another three or four dozen milled about, fetching items and bringing refreshments to the guests who had spilled onto the back lawn of Meadowbrook.

And still she would be hard-pressed to say there were enough. The earl had hired a hundred more staff to help with the two-month tournament. Caroline had peeked into the estate ledgers and nearly swallowed her tongue at the expense column for the past week. And there were to be seven more?

Caroline walked with Sarah among the guests who were outside enjoying the day and taking advantage of the opportunity to curry favor with members of society who might just be moving *up* in the world. Some of the more serious contestants had retired to prepare, while others frolicked among their admirers.

It was hard to discern what was more the spectacle at the moment; the anticipation of the next game—a fencing competition that would take place in a couple of hours, with the contestants lapsing from boastful to nervous—or the social game being played in the halls and on the grounds.

A furious cricket match raged on the small pitch, with pall mall, quoits, and lawn bowl events taking place on the sides. A small minority of the women had joined in the latter three games, while a larger group cheered the cricket players. Others gossiped, sewed, painted, or put themselves on display. The remaining gentlemen were interspersed among them, exclaiming over art or the exquisite bearing and apple cheeks of a particularly attractive specimen.

"The house is fairly bursting," Caroline said. "I wonder when the earl will start putting guests in the cottage or the stables."

Sarah laughed, hand tucked into Caroline's arm. "Or double them up. Can you imagine?"

"No. I heard Mr. Tenwatty is renting rooms to reporters from the *Times*. Mrs. Tenwatty will drain the gossipmongers dry."

Sarah laughed. "I daresay you are correct." She tipped her head suddenly.

"What?"

"Oh. I thought Mr. Deville was looking this way."

Caroline's heart sped up and she stepped forward a beat out of sync with Sarah. "Is that remarkable?"

"When he is wearing an expression like that, yes."

"What expression?" she asked with as little concern as she could muster.

"One like a cat devouring a canary."

She waved, trying to keep her face from showing any of her unease. "Probably watching Mrs. Noke."

"But Mrs. Noke retired ten minutes past in order to change."

Caroline looked up at the windows seeking inspiration. A curtain blowing in an open window gave her none.

"Oh, there he is looking again," Sarah said, craning her head to find the source. "It's enough to make a heart leap."

Caroline determinedly kept her eyes forward. "Let's take a turn around the cricket match."

Sarah gave her a startled look—they'd just come from that direction—but let Caroline lead her forth again.

And there was Sebastien Deville, in their direct path, idly pretending to watch the match.

She switched directions, tugging Sarah around. "We should talk to Mr. Copley."

Sarah blinked, but followed.

Mr. Copley was a charming gentleman, but he seemed more interested in discussing philosophy and taking thoughtful pauses while staring into the distance and perhaps contemplating life than in making inroads with the bride. They moved on.

An indolent body and cleverly arrayed head of hair moved into their direct path again, and once more Caroline moved diagonally. "Perhaps we should talk with Mr. Copley."

"We just spoke with Mr. Copley, Caro. Whatever is the matter with you?"

"Silly me, I meant Mr. Yarking."

Mr. Yarking was a boor, a twiddle poop with a monotone voice and condescending attitude, who enjoyed listening to himself. If she weren't pretending so hard to pay attention to him in order *not* to pay attention elsewhere, Caroline wasn't sure she could have held as silent, nodded along so automatically. It made her even more annoyed with Sebastien Deville. To soothe her general irritation, she put Yarking on her incapacitation list, though she had a feeling she might as well not bother. Mr. Yarking wasn't a serious contender to win the tournament. He'd probably never leave his chambers if she installed a few servants there with the express purpose of asking him questions about himself.

Sarah gripped her arm in a sort of I-need-to-leave-before-I-scream manner, and they made their excuses and beat a hasty retreat.

"Well, my dear, if you marry Mr. Yarking, I can't say that you need be worried about extramarital affairs. Unless you consider him having an affair with himself as adultery."

Sarah snickered.

The cricket match ended, and they walked to view the quoits challenge. Blue-green eyes caught hers across the crowd, and she shivered. He was stalking her like prey, and she had no idea what he would do with her once she was caught—and it was only a matter of time. Even with the hundreds of guests and servants milling around the grounds, it felt like an intimate gathering whenever his eyes met hers. Would he boast to those assembled that he had had his wicked way with her days before? Or would he simply bend her back and repeat the experience again?

She bit her lip and tried to focus on something other than one particularly handsome, demonic contestant. Perhaps a tool to smite him instead.

She needed to find something, some overriding element that she could use to explain away future mischief. Something that she could use to take him out of the competition before he took her out of play.

Sarah began talking to one of the young women who had just arrived. A respectable, age-appropriate companion, unlike the women who had first made an appearance.

Caroline looked up at the open, curtained window with its flowing movement and diaphanous material. A ghostly form embracing the breeze.

A smile curved her lips. Brilliant. She slowly sidled over to a group of older women. All it would take was a seed, a little water, and then to sit back and watch the bloom.

Two men passed her as she neared the women, and she wrinkled her nose. The men weren't dressed as grooms, but their smell indicated a trip through the bowels of the stables. Her attention returned to her plan—something infinitely more exciting and better smelling.

Sebastien entered his room and immediately set to work on his cravat with one hand, while he shut the door with his other. The heavy, glittering colors surrounded him. The navy urging him to be upright and priggish, the gold loudly whispering about the opulent wealth that could be his, the burgundy pressing into him with its stunted sensuality, jaded and oppressed. He pulled the cloth away from his neck and threw it onto the chair for his valet, whose absence was unusual, especially when the man knew the schedule of the games. The second game would begin in an hour.

"Grousett?"

He walked toward the sitting room, stopping dead after five steps. The telltale smell of the stables, dirty and foul, hit him. He could hear his heart beating in the stillness, picking up speed.

He cursed loudly and sprinted to his locked chest. He fiddled with the lock, retrieving the hidden key, and threw back the lid. Pawing through the papers, he sighed in relief. They hadn't gotten in.

But the smell persisted. He spied loose papers on the side table, and his lips tightened. Standing up from his crouch, he walked toward them, somehow finding himself in front of the papers without feeling his legs move. The smell grew worse. His fingers hung an inch above the overturned top page, hovering. He curled his fingers into his palm. He didn't have to inspect them to know what he'd find.

Streaks drawn into the grooves and curves and lines. Into any letters. Into the fabric of the drawings.

A furious tapping finally registered.

He gave the ruined drawings one last look, then turned away and walked to the wardrobe. He yanked it open and a man and woman tumbled out, hands bound, rags in their mouths.

He tugged the rag from his valet's lips.

"Won't happen again, Mr. Deville," he said as soon as the cloth was free.

He narrowed his eyes and took in the maid's state of undress as well as his valet's. "You know what needs to be done, Grousett."

"Yes, sir."

Sebastien cut through his bonds. "When?"

Grousett untied the maid, and as soon as she was free she ran, stumbling toward the door, crashing into it before yanking it open just wide enough to slip around and slam it back closed.

"About half an hour ago."

Anger that had gone beyond heat and into ice collected in every limb of Sebastien's body. The perpetrator had either known he wouldn't come up until later, allowing the men to get a drop on his valet, or they'd meant to shove him into the wardrobe as well. Either way, the intention would have been to put him off his stride for the next game—or out of the game completely.

"Cheeky sons," the valet said, already putting his clothes back to rights. "I know exactly where to strike."

"Good. See to it. I'll take care of their master myself. Without subterfuge." He didn't have to ask who'd done it. He knew who'd done it. He knew how to fight back. Too many similar incidents at Harrow had hardened him, and taught him well. "Oh, and Grousett?"

"Yes, sir?"

It had been a sloppy job and far too familiar. The man had no style, though he certainly had an unerring accuracy for finding his weak spots to exploit. Probably had chuckled maliciously and thought of it as a warning. He should have remembered that Sebastien had stopped delivering warnings years ago. "Try not to be so far inside a maid next time as not to know what is happening around you."

"Lovely bit of muslin, sir. Hard to resist."

"No woman is worth that much attention." Forgetting gender, *nobody* was worth that much attention as to forget one's primary purpose. *You always have to look out for your own skin first. No one else will.*

"But the legs on that one—"

"Grousett?"

"Yes, sir. I know, sir."

No one would interfere with his goal.

* * *

Fencing was an art. One that was not Sebastien's best. But he had always admired the grace, speed, skill, and trickery involved. Sloane, with his renowned personal fencing master, was exquisitely gifted at the sport. Not even Benedict or Everly, with their own access to similar resources at Angelo's School of Arms, could compete on the same level.

The audience assembled around the twenty-foot square to assess the combatants and place bets as the competitors limbered their wrists, executed parrying and reposte combinations, and engaged in intricate footwork drills.

The Marquess of Sloanestone had an undeniably smug expression as lots were drawn for brackets.

Sebastien drew a lot from the heavy gold chalice; the oppressive lip of the metal formed spiked talons that led into eagle's claws along the sides. The parchment read "Troubadours" in a long script. Sloane's bracket. Bad luck, that.

But there were ten games to the competition, and every gambler knew that sometimes you had to lose a pot in order to gain a larger one.

He moved to the rear, watching as each man withdrew a lot in turn, grimacing or grinning as they compared them.

"Bards, over here. Troubadours, there."

Sebastien shifted to the left, eyes focusing on the women walking inside the room. On first glance, the large group appeared united, but a deeper look revealed a definite hierarchy, a slight splitting of the ranks, and Lady Sarah seemed to be separated near the back with the blonde at her side.

The women wouldn't be so blatant as to dismiss Lady Sarah outright, but the spillover from the season appeared in full effect, the heiress making little impact on either gender in her social circle yet. But here she walked a little straighter, seemed more at ease. He wondered if it was the blonde's doing. She seemed to carry an extra pole just for shoving up someone's spine.

Benedict, who was looking distinctly dark under one eye and sporting a cut lip to go with it, Bateman, and Everly all drew Bards. Parley, Sloane, and Timtree drew Troubadours to join him. The others, though some more skilled with a foil than his main competition, were mainly fodder. Even if they did well here, it would matter little in the overall context of the games.

Tough luck not to duel Benedict. Everly would surely win the Bards side of the draw and then battle Sloane in the championship bout. He'd have to continue their vendetta later.

The game began in earnest. One person from each side drew a name from the cup. Each bout was important in a single-elimination tournament.

Bateman, who used a bent-arm attack and exposed his target too often, went down quickly to Everly. Sloane took out Timtree.

"Two of them down." Parley's satisfied smile took on a sheen of smug superiority. The gold shimmers, the ostentatious glittering, reflected off his normally dull brown eyes.

Sebastien narrowed his eyes. A game within a

game. And the favor of this one to the legitimate progeny at four to two.

Sebastien reached into the remixed chalice and saw the scripted P along the edge of one folded piece. He drew the paper, handing it to Cheevers without opening it, his eyes seeking his prey.

"Deville versus Parley."

His eyes never left Parley as he smiled, the flattened, dead smile of a reaper simply doing his duty. Parley fumbled his priggish grip for a second, and Sebastien's smile grew.

"One to go, eh, Parley?" Sebastien whispered as he clasped the other man's hand in a too-tight grip. He abruptly let go and signaled with his blade. Parley held his at ready, only a small tremor showing his nerves.

Parley was a decent swordsman, but with none of the flair of Everly or the outright technique or skill of Sloane. He relied too much on fundamental postures, stances, and basic attacks, showing no individual style. Although his footwork showed adequate speed, he often moved forward without extending. Parry, parry, thrust, thrust. Sebastien started toying with him, darkly amused by the anxiety in Parley's eyes as it became more apparent that he would be the loser. Perhaps next time the man would think before he spoke.

Sebastien changed rhythm, moving forward on attack and catching Parley off guard. A flash of light suddenly caught the edge of his awareness. He parried Parley and made to thrust when the light caught him dead in the eye, momentarily blinding him. He could feel Parley step closer, could sense the crowd tipped in anticipation of a score, but the movement in front created a starburst of color surrounding a circle of white.

Something split the air, the blade slicing through the corona, and Sebastien feinted left, Parley's blade an inch from sliding along his stomach, hitting the air where he had just been.

He pulled his epee up and tagged Parley, the movement sending him out of the beam of light. A trick of tilted glass from the window, or something more sinister? He stepped back, allowing Parley to advance upon his seeming retreat. He allowed Parley to continually thrust him back, until the light hit Parley's face. The light was yanked away. Something more sinister then.

Sebastien stepped in for the kill, tagging him a final time, wishing, just a little, that the blades were untipped.

Parley ripped off his gloves at the sidelines as the next two took their positions.

"It wasn't fair. Something tried to blind me."

"Something *did* blind me, Parley. Get past it."

"You pushed me in the direction of the light then," Parley said, accusation and defiance dripping from his words.

"Of course I did," Sebastien explained in a way that a two-year-old might understand. "When you fight you use every tactic to your advantage. Someone deliberately reflected the light onto me. You simply moved into the path that was already there, just like a window's light. Your inattention was your disadvantage."

Parley's face turned even more mottled.

"What did you see?" one of the women asked the prig.

"White. Like a mirror."

"The ghost," she whispered. Another woman tittered.

Ghost? Women were such odd creatures sometimes. "It wasn't a ghost," Sebastien said. "It was treachery."

"The ghost was trying to disorient him," the one woman said to the other.

Sebastien clenched his fists, his patience nearly evaporated. He turned his attention to the pair dueling as the women whispered about spirits.

The competition continued on, weeding through the brackets, and in the second to last round, he finally met Sloane, who scored a preponderance of hits, and bowed out to him. Benedict was beaten by Everly on the other side of the draw, as expected. Benedict eyed him in mutual dislike. He and Benedict would be declared third and fourth depending on which man won the last bout.

The match wore on for what seemed like hours, Sloane gaining a single point while Everly claimed none. Sloane was clearly toying with Everly, evaluating his strengths and weaknesses. Sebastien leaned against the wall waiting for Sloane to win so that he could collect third. Another win to a bastard son. Another small victory, even if he wasn't the one to gain it. He saw the reflections on the other faces. The eagerness versus the tight-lipped disgust.

His eyes shifted to the blonde, watching with Lady Sarah in the corner. Her face held a look of fierce concentration as she watched.

All of a sudden a crack sounded, and Sloane's blade separated from its guard, clattering to the floor.

Everly attacked with hot greed, plunging in and striking Sloane for the point, taking advantage of his opponent's misfortune.

Sloane looked down at the broken epee in amazement. People began murmuring on the sidelines. Some arguing that Everly shouldn't be rewarded the point, others saying whatever it took to win was acceptable. Most seemed to agree with the latter.

"He's a cheat," Bateman slurred.

"He's the son of an earl!"

"Sloane is the son of a marquess. That trumps an earl."

"He's a bastard. And if there is any cheating going on, then it is on your side. Bastards all cheat," Parley proclaimed.

"Bastards all cheat? What is this? Wisdom from a third son, no better than a dog," one of the lesser-known contestants said.

Parley shook his fist. "Better than you, you mangy bastard."

"And what is this about 'our side'? The thirds and fourthies trying to stake a 'better than thou' claim on the competition?" Timtree cocked his head.

"Better than you," Parley said, looking ready to draw blood.

"How tiring you've become."

The fathers watched avariciously, which did little to improve Sebastien's mood over the ire already incurred by the legitimate sons' taunting.

"Everly won," yelled a contestant Sebastien had barely spared any mind.

"Everly scored a point, you dilettante fourthie, he didn't win," Timtree countered.

Irritated and annoyed by it all, Sebastien stepped in and handed his blade to Sloane. "Here. I've checked mine; it seems to be fine."

"Maybe you were the one who weakened his blade," Benedict said.

"Don't be an ass. As if I would sabotage Sloane instead of Everly, some cock-kissing third." He looked directly at Benedict, who went puce.

Voices erupted again, chaos embracing the room.

Caroline walked down the steps of the squire's house, a basket full of lemons in her arms, plans for the village celebration in her head, and sketches for the final two games dropped off with the assignments. There was extensive planning needed for both. They had successfully scheduled the village festivities to take place during the two-week break in the tournament. Cheevers had assured her that most of the guests would leave then. She hoped so, otherwise their small village celebration would be overrun with society guests, who had no business being there.

The party tonight would be overflowing with such people.

She grimaced. More and more she could see how the notoriety would help Sarah's social status in the future, but the idea that she could be saddled with someone like Deville for a husband didn't sit well.

No, she'd not argue the tournament outright,

but she would continue with her plans. First the saddles, then the blades, then the mirrors, then the ghost, then the trousers, then the . . .

She kept up a steady stream of planning as she walked through the valley and up the hill, looking at the ground in front of her without really paying attention. The well-traveled path from the village to her cottage was automatic. Her feet knew the path without her having to think about it.

It was a dangerous road she trod by altering the games. The first game had been a lark, a test. The earl hadn't so much as looked at her strangely when he'd talked about pranks or the switched items—he sometimes terribly underestimated women, which was to her advantage.

And with others sabotaging as well, and in more evil ways than she could ever dream, the culpability and guilt was spread.

She approached the Roman ruins near the top of the hill, tripping slightly over a small stone, her mind not on the path in front of her. A lemon rolled from her basket and hit the ground with a plop, a spurt of juice indicating a tear in the rind. She sighed and bent down to pick it up.

"A lovely view, but you'll lose them all, if you aren't careful."

Three more lemons spilled as she jerked upward to see Sebastien Deville lazily lounging on top of one of the stone arches above her. Shock tore through her in the same way the lemons split upon the rocks. Every memory, every touch and sigh, played through her mind. She forcibly strangled them into submission.

She swallowed heavily, gathering her defenses to the fore. "Have you no shame, sir? Those arches are over a thousand years old."

One leg swung indolently like a pendulum in need of winding. "As old as all that? Were you alive to see them built then? An old maid such as yourself?"

She narrowed her eyes. "Get down."

"Perhaps." He smiled, swinging his leg, relaxing on one hand. "I've been waiting for you, and now that I have this lovely view, just able to peek down the valley of your dress, I'm not sure I want to relinquish my vantage point in the least."

Her free hand automatically pressed against her chest. Everything in her that was sane told her to run, but her limbs seemed lethargically frozen in a parody of immobility.

He leaned forward, his hands splayed to the rock on either side of his thighs, rich brown hair falling into his eyes. "Now that wasn't a very nice thing to do to my view. Should we cast bones to determine whether I hop off or whether you resume the show?"

"I believe I shall abstain."

"From which?"

"From *both*."

"Perhaps you'd rather climb up here? We could test the sturdiness of the arch together." One side of his mouth lifted. "You put in quite the effort on the bench the other night."

Her cheeks burned. She reached down to gather the broken lemons. "I don't know to what you are referring. Good day, sir." She stepped forward.

"Do you really wish to leave?" he asked in a voice full of humor. "I'll just have to ask again in front of a crowd at the manor."

She stopped and turned back. "I can't believe I— You are a *wretched* man."

He smiled devilishly. "I believe you mean a *wonderful* man. I helped you with your sketch, after all."

"You took advantage of me."

"Such an ugly phrase. I prefer to think of it as persuading you to use my heavenly body to *your* advantage." His eyes dropped to her lips. "Which I'm pleased to say you did."

Her mouth dropped. She tried to utter any number of set downs, but nothing emerged.

"Catching the butterflies again?" He whipped the hair from his eyes with a jerk of his head. The lock slowly slid back. "Which shall it be? Are you coming up or am I going down?" There was a wry tug of his mouth. "I must say that both options sound appealing. I believe a toss of the dice may truly be in order."

"I dislike gambling," she said automatically.

"Dislike gambling? It is our country's favorite pastime."

"Indeed. Perhaps you should return to the house; there are plenty of horrid men there who will wager with you. Gambling your lots away." Gambling her *friend* away.

His fingers played over the stone. His eyes turned heavy and jaded. "A Puritan, Miss Sculler? Against all sorts of things? Like gambling, alcohol, the manner of one's birth?"

Anger pulsed through her, but at least he hadn't learned her name. Surprising. *"Mrs."*

"Married? Even better." One edge of his mouth curled.

He was in fine form today, as if truly happy to see her, which was ridiculous—he could no more care for her than she for him. His eyes were still shadowed and cynical, thankfully, which kept him from being undeniable. His flashes of spark and creativity intrigued her, but the set of his features, which promised he could turn derisive and cruel—his reputation only confirming that to be true—repelled. He reminded her too much of Patrick before he'd gotten himself killed by a vengeful husband. A charming scoundrel turned bitter and jaded, looking to move to greener pastures.

"Widowed," she said tersely, immediately irritated she had said anything at all.

"The news just keeps growing lovelier." His smile curved further. "And since you mentioned all of us sinners at the house, I can only presume to have the pleasure of the company of Caroline Martin, a long-distant relative who lives on the edge of the estate. Not much of a scullery maid after all."

So much for him not knowing her name. Her lips pinched. "Very good, *Mr. Deville*. Now if you don't mind, my Puritan spirit would like to return home."

A sinful pull of lips followed. "Now that we are all introduced, it would be a shame to part ways so quickly."

"I wouldn't find it a shame in the least."

"I'm not sure I believe you. Not after your body's reactions at Roseford." He stretched, his shirt pulling across his chest. "What is so important that you have to return home posthaste? Perhaps I may be of assistance."

Since she was plotting ways to destroy him, she doubted it. "I'm planning a midsummer celebration for the villagers. Do you care to speculate on the placement of the poles?"

A gleam entered his eyes. "I can speculate quite a bit on the placement of a pole."

She narrowed her eyes. "You are not a gentleman."

His smile grew more deadly, and his eyes hooded. "Never."

He stared at her. She stared back. She shifted but did not relinquish whatever battle of wills they were playing. "Was there something you wished, Mr. Deville? Or do you simply plan to annoy me this afternoon?"

He vaulted from the top of the arch and landed on cat feet, stealthy and sure. She scrambled backward, lemons scattering. Two steps brought him closer to her, and she stopped herself from taking a step back like a hare hunted by a fox.

"Have I frightened you, Caroline?" he asked innocently, but his eyes said he knew better.

"What a silly question. And I did not give you permission to use my name."

She crouched to collect the fallen fruit, never letting her eyes stray from his as she lifted each one.

He stepped closer. Lethal blue-green eyes

pinned her. Stalking her like prey. "You seem unsure of my presence. I seem to have a rather unsettling effect on your nerves."

"My nerves are perfectly steady." Her hands gripped the last lemon in one hand and the basket in the other. "I am simply tired, and being in your ghastly presence has made me long for a year's nap."

He put a hand over hers. She tried to pull hers away, but it was trapped in silk.

"Then why are you still here?"

"Your threats bullied me into staying. It is impolite of you to suggest otherwise."

"Excellent." And suddenly he was mere inches in front of her, leaning into her, a finger tipping her chin up. "Then if I were to kiss you, it would be impolite to resist."

The pad of his finger held her chin tipped toward his. Zings of sensation pulsed from the point. Trapped like the hare in the fox's net.

Her brain screamed for her to move. His face came closer, the aquamarine of his eyes glowing brighter as his head blocked the sun from view. A feeling beat in her throat, throbbing downward to deep within her belly, a conduit of charged lust and anticipation. A feeling that had long lain dormant before he had entered her well-regulated life, and had revived tenfold in magnitude.

"Mmm . . . I don't think you quite understand the picture you make at this very moment." His lips were a breath from hers, his voice low and deep. "Your eyes are nearly black with desire, the blue all but swallowed from within." The finger traveled down her chin, down her neck, to the hollow of her throat. Her head stayed perfectly still, as if he had sculpted her to the position.

His cheek brushed hers, his lips barely touching her ear. "Don't you wish to unlock that passion again, Caroline?"

"No," she whispered, unsure how she'd managed to do so.

"Are you sure?" The little whispers of air made every small hair in her ear and on her neck stand on end.

"Quite." Her heart thumped an erratic beat.

He pulled away slowly, the look in his eyes satisfied. Clearly disbelieving her. "I think I could take you here. Prop you up against one of these ancient pillars and drive into you until you bucked and screamed to the ancient gods for release. I think you would simply tip your head back and let me do untold things to your body and mind."

"Never."

He hummed something. "Yes, of course you wouldn't be passive. I'd hardly be interested in driving you against those pillars if you were."

She squeezed the lemon in her hand. "I meant that your scenario will never happen."

"That sounds like something of a challenge, Caroline. Are you attending the party tonight?"

She tried to hide her anxiety. An entire night of this cat-and-mouse game loomed before her.

"I'll take that as a yes." He smiled slowly and backed away step by step, still looking at her. Even stepping *away* from her, he was still the hunter, she the hunted. "See you tonight, lovely."

Chapter 7

Grown women were seen crying in the streets when they did not receive an invitation to the first ball of the tournament, which takes place tonight. It was this author's delight and distress to see a countess of great magnitude break down in the most fashionable Chattery Hattery milliner shop when informed that she had not made the list. Scandalous deeds are surely afoot tonight as the dark and charismatic personalities headlining this competition mix in social pursuit . . . where wolves and lambs play in a game where the lambs rarely win . . .

The local gentry and Town fashionable had turned out in full force for the gathering. Judging by the calculating gazes on the faces of the participants, Caroline had a feeling that a number of the more carefree country girls were going to be in for a tumble or two, if they weren't careful.

"Lady Sarah. It is a lovely evening."

The redheaded man sidled up to them, but his eyes never left Caroline, even as he addressed

Sarah. The earl's mocking words ran through her head once more.

"Mr. Everly," Sarah said, with the insipid smile she could never completely get rid of in social situations. "May I introduce my cousin Mrs. Martin."

He bowed, his eyes staying on hers. "Charmed."

She curtsied back and pasted a smile on her face. "Likewise, Mr. Everly."

"I saw you at the racing and fencing competitions with Lady Sarah, but don't believe I have had the pleasure before."

"I rarely venture to London." The poor choice she had made in running off with Patrick had guaranteed little reception in social circles. Only the earl's force in making Patrick marry her let her move in them now at all.

"No season then?"

"No, I married before my season might have taken place." She likely wouldn't have had a season anyway if the earl was to be believed. He hadn't been in the country at the time, part of the reason she had been able to make the choices she had.

"Ah. And your husband . . . ?"

Her pasted smile grew more strained. How she hated these games. And that this man was starting one in front of Sarah spoke volumes about his character. "Deceased."

He looked about as sad at that statement as she had expected. She increased the intensity of her smile. "So how do you come to find yourself at the estate playing for a chance at Lady Sarah's hand?"

His fake conciliatory look fell into surprise,

then discomfort at the switch of the conversation. "The fair lady Sarah is the most splendid prize," he said with a feigned smile.

"Very true, Mr. Everly." She smiled at Sarah, who was looking awkward and miserable. "Those who discover the truth of that statement will win a prize indeed."

Caroline feigned a look toward the other side of the room. "Oh, if you'll pardon us, Mr. Everly, Lady Tevon seems to need our attention."

"Of course," he hastened to say, suddenly looking quite eager to get away.

Sarah hurried alongside her as they walked away from her "suitor." "Oh, Caro."

"Hush. Come, let's find better company."

"Hardly possible in this crowd," her companion muttered.

"Poor Everly must be in terrible straits tonight to have chased you away that quickly, Lady Sarah, Mrs. Martin."

The dreaded voice.

They pulled to a stop and turned to see Sebastien Deville leaning against the back side of the pillar they were passing, hidden from previous view. A perfect spot from which to spy. A brandy snifter dangled from his fingertips.

"Good evening, Mr. Deville," Sarah said

Deville bowed low to her, giving her his full attention, unlike what Everly had done. "And a good evening to you, Lady Sarah. It's been weeks since I last saw you in Town. You are looking lovelier than ever."

Sarah's cheeks flushed with delight. Caroline

could feel her own heat in anger. Sarah did look quite lovely tonight. Lady Tevon, for all her other faults, had a marvelous sense of style and had done a nice job picking out a new wardrobe for her charge.

But how dare he attempt to work his false charm on Sarah.

"Thank you, Mr. Deville. You are looking in fine health yourself."

He smiled, a smile not quite edged in the same way as the ones he gave her, but she could see Sarah's color heighten further. "I find a good hunt will do that." Aquamarine eyes suddenly turned to her. "Mrs. Martin."

"Mr. Deville."

"I hadn't realized you two had met," Sarah said, switching her gaze between them.

"We haven't," she said in a clipped voice.

Deville smiled in a lazy manner. "Haven't we?"

"No."

"Pity."

"Come, Sarah, let's find Lady Tevon."

"Yes, *run* along."

She bristled, but pushed Sarah forward. Sarah didn't stumble, the innate grace that she had when she was comfortable saving her. Concentrating on Caroline, she had obviously forgotten to be nervous.

"Caro, what is going on? How do you know Mr. Deville?"

"An unfortunate circumstance, I assure you."

Sarah stopped in the shade of a potted plant, her knowledge of the ballroom giving them a mostly secluded spot. "Tell me."

Caroline waved a hand. "Our paths crossed. Foul luck, that."

Sarah's eyes searched hers. "Oh, Caro, you aren't falling for him, are you?"

"Pardon me?" she asked, shocked into immobility.

"Falling for Deville? Lord knows you wouldn't be the first."

"Sarah, dear, I would as soon fall for that Mr. Everly as Mr. Deville." She injected just the right amount of sincerity. She nodded internally.

"No." Sarah shook her head. "I don't think so. They are little the same type of animal, though Everly wishes they were."

"You *know* that I would not fall for Mr. Deville's sort."

Again went left unsaid.

Sarah worried her lip. "Of course, Caro, of course. But Patrick—"

"Was a mistake I do not intend to repeat. I've told you that." She turned to walk in the other direction, behind the row of plants, and found a man standing farther within the shadows, watching them.

"Can we not get away?" she muttered under her breath, though not low enough, it seemed.

The man held up his hands in surrender. "Forgive me, I didn't mean to eavesdrop, but I was here before you stopped."

Sarah's chin lifted. "That is—that is little reason to continue to eavesdrop."

Caroline, pleased with this reaction from her friend, watched the unknown man step into the light. He was pleasant-looking, straight brown hair, brown eyes. Friendly enough, if any of the men at this event could be deemed such.

"True, but I found myself most intrigued."

"Curiosity is not an excuse for ungen—ungentlemanly behavior." Sarah's chin stayed firmly in the air.

The man smiled and held out his hand. "I find myself without someone to introduce me, and a most firm desire to be introduced despite the impropriety. William Manning. My abject apologies, Lady Sarah."

Sarah gingerly took his hand. "Mr. Manning."

"And Mrs. Martin."

Caroline's irritation decreased a notch as the man returned his attention to Sarah. She couldn't detect any subterfuge coming from his quarter, but she would remain alert. Fortune hunters were always on the prowl, and she would have to discover his motive before any trust formed.

"Out of everyone here, I was most interested to meet you, Lady Sarah, and I see that interest was not misplaced." The words put Caroline on edge, but she still couldn't detect anything but sincerity from the man.

"Why would you find yourself interested to meet me?" Her friend looked baffled.

"You are part of the inspiration for this competition, are you not?"

Sarah lost a little of her spark. "I believe I am more of a side note."

William's head cocked to the side. "But not as far as the King is concerned, no?"

She looked startled for a moment, then her eyes

narrowed. "And why would you think that?"

He smiled. "I am merely an observer. An impartial judge, if you will."

Caroline had never seen William Manning before, but there was something familiar about him. She couldn't place her finger on it.

"You are not a competitor then?" She hadn't seen him in the ranks, but who knew what new deviltries were in store.

"Alas, no." He smiled.

This man was dangerous in a much different way. There was a feeling of peace about him. Of settlement. That he had searched inside himself and accepted what he'd found. And with those friendly eyes, he was the type of man to whom you spilled all your deepest secrets.

Sarah seemed to understand that too, as her face vied between wariness and hope. Wariness built from years of crushed interactions. Hope for another friendly face in this madness.

William's smile widened. "May I escort you ladies to your destination?"

Caroline made the decision based on instinct. "Yes. Perhaps you would escort us near the dance floor? The music is about to start."

And if he hurt her friend at all tonight she'd rip off his arms.

The humor in his eyes seemed to say that he understood this fully well. It increased her wariness as well as her comfort. An odd combination, to be sure.

He held an arm out to each of them.

"From where do you hail, Mr. Manning?"

"From London, but most recently from the Americas. Diplomatic matters for the King."

The room grew more crowded as the musicians tuned their instruments.

"How intriguing. Where did you travel?" Sarah asked.

Caroline kept an eye on her friend and their new acquaintance; at the same time she was searching the crowd, categorizing the behaviors of all the "suitors." Which ones needed to have a further eye kept upon them, which were inclined to drink or behave badly.

A long violin note heralded the start of the music and dancing. William Manning asked Sarah to dance, and they went merrily into the throng. A young man asked Caroline as well, but she declined, sinking into a chair near the matrons' area. A place to watch charges and catch up on the gossip.

A perfect place to make sure the flames of her plan were fanned.

The elder matrons rose, and a number of the more salacious middle-aged women took their places. A cross-section of neighborhood gentry and women of the town. All slightly scandalous.

"A good choice of suitors for Lady Sarah. Can you imagine Sloane as a peer? Any woman's dream husband."

"Sloane? No, Sebastien Deville." Another voice tittered. "Can you imagine what he would be like to come home to every night?"

"Except if you were married to him, it would be highly unlikely that *you* would be the one he would come home to."

"But having all of that attention on you even for an instant . . ."

"An instant is all it would be. Deville gives, takes, and goes on his way."

"I've heard that the giving and taking is worth every amount of the resulting pain."

"You should try him then, dear. Although he is very choosy. Surprising, given his avaricious nature with the debutantes."

"I can speak to his talents," said a sensual woman whom Caroline disliked on sight. Bold. The type of woman who attracted or repelled. "And I will speak to them again soon."

"Harriet, your overconfidence is tiring," another woman said. "I haven't seen him so much as look at you tonight. I think he has other prey."

"Who?" Harriet looked around as if there wasn't another option to her beauty or skills. She met Caroline's eyes for a second before moving back to the conversation. "Besides, he is going to win this competition. And I for one intend to ensure a place near him."

"Why?"

"Do you know what a man like that will do with the title and power he gains?" A thread of desire and greed wove through her words. "He'll move mountains."

"When has Deville shown any desire to be part of society? He loathes it."

Harriet shrugged, a secret smile curving her mouth. "You don't look beneath the surface. He'll win. Nothing will stop him from it."

Caroline begged to differ. She had a few well-placed plans to stop Sebastien Deville from winning.

"I still think Sloane has a chance. And Lord Benedict has just as much of a reason, if not more than Deville to win."

"And don't forget Timtree."

"Amanda, you just like Timtree because he tupped you in the rose garden."

The woman's cheeks tinged pink, but she held her head. "He showed good sense in the horse hunt."

"Yes, but what would he have done had the rings been in the right places? It takes more than cunning to win this type of competition."

A woman near her turned to another. "What is this about the right place?"

"The rings were not positioned as they should be. Declared to be a prank."

"Oh! And the epees too?"

"Likely a prank as well." The one woman turned back to the main conversation, but the other, the one closer to Caroline, looked thoughtful.

Caroline leaned toward her. "*I* heard it was the Cheevers ghost," she confided.

The woman's eyes widened and she looked around. "The ghost? The rumors are true?"

"Only the *best* houses have ghosts, of course. A mischievous spirit. I heard from one of the maids that she saw the ghost touching the blades and flashing a light. Lady Tevon said she heard it was spotted on the grounds of the hunt. And Mrs. Dalworthy mentioned seeing something ghostly in the halls."

None of them had said any such thing. Though that wouldn't matter an hour from now. Not with the setup she had created earlier, before the fencing competition, planting the seeds. A little water here and . . .

The woman's eyes turned speculative. "Of *course*. That must be what I saw last eve. And it makes so much *sense*."

Caroline nodded solemnly. "Be careful."

"Oh, I *will*."

And within fifteen minutes the conversation rippled through the assembly. "Have you heard? The house is haunted, it's true. More than ten sightings already. Mrs. Kitchner says a spirit was in her bedroom. And that it moved her silver brush while she was sitting *right* there."

Perfect.

The woman who had "started" the rumor had long since left and another had taken her place. She turned to Caroline. "A ghost. My word!"

Caroline put a hand to her chest. "Incredible!"

And the night continued on. She turned down dance after dance, while Sarah continued to accept them. It worked just as she planned, with the men who were coming to ask her to dance turning to Sarah instead. With her gentle movements and pinkened cheeks, courtesy of their new friend, Mr. Manning, who kept showing up at random intervals to spar with her, the other men began watching Sarah speculatively on their own.

The look on her face said that her London unhappiness was all but forgotten, at least for tonight. Good.

But Sarah's future happiness was worrisome. She bowed to her father in everything, and would never risk his wrath. As she partnered with William Manning for a second dance, Caroline's anger at the earl grew. He would never *let* someone landless and title-free marry his daughter. And he would never release her from this competition. Further, Sarah would never leave.

She watched the activity from the shade of Manning's pillar after she returned from another bout of ghost gossip in the retiring room. She had to commend Manning—it was a great spot to see without being seen.

A low hum of vibration thrummed through her as someone stepped behind her.

"Aren't you going to dance?" a voice whispered in her ear.

She watched the dancers come together and fall apart. She tried to keep her breathing steady. "No."

"Pity." The edge of his coat brushed her shoulder and the back of her bare arm as he rounded her. She kept her eyes on the dancers, the whisper of a wild wind at Roseford brushing through her mind.

"I notice that you haven't been dancing either, Mr. Deville. A weak area for you?"

"Is that an offer to find out for yourself?"

"Merely an observation and a question."

"Coward."

There was something heavy and sensual in the air that blanketed her ire, unwillingly pulling her toward him. "You have been much on the lips of the guests. They say you prey on debutantes and discard women like tattered handkerchiefs. I would do well not to speak to you at all."

"Oh, I won't discard *you*, Caroline."

The blanket of heavy air rubbed along her bared skin. "I am hardly going to allow you the opportunity." She edged out of the shadows so that she could be seen, stepping away from the suddenly weighted air.

"Worried for your reputation?"

"Perhaps you should be more worried for yours."

He smiled dangerously. "But where is the fun in that?" He withdrew a cheroot from his coat.

"You surely do not intend to smoke that here."

"If I desire to do so, yes." He tapped it against his sleeve.

She pinched her lips together, her irritation crisper the farther away from him she traveled. "You are no gentleman."

"I believe we have already established that. And it is a good thing, as I don't believe you would have much interest in me if I were."

"What a ridiculous comment." She cleared her throat, suddenly hoarse.

"But true, is it not? Your knees are firmly locked in the presence of such men as Everly and Manning. Too poncy or too gentlemanly. Oh, but then you *like* gentlemanly behavior, don't you?"

He lit the roll of paper and cloves. She stared at him in disbelief as he exhaled.

Smoking. In a ballroom.

True, no one could see him at present, but she somehow didn't think an audience would make one whit of difference to him.

"I do, and gentlemen don't smoke in ballrooms. *Ruffians* don't smoke in ballrooms."

"I guess that makes me a saint." He smiled and leaned against the pillar, crossing one leg over the other at the ankle.

She crossed her arms. "In a sinner's world, you would be revered as one."

"Then welcome to paradise." He extended his hands, waving the cheroot in a mock-blessing gesture.

"You choose to be difficult."

"I think we have established how utterly trying being good is."

"Why is that?" She cocked her head, frustration at the feelings he produced, totally at odds with her good sense, causing her to lash out. "Trying to get revenge against your brother?"

His eyes narrowed, his crossed foot tapped a jarring rhythm against the floor. A sliver of smoke curled into the air.

"To gain society's attention?" she continued.

The whispered confession of a man saying that long ago he had desired to turn into a sparrow and fly away echoed in her mind. A desire she could more associate with the persona he had presented at the Grange, but not one she was comfortable reconciling with the smooth social demon in front of her.

"Hardly."

"To gain your father's attention then?" She needed him to stay away from her, to stop muddling her thoughts.

Something glittered in his eyes that she couldn't

read. "I didn't realize what a creative mind hid behind that icy exterior, Caroline."

Her name stretched out on his lips irritated her further.

"There is always a kernel of truth in the rumors. And they say that your father is forever cleaning up your affairs. You risk little through your be- · havior except to drive attention."

He laughed, a brittle, ugly laugh. "Silly girl. Is that what you hear? A kernel of truth to the rumors?"

He pushed away from the pillar, and suddenly she found him directly in front of her, pressing an invisible wall against her chest. "Well, I hear you are a frigid princess." The sibilant last syllable hissed from his tongue. "If it weren't for the way you *performed* last week, I'd believe it too."

He leaned back and flicked ash into the potted plant hiding them from main view.

Every disk in her spine tightened and snapped into place. She nodded sharply, pivoted and strode straight back to her spot near the dance floor. Another set was forming, and Sarah had a partner. The biddies and matrons were gossiping like hens, probably waxing on about Sebastien Deville or something equally horrifying.

A man stepped into view next to her. "Mrs. Martin, would you care to—"

"Yes," she snapped, grabbing the startled man's arm. He recollected himself and hurried her onto the dance floor.

The first steps of the quadrille began, each turn giving her a perfect view across the floor and into the eyes of a demon surrounded by a cloud of hellfire.

Chapter 8

◦◦◦◦

Dear Reader, when we have discussed the personalities of this tournament, much has been said of the relationships between the men sponsoring it and their offspring in pursuit of the victory. Much has been shared in this column in the past—the on-dits concerning the various members of the Tipping Seven and their progeny in particular—but something must be said about those members who have chosen to encourage both their latter-born legitimate sons and their natural sons to compete against one another. Such is the mark of an epic battle at its finest, and one wonders what sparks such a man that would light the flame beneath . . .

Sebastien stubbed his cheroot into the dirt of the plant, exhaling in irritation as the dancers twirled once more and he caught a glimpse of a shining blonde head.

"There you are." Timtree strode over to him. "Card game in the back."

He lifted a brow. "And?"

"And the stakes are good."

Sebastien doubted that, but as the quadrille was going to last ten minutes more, and he didn't much feel like seeing his prey in the arms of another, he followed Timtree. "Why include me?" Timtree had negative luck against him at cards.

"Oh, I'm not playing." He sent him a sly look. "But Lord Benedict is. And the duke. He was just announced a few minutes ago. Returned from London a day earlier than planned."

He had missed that. Must have been when he was talking to Caroline.

"Well, that just makes my night, Timtree. I can't express my gratitude for you coming to get me immediately."

"Yes, yes, enough." His sly eyes turned. "But with the people gathered in the room . . . there is ample opportunity for a memorable occasion."

Timtree was nothing if not an instigator. Possessed of a cruel streak, he could be an excellent ally or a ferocious enemy.

There were already six full tables. Sebastien lit another cheroot, safe now to do so in the bastion of the game room. Though it was not as much fun as seeing Caroline's shocked and appalled face.

A table with Benedict, the duke, Cheevers, and Petrie was already in progress. Benedict and Petrie were partners. Sebastien withheld a grimace and gave Timtree a look that he returned with an unabashed grin. Timtree had known then how this would end up. The bastard.

Sebastien stuck his free hand into his pocket and leaned against a wall of books, waiting. He smoked while Timtree kept a running dialogue of the night, both of them playing their parts as they waited for the next act to begin.

There was a movement from the duke, and Petrie excused himself. The duke beckoned Sebastien over, heavy signet winking in the lamplight as always.

Timtree smirked and strode off into the smoky gloom as Sebastien moved forward to join the table.

He seated himself across from Benedict and saw the irritation and anger in his half brother's eyes. Sebastien smiled in response, causing Benedict's anger to darken further.

Cheevers overturned four cards to determine the deal. "How is Lord Grint?"

Sebastien watched his partner's face. If there was one person that Benedict loathed as much as he hated Sebastien, it was the duke's heir.

"He's doing quite well. I would have been quite happy to have him married to your daughter, but for his determination to root himself in Parliament first. Boy has a fine head on his shoulders for politics."

Cheevers nodded. "You should be quite proud of him." The implication that he was the only one of which the duke should be proud wasn't lost on Benedict, and Sebastien watched his shoulders tense. Feeling just the tiniest bit of sympathy for him, tiny as a mote of dust, but there all the same, he dropped his cheroot below the table edge and ashed onto the expensive rug, grinding it in with his boot.

"As should you with your own heir. Boys can be quite difficult."

Sebastien tossed a card onto the table and ran a few numbers in his head about how much his newly scrubbed persona would take a hit if he tossed a few fingers in their directions instead.

"At least you have all male children, however misbehaved, instead of blasted females," Cheevers said.

"You have one daughter, Cheevers, and a model of meek propriety at that. How bad can it be?"

He waved the hand holding his card before playing it. "Birth one, then tell me."

Sebastien's eyes met Benedict's accidentally, their reflected emotions quickly morphing into dislike.

"Lady Sarah is a very nice young lady," Benedict said diplomatically. The bootlicker.

The duke played his card. "Yes. She is an asset to the competition, Cheevers. Pliable and good-natured."

"She does as she's told, but you can never be sure of the female mind."

"Sometimes it is the quiet ones that make you the most nervous." Sebastien followed the play, scooping the trick. "They could be plotting the destruction of England and you'd never know it."

Benedict sneered. "No, you'd be too busy beneath their skirts."

"Really Benedict, you show your breeding so poorly," he said as he examined his cards for effect.

The duke raised a brow.

Sebastien simply raised his in response and threw out his lead. "Lady Sarah could be plotting the end of the world right this minute."

"She'd be purely following directions, if so," Cheevers muttered so low that Sebastien wasn't sure that was exactly what he'd said.

Benedict's face couldn't contain his spike of glee on the card play as Cheevers followed suit. Really, was the man a complete mutton head? No, he already knew the answer to that. Of course Sebastien was going to lead that suit after Benedict's play three tricks ago. Regardless of his dislike for his partner, Sebastien knew how to win. And if he was unwilling to let Benedict beat him, he was doubly unwilling to let the duke and Cheevers win.

Benedict wasn't a terrible cardplayer. Sebastien had witnessed him playing against others and he wasn't half bad. But he lacked finesse, and he played poorly against Sebastien, letting his emotions rule, the strength of his cards easy to see on his face and in his actions.

"Have you completed your betting sheets?" Cheevers asked the duke.

"Yes, I have."

"And what did you bet, Father?" Benedict asked, stupidly. Sebastien could have reached across the table and slapped him for falling right into the trap.

"I bet on the outcome of the competition."

Benedict opened his mouth, and Sebastien couldn't take it. "Benedict, don't ask any more questions unless you want to know how little you matter in the scheme of the duke's life."

"Really, Sebastien. You hardly know what he was going to ask, or how I would answer," the duke murmured, anger in his eyes. Upset at his little game being spoiled.

Sebastien lit another cheroot. He wasn't going to be able to breathe for a day after smoking nearly nonstop tonight. He was going to maul someone otherwise though. He waved the cloves toward Benedict. "Have at it then. You've never been one to know good advice from a pile of sheep manure."

Benedict shot him a nasty look, then turned to the duke. "Who did you bet on to win?"

"Sloane."

Benedict obviously wasn't expecting this. Probably had thought the duke would either pick him, or taunt him and pick Sebastien. He opened his mouth, then closed it again. "Sloane?"

"Of course. Odds-on favorite."

"But he's a bastard."

Sebastien snorted and blew a ring toward the gilded ceiling.

The duke shrugged. "The status of birth doesn't matter for these few months."

Benedict looked shocked. He opened his mouth to say something stupid or pleading. Sebastien leaned back and let the hard toe of his boot hammer into the other man's knee. Benedict buckled, his cards showing briefly. Sebastien switched the card he was going to play, accordingly.

The pain didn't seem to stop the conduit between Benedict's bottle-headed brain and his mouth, however. "Why would you bet on another's son? At least if you bet on Deville it would explain—"

"Explain what? I bet on the favorite. If you think to win, prove the books wrong."

Cheevers nodded at the duke's comment and motioned toward Sebastien. "Deville hardly looks bothered. And he's a bastard on top of it."

Sebastien shrugged, the easy, dark smile never

leaving his face as he dropped his cheroot on the rug beneath the table, letting it burn a bit before grinding it into the nap. It wouldn't be found for weeks by the time he had worked it in. "Why should I be bothered?"

Benedict looked even angrier, if such a thing were possible.

Sebastien would wager ten thousand pounds that the duke had *not* bet on Sloane. Benedict had never understood their father, though.

Being born as a duplicate of a man like the duke helped Sebastien understand exactly how the man's mind worked. And sometimes that was the worst curse of them all.

"Mrs. Martin, you don't appear to be enjoying yourself."

Caroline spun to see William Manning on the terrace. "On the contrary, Mr. Manning, I am having a pleasant time." She flourished her hands in invitation at the spot next to her overlooking the grounds.

He leaned back against the stone rail to watch the ballroom, the dancing bodies and glowing faces. Partygoers sifted in front of them, gossiping about the competition and seeking relief from the heat inside.

He turned his head toward her, searching her expression. "You do not approve."

She examined him. She had just met him; she could hardly trust him. Yet there was something about him. She crossed her hands on the stone. "I do not."

"You are not alone." Friendly brown eyes were piercing as he leaned back farther, propped against the railing.

"Why then are you here, Mr. Manning?"

"I assume for the same reason that you're here."

She cocked her head, intrigued.

"To protect interests," he said.

"And whose interests are you protecting?"

He smiled, a friendly smile that invited secrets. "That doesn't matter. But we are perhaps after the same goal."

"And that is?"

"To see the best man win this competition."

"I do not think that possible."

"Oh, come now. At least one or two of the men must be respectable. Sloane, at the least."

"He is respectable, but he is not for Sarah."

He cocked his head, mimicking her pose. "And why not?"

She watched Sloane, who stood just inside the terrace doors, effortlessly charming the women around him. "He would treat her well enough, but he'd never understand her. She'd be another bird in a gilded cage."

"And what is wrong with that life?"

His tone was genuinely questioning, so she spared him the glare she would have given otherwise. "The bird's spirit withers and dies." A memory of the earl's wife flashed in her head.

She glanced at Sarah through the glass, dancing again, for once looking as if she was enjoying herself at a social event. A few of the competitors were casting her second glances. But interspersed with the second glances were lustful looks at the fallen ladies in their midst.

Men were not faithful. It was part of their society. And if that was just what it was, then she might possibly be able to stomach it. But to make a woman believe that she was the sun rising and the moon glowing and then to turn those eyes elsewhere . . . the hurt, the pain . . . to wonder what deficiency one possessed . . .

No, she didn't want that for Sarah.

"You think that she needs a man who understands her in order to be happy?" William asked.

Caroline pressed her lips together. It sounded horribly cloying when put that way. "I think that she is still young enough that she defines herself by the way others treat her."

"Ah. And you are too old to do the same?" His tone was gentle.

"Too jaded, I suppose."

He acknowledged her statement, but said nothing either in affirmation or in denial. She relaxed against the railing. Here was someone who might just let her *be*. The night began to take on a steadier hue. The activity whirled around them—the chattering, the music, the sounds of feet clomping to the twirling beat.

She felt calmer. "Why are you here, Mr. Manning?"

"To observe, as I told you."

She turned to him, one hand relaxed against the stone.

He stayed quiet beneath her regard for a peaceful minute. "To observe that the competition proceeds in a manner the King approves," he said.

Her heart picked up speed. "You are the King's watcher."

"Yes. I'm not to interfere unless something significant occurs."

"Oh." Another stick in her sabotage plan—one that could have significant repercussions. She laughed as lightly as she could manage. "Sounds like you will be quite idle during your stay then."

He looked at the crush inside and the fellow revelers on the terrace. "There is a lot that could happen. So much at stake here."

She frowned. "Yes, for Lady Sarah."

His eyes met hers. "For everyone involved. Do you understand what this competition is about?"

"Prizes and glory. Pride and greed."

His eyes were gently chiding, and her cheeks heated. "For each man competing, this is a dream, and a nightmare."

"How so?"

"Imagine having everything you've ever wanted dangled before you—everything you've aspired to, everything you've been denied."

"I don't understand how that can be a negative for them."

"Your most fervent dream—in front of your eyes? Terrifying."

"So you believe most of the men are scared?"

"No. But it is not as carefree an event as you wish to make it, Mrs. Martin."

She swallowed. "I don't want to see Lady Sarah hurt."

He smiled. "Admirable of you. You are a good friend to her." He grew sober. "There is little you can do to stop the machine, though. Help her to adjust instead."

He looked inside once again. "Ah, it seems our time is at an end. Until later, Mrs. Martin; it was a pleasure."

He smiled and slipped back through the doors. A figure, dark and handsome, walked past him in the frame. She grimaced and pushed from the railing, ready to follow William's route.

"Running already, Caroline?"

"Mrs. Martin," she corrected sharply.

"And feeling unnerved. I must have done something right earlier." He reached her and took William's spot, reclining in almost the same position, but whereas William had made the space comfortable, everything around Deville crackled.

"Doubtful."

"Miss me?" Straight teeth mocked her.

"Actually, the night had been getting steadily better since your disappearance."

"I'm hurt, Caroline, truly."

"Are you trying to convince me you have a heart?"

"A wretched, lonely one." He put his hand to his chest, another spot-on impersonation of Kean inviting her into the joke.

An unwilling smile tugged at her lips. "Wretched indeed."

"Pierced."

"It is doubtful anything could pierce that shell of arrogance."

"Dance with me." Not a question. A command. Her heart quickened. "No."

He stepped in front of her, blocking her from the view of the others on the terrace. His fingers curled around a lock of her hair, and she forgot how to breathe, how to move. "Dance with me, Caroline."

Heavy tendrils of spice and desire echoed the plaintive hum of a violin. The low note of the answering viola wrapped an intoxicating brew of longing around her limbs. To let go, to be free, to let him bind her in his grip.

She broke the spell and pushed away from him, stumbling inside among the dancers moving toward the floor.

A hand spun her. Her breasts pushed against his chest, connecting them, as the rest of her body roughly pulled against his. His fingers wrapped around hers, the touch exploding through her, shooting up her arm, down her spine, coiling below.

"What do you think you're doing?" Her intended hiss came out on a caught breath.

"Dancing with the loveliest woman in the room." Strong arms pulled her onto the floor, leading her skillfully as the tempo increased.

"I'm not dancing with you."

"I think you'll see that you are." He twirled her, keeping her close to him inside the other couples on the floor.

She swallowed, looking at the haze of faces as they moved past. She could pull away from him. Leave him on the floor. Cause a scene.

His lips lowered to her ear. "Would you?"

She concentrated on the colored shapes and animated faces whirling by.

"Ignoring me. I'm offended."

"I didn't want to dance with you." She didn't want to be this close to him *at all*.

"But you do, Caroline." His lower half connected with hers, sending alert signals to all parts of her body.

Just because her body was attracted to his, it didn't mean anything. His fingers stroked the back of her hand, causing her to catch her breath. Desire was entirely different from true emotional feeling.

"You think all can be solved with a tup and a smile, don't you?"

"Mmmm . . . that is certainly a naughty way to put it." Mercurial eyes rapidly changed—she caught none of the emotions, only their changing nature. "I think we'd solve one of your problems, Caroline, with that approach. Thaw you out a bit."

"I need no thawing."

"You are melting right here."

"I'm a puddle from your limp leading."

"Limp?" He pulled her against him again, hardness pressing.

She stepped on his foot.

"Your actions wound me, Caroline."

"That was the intention."

"My poor, forsaken heart," he drawled.

"You are the last man in this room who I would say has a heart, Mr. Deville."

He pulled her fingers to his chest, the steady beat thumping beneath her pads. She cursed herself for not wearing thicker gloves.

"No?" The whispered words caressed her ear.

A break in the music came, and she tore herself from his arms. "No." And with that she bid a hasty retreat.

She strode away, hips swaying. Her posture, her actions in dismissing him, fired his blood. The icy exterior hiding the fire beneath.

He was reacting in a way that wasn't his usual style, but then she wasn't his usual mark. He hadn't had a true challenge in so long—that was all. And the farther they fell, the more they pleased him.

Benedict stepped next to him on the edge of the floor, breathing hard, smirking. "Someone you can't get, Deville?"

Sebastien smiled lazily, wondering how much Benedict had overheard—he'd obviously been dancing. Quite possibly near them the entire time, because for once Sebastien hadn't paid a whit of attention to his surroundings. He had been concentrating on *her*. He watched her strong walk as she disappeared into the crowd. "That person doesn't exist, Benedict."

He smirked at his half brother, turned, and walked through the terrace doors, Benedict close on his heels.

"You rely on women, Deville, because your lack of respect gets you nowhere. Once you lose your looks and charm, well, then where will you be?"

"About the same place the duke is, don't you

think?" The duke was consistently surrounded by admirers and mistresses. "Seeing as I, at least, look exactly like him."

He turned in time to see the rage poorly hidden behind Benedict's superior expression. Slow boy had walked right into that one.

"How about a bet, Deville?"

"Don't you think there has been enough talk of betting tonight? Poor little ralph spooner, you were terrified of not receiving Daddy's love earlier."

Benedict didn't take well to the reminder of their card game, or to being called an idiot. Which was too bad, really, as he excelled in defining one.

"Street language. You belong in the gutter, Deville. I doubt you can even get that woman to kiss you of her own will."

"You bore me, Benedict, as usual."

"Scared, Deville?"

Timtree and Everly sidled up to them, a few of the others who had gathered on the terrace following. "What's this?" Timtree asked.

"I'm asking Deville to make a bet. On a woman."

"Which woman."

"The blonde." He pointed to her through the huge glass panes as she stepped next to the heiress.

"A fine piece, that one, though sharp-tongued," Everly said, his face crinkling.

"I saw how well you handled her earlier," Sebastien drawled.

Everly's eyes narrowed. "I'd bring her to heel soon enough. Perhaps we should include her in the overall stakes."

"Yes, a mistress to the winner," another man added.

"And how exactly does that work? I believe the woman gets a choice in the matter," Sloane said. Sebastien knew there was a reason he liked the man.

"Damn, man, leech all the fun away."

"She's a widow. No young ones hanging on her skirts. Maybe she's barren."

"Perfect mistress, if so. A rounded belly on a woman is fabulous, but you don't want to have to climb a hill. And the damn emotions. Last one nearly broke my head with a vase. No, a barren mistress is a godsend," another man said fervently.

"No more extra mouths to feed either. Deville probably can't handle any more bastards."

He sent the man a condescending look. "I don't have any bastards, Petrie. Unlike you, I prefer to avoid the squalling pukes and the pox."

"Right, as if you care where you stick your rod."

Sebastien lifted his glass, ignoring him.

"So are we going to include her in the overall bet? I'd love to see where else that blonde hair grows," Everly said.

The grip on his glass became painful. He made his fingers relax. He had already marked her as his prey; that was the only reason for his anger. "No. The bet was for me alone."

"Come now, more interesting for all of us. A side bet to the competition."

Benedict was watching him. Sebastien had to

be careful in his handling of this or else Benedict would have a weapon to use against him.

"Benedict is putting up the money for the bet," he said casually. "What does he have to say?"

Benedict tried to hide a grimace at the word "money." Perfect.

"A bet between the two of us; sorry, fellows."

There were a few groans. Timtree looked between them, a knowing look on his face. "Why is that?"

"It's for a Grandien heirloom."

The group quieted, a queer tension gripping the space. Sebastien took another drink, flexing his fingers again. He let his empty glass hang between his fingers.

"And what are the terms of this bet?"

"You have to bed her, of course. And we'll require proof."

"How schoolboyish of you, Benedict. Requiring proof that I've had her."

Timtree raised a brow. "As if we need proof that Deville can toss a skirt."

The other men laughed, and Benedict's features tightened. "Make her fall in love with you then."

The laughter stopped, a few of the men looked intrigued, a few looked cheated out of their voyeurism.

Sebastien lit a cheroot to hide his unease. "What an interesting proposition, Benedict. Love? Who would have thought you a romantic?" The last syllable clipped from his tongue. "What do you get out of this, young Eros in the making?"

Benedict could barely contain his anger, but

there was something manic in his expression as well. "Ten thousand pounds. A mere pittance. The great joy and real prize will be in watching you fail."

Sebastien lifted a brow as he blew out a stream of smoke. "Imprudent of you. What makes you think I'll fail?"

"No one could ever love someone like you."

The tension heated.

"Interesting. I know a great many women who would disagree."

"I don't see any of them running off to the altar with you."

He smiled darkly. "I've never asked nor wanted any of them to."

"You expect me to believe that?"

Sebastien flicked ash to the side. "Believe what you will, Benedict. I don't much care."

"So you'll do it?"

"What heirloom?"

Benedict tapped his finger against his hip. Sebastien understood the message. The Patiere watch. It wasn't worth ten thousand pounds, but the intrinsic value of the heirloom and how the duke valued it made it worth more. He had given it to Benedict when he'd reached his majority. Sebastien had received a fine bottle of claret on reaching his—a disposable gift that he'd summarily tossed to a beggar he'd passed on the street. The duke's third son was obviously at the end of his rope if he was extreme enough to bet the watch. Either that or very sure of himself.

The silence stretched. The other men broke into

side conversations, but Sebastien smoked and contemplated Benedict.

Benedict ran a hand along the rock wall and leaned forward, his head parallel to Sebastien's. "I suppose I can open the competition back up to everyone," he whispered.

Caroline swished by the windows with another man, flanking the heiress. Everyone watched her. Benedict leaned back, once more a part of the circle. There was something in his eyes, something that didn't sit well with Sebastien. As if he knew a secret. But he didn't want to countenance that Benedict could concoct so much as half a cunning plan.

"Are you in?" Benedict asked.

Sebastien took another drag. If he claimed her now, it would keep the rest away. It was unacceptable for the rest of them to be after his prize.

And love? What did Benedict know of it anyway? Desire would suffice. He could easily accomplish that. And there was little downside. Benedict might need the money, but Sebastien could afford to part with ten thousand pounds—not that he planned to.

It would be sweet to have the watch, to take one more thing from Benedict. For Benedict to disappoint the duke yet again. And seducing Caroline was already in his plans. Desire was so often confused for love. In every instance of observing people in "love," he had seen focused desire instead. And desire waned. True love? He nearly snorted.

"Yes. Prepare to part with your treasure."

Chapter 9

*It has come to our attention that foul deeds
are afoot. We are quite speechless that someone
would try to poison half the field of competitors. Equally abhorrent are the reports regarding the destruction of personal property,
kidnapping, and even one stabbing! A stabbing, Dear Reader! What will be next? With
the first cut of the tournament approaching we
can only imagine that truly appalling times are
ahead for those who cling to the edge. What
might they be driven to?*

*It is a fact, Dear Reader, that some people
will do anything to win a game or a bet . . .*

Caroline carried her supplies into her yard and
stopped abruptly. A man was lying on her
garden bench, one bent leg up.

She knew that leg. She might never have seen it
before two weeks ago, but she well knew it now.

A paper lay on his stomach, and a forearm covered his eyes.

She crossed her arms and tapped her foot. He
didn't stir. What on earth was he doing at her cot-

tage? She snorted. No, silly question. He was obviously there to make her life miserable.

She cleared her throat. No response.

She put her supplies down and stepped toward him. Still he didn't move. His left arm hung loose, fingers touching the tips of the blades of grass there. Something was clutched in the hand attached to the arm covering his eyes.

What was it?

She changed tactics, tiptoeing around the bench in a wide swath, checking that he didn't wake. She couldn't discern what was in his fist. The paper, though, was free. She crept closer and crooked a finger beneath the paper's edge. Slowly she lifted the corner, peering beneath.

And found herself flat on her back on top of him.

A gurgle worked its way up her throat as his arm formed a band across her breasts.

"If you had just told me that you fancied yourself on your back, I would have been much obliged to help," he whispered in her ear.

She struggled, and after a few seconds of maneuvering found herself free. She pushed off, not even thinking about where she placed her hands as a soft "oof" issued from him, her hand sinking into parts better left untouched.

She whirled around to see his hand protectively covering himself. "Very close there, Caroline. I'll start to think you really do fancy yourself on your back."

He pushed himself into a seated position, the paper quickly crumpled in his fist and tucked into a trouser pocket. He scrutinized the ground briefly before returning his attention to her, smiling charmingly. "Good afternoon."

"What are you doing in my garden?"

"Just finding a beautiful spot to relax and think."

"Think? What does a man such as you have to think about?"

"The beautiful woman who owns this lovely spot?" he waved his hand expansively.

She refused to let him charm her even as the words did funny things to the inside of her stomach. "What do you have there?" She pointed to the paper, the edges sticking out of his pocket.

An angelic expression overtook his face. "I have no idea."

"That paper in your pocket."

"What paper?"

"That one." She pointed more ferociously.

He looked down, eyes moving over his trousers, over the paper. "I have no idea what you are talking about."

"Of course you do."

"No, I don't. You'll have to show me what you mean." He leaned a hand on the bench and cocked a brow.

Her lips pinched. "Why are you in my garden, Mr. Deville?"

"Call me Sebastien. 'Mr. Deville' is quite formal for a man who has had his hand up your skirt, don't you agree?"

She was speechless for a second. And thankful that her day maid from the village had left earlier.

She shuddered to think what the villagers would have said to that juicy piece of news. "No. And the formality is precisely why I plan to continue its use. I hardly know you, Mr. Deville, despite where you might have placed your digits. And what I do know of you hardly entices me to use your given name."

"You wound me, Caroline. A near-mortal thrashing."

"Well, then you should make haste to bandage it. Hup, Mr. Deville. The midwife will be happy to see you."

"Perhaps later." His lazy gaze took her in, an entire cataloging of her body that left her out of sorts and irritated. "Just back from your tasks? Dealing with the commoners?"

"*I* am a commoner, in case it failed your notice."

The cataloging of her body continued. "Nothing common about you, darling."

"What do you *want*, Mr. Deville?"

She expected a smart rejoinder, but something passed over his face that might have been vulnerability, had she thought him capable of such emotion.

A smile split his face, the moment gone as if it'd never happened. "How about a cup of tea?"

"No."

The wounded look on his face was so overdone that she almost smiled. Almost.

"Please, Caroline. I'm a dying man just looking for a cup of your regard."

She was ten kinds of a fool to be taken in by that

look, especially after he had purposefully tried to shock her, and had succeeded. He turned up the expression, the pleading in those aquamarine eyes.

A phrase of refusal was on the tip of her tongue, but a watchfulness appeared just behind the sheen of color in his eyes. As if he was already prepared for her rejection.

No structure is just *a building. Just like no man is* just *a man. There is an identity to everything. Look at the loneliness in the peak. The way it tips toward a lost support. Calling for that which is missing. Rubbish to call it just a structure.*

This was the same man as the one she'd encountered at Roseford, the one who had shown a glimpse of something beneath the smooth veneer.

"Fine. One cup," she said, already unnerved with herself for giving in. She pivoted and entered her cottage, half expecting him to follow her inside, to push his way in. But he was still sitting calmly outside when she returned. He held out a hand to take the cup, long fingers curving around the base.

She sat primly on the other garden bench, another cup clutched in her hand.

"Thank you, Mrs. Martin."

Her head shot up at the address. Terminal innocence cloaked him.

A smile broke unwillingly across her face. "You are such a rascal."

"Yes. And I need to be brought to heel."

She shot him a look over the edge of the cup. "You do at that."

"I throw myself upon your mercy. If you will

but teach me the way." A lock of hair fell across his eye and he flipped it back, the strands arcing.

"I think you get by purely on the way you flip your hair back sometimes, Mr. Deville."

One corner of his mouth lifted. "It's a truly magnificent head of hair, is it not?"

"It is not."

"Now I know you are simply being difficult." He stretched, watching her. "What are you making?" He motioned to the supplies.

She pulled the colorful banner into her lap. "Trimmings for the tournament. Nothing very exciting."

He examined them more closely, causing her to ball them tight. "Something secret? They look like medieval decorations."

"They are nothing for you to worry about."

"But I may lose a fair amount of sleep now wondering how on earth I'm going to sew a banner before Lord Benedict completes his. I daresay he has more skill with a needle than I."

A smile tugged at her mouth. "I don't believe you need to worry on that score."

Her clock chimed inside, indicating the late hour. She had thought to do a bit of work on the banners in the warmth of the garden sun before her appointment in the village, but had underestimated the time. "You must excuse me, Mr. Deville, but I'm needed elsewhere." She started to rise.

"I could say you are needed right here over my lap—"

She stumbled in her skirts. Hands suddenly gripped her waist, steadying her.

"—but I know when to return to fight another day." The words brushed over her hair as he held her against him.

She expected him to use their position to his advantage, but he stepped back, eyes wide and guileless, only the slight curl of his mouth proclaiming his dearth of innocence.

"Until later, Caroline."

His fingers slipped away from her waist, the rounding of her hips. He smiled enigmatically, a promise in those sinful eyes, before he sauntered off down the cottage path.

She looked down, baffled to see smudges across her dress. Just as at Roseford. Her head whipped up. She watched Deville pass from view. Watched the paper sticking out of his pocket disappear with him.

A quick search uncovered a chunk of black chalk lying near the bench. She picked it up. What had been on that paper?

The next week passed in a haze of games and verbal fencing—both with Deville and among the other guests. Sarah and William sat together more often than not to watch the proceedings. Caroline was in full havoc-wreaking mode and often needed to excuse herself to initiate a new maneuver or to find a solitary retreat in which to release her laughter. Games proceeded apace both for the competition and within the ranks of the houseguests.

The archery game had been an especially fine work of art with bows splitting, targets falling apart, arrow feathers bent and misshapen. Deville's pure determination in shooting, even with a broken bow, had almost made her feel guilty. Almost. Damned if he didn't come close to winning that game anyway.

The cautious, edgy looks that the contestants—and some of the fathers—wore made her feel quite smug. The sabotage couldn't be laid solely at her feet though. And that allowed her to stay out of the earl's eye. She had been with him twice when timely mischief had taken place.

Other pranks out of her control had been purely diabolical—multiple poisonings had resulted in each contestant using a servant to test his food. One man had been locked in a cupboard for hours in some barely traversed wing of the house. Another had been systematically stripped of his wardrobe—one piece at a time until there had been only a few changes of clothing left. The last she had observed of that debacle was the man's valet running down the drive as if the devil nipped his heels.

Rumors swirled about some property of Deville's being ruined. Lord Benedict had conspicuously sported a black eye when the tale had circled. No one had been disqualified yet, but as a result of those types of occurrences, eyes were firmly focused on the men as the responsible parties.

The boxing matches weren't to her taste, but she was given an excuse to see the results of her latest handiwork as the women gathered to watch, titillated at seeing the men dressed in fewer clothes in the summer heat and speculating about their lack of clothing beneath. Someone had tampered with the men's drawers—itching powder or some such thing—causing most of the men to go without. Or so the rumor went. She didn't think anything could be more perfect.

"Such a true test of character and strength," one woman said, fanning herself under the shade of the large umbrellas placed outside for the guests.

Caroline exchanged a glance with Sarah.

"A manly pursuit," another agreed.

"Only the bravest and truest men can prevail."

Rip. The sound of stitches straining and tearing echoed through the courtyard around the constructed ring.

The man's trouser mishap—split right down the middle of his backside in a neatly executed fashion—saved Caroline from retching into the bushes over the woman's fawning.

The crowd gasped. The man's eyes widened, and his hands flew to his backside. His opponent took full advantage of his lack of concentration, and a small spray of spittle shot to the side as his head whipped from the blow to his cheek. The struck man seemed to barely register the blow though as he hobbled over to the sidelines, hands glued to his back seams.

He hastily stepped from the ring and into a long coat that his valet violently shook in encouragement.

"Forfeit!"

Another ten minutes elapsed before the crowd was so gifted again. *Rip.* The man's trousers must have been a bit more used, as the path of the tear zigged off in a new direction from the seam. The hapless man looked equally mortified at exposing his glowing wares and ran to his valet on the side. The other valets were wildly searching for garments to cover their masters.

"Forfeit!"

Snickers began like small sparks turning into a raging brushfire. A few men tried to unobtrusively feel their rears. Two of the contestants, who were to fight later in the lists, sprinted off toward the open doorways of the manor, likely trying to avoid the others' fate.

Caroline smiled smugly as Deville entered the ring

The women's laughter was replaced by widespread ohs and ahs as he bounced from side to side lightly on his feet, jabbing the air, and warming his muscles.

Minutes after the bout began, Deville's trousers made a tearing sound much worse than the others. *Riiip.* One entire white cheek blazed through under the afternoon sun. The tittering of the ladies reached new heights. Instead of darting to the side, stepping from the ring, and forfeiting, Deville just flashed a smile to the ladies. He bowed away from them, his eyes still focused on his rival, allowing the women to see even more cheek; and then promptly knocked his opponent to the ground in a spurt of spit and ungentlemanly blood.

Caroline's mouth dropped, and the snickers turned into admiring whispers and a few yells of encouragement.

After Deville's display the men made it a sport. They seemed to find it a boon to hear the sound of tearing linen, smiles lighting their red, sweaty faces. They made a game of flashing their unsightly wares in every direction, and Caroline was just glad that the younger women had been hustled off after Deville's show. The men who had forfeited were noisily trying to reenter the lists, modesty for some reason not an issue anymore. She thought it might be best if she gouged her eyes out afterward.

The boxing matches took on a more serious tone as the clothing stopped tearing. Caroline tried to watch with detachment as Bateman pummeled his challenger with far more force than a gentleman usually employed, a gleeful smile on his face as he landed each swing. Disgusted murmurs swept the crowd. With a strong right hook his opponent crumpled to the ground.

The man stayed in the soil for a few seconds, his face pure white, but for the blood staining it. He picked himself up, hands shaking as he did so. Caroline wondered on it until she saw the older men clustered together, shaking their bent heads. One of them, the man's father, looked at his fourth son, disappointment etched in every line of his face.

After a few seconds of conversing, Cheevers turned to the gathering. "I regret that Mr. Toupnep will not be continuing in the competition, as he has failed to earn the necessary points."

Toupnep stumbled out of the ring, hardly comforted by the pats on the back he received from the more cordial competitors. Bateman snorted, and more than one eye blasted fire in his direction, most of them from the legitimate sons, but a few of the bastards looked disgusted as well.

Toupnep's father chased after him, as the defeated man stumbled back to the manor.

Thirty minutes later another man, shaking and white, left the competition as well. Three others looked ill. Caroline recognized them as the lowest point holders now that the bottom two were gone.

Deville finished off the second round of boxing against one of the three men, one of the illegitimate sons. It was easy to tell which of them would be victorious after only a minute of sparring.

The man momentarily dropped his hands, leaving himself wide open, an easy shot that no one with a modicum of skill would miss.

There was a tinge of—was it regret?—in Deville's eyes, before it was wiped away behind a blank facade, and he took one last swing. The hit was designed to fell the man, but not concuss him or leave him damaged. She had to admit that Deville was one of the more gentlemanly boxers, surprisingly enough.

The fallen man looked at the ground, then resolutely pushed himself up, shaking Deville's outstretched hand, a strained smile in place.

Caroline was too far away to hear, but something about Deville's tightened eyes and the words he was speaking made the man's shoulders relax an inch. The ousted man gave a swift nod and returned to the group; more pats on the back and another irate father joined the mix.

She bit her lip. She hadn't directly sabotaged the men at the bottom of the standings because they had posed no threat to winning the competition. She actually wanted them to do well, since if she could manipulate everyone to share in the points, she might be able to keep *all* of them under the limit to advance farther down the line. The likelihood of that was low, but when dealing with something that she had so little control over, she simply had to hope. And cause universal havoc.

Besides, a few of the men making their exits were the more genial contestants. The less hungry, really. She would need to step up her attacks and be more devious with those at the top, just as she had with Deville in the fencing competition. Maybe the men would just decide that the prize wasn't worth the hassle.

Wishful thinking at its most keen.

She shivered thinking of Deville's reaction should he ever discover that she was the one responsible for most of the attacks directed toward him. If he was intense now, she could only imagine his reaction then.

"These schoolboy pranks must stop." The color in Cheevers's cheeks was high. "Ridiculous. This is a respectable tournament. We seek a winner who deserves the title."

Sebastien fought the eye roll that came so naturally. The anger at the events he had just witnessed still thrummed through him. *They won't win.* He had made the promise to the fallen man. He'd be damned if one of the legitimate sons prevailed.

He had started playing a part in the company of the older gentlemen. Showing his promise as the potential winner. That he would get in line and become respectable. A bluff just as when playing cards. His revenge and fury caged and prowling.

"How has the blighter not been found?" Benedict asked.

Sebastien shot him a mocking look, and Benedict's color rose. As if he didn't know some of those involved. That there was more than one person responsible for the mayhem was obvious. Why Cheevers and the others had either not picked up on it or not chosen to say anything was something that made him think twice about Cheevers's *ire*.

"We have people watching each game—"

"Well, up the guards, man!"

Cheevers shot Parley a look so menacing that Parley actually backed up a step. Idiot.

Sebastien watched the other competitors. Benedict was a prime candidate for saboteur—especially since a lot of the doings were aimed at Sebastien, more so than against any other contestant. But . . . something just didn't ring true for Benedict's guilt. The school pranks, those were Benedict's style. The ingenuity involved in setting up the mirrors and strings for the fencing competition, the irreverence in the split trousers . . . that was someone else.

No one looked particularly shifty. Well, no more shifty than usual. The problem was that everyone present had a motive and most of them had opportunity. Besides hiring a number of guards to watch his objects and backside, he would just have to rely on his instincts and stay watchful.

Petrie's color was high as Cheevers continued his rant, and he had no doubt that Petrie had pulled some of the pranks, yet Petrie had been deeply mortified when his trousers split earlier, and that had the stamp of the person targeting him—his trousers had ripped far further than any of the others. No, it wasn't Petrie.

Bateman was almost assuredly responsible for the poison. Sebastien might scoff at men who deemed themselves gentlemen, but there were certain lines no man should cross. Bateman was malevolent. But the more evil doings like the poison had been targeted broadly, and Bateman simply did not possess the creativity needed for some of the more clever pranks.

One of the fathers had been needed to pull the time switches on two of the games, which had affected Sloane, Benedict, and Everly the most, since they had rooms farther away from the others. If he had to gamble, he'd bet that one on Timtree's father, Baron Tewks.

The ladies drew his attention, and he watched Caroline, who kept glancing at the heiress while fending conversational salvos for her and protecting her.

The idea wormed around, the types of pranks that had occurred cycling through his mind. Broad pranks aimed at everyone. Specific treachery targeted on the leaders.

Protection. And with a firm reason to target him specifically—she'd been appalled and frightened to see him again after Roseford, of that he was sure. She had both the will and opportunity to implement a strategy, and a quick mind at her disposal to carry it through.

Now that he considered her a suspect, no one else made sense as the culprit. Every betting instinct in him said she was the party responsible.

Caged anger lashed outward and he struggled to keep his face blank.

There was more than one way to fulfill a bet. Poor, dear Caroline . . . was in a lot of trouble.

Caroline gripped the last stake and pulled as hard as she could. Still it wouldn't budge. She could have asked a servant or villager to help, but once she had realized the extreme nature of punishment should anyone be caught in the act, she had tossed the idea. She'd only had help with the stable prank, and she had regretted enlisting others ever since. The targeted pranks worked much better anyway. If she perhaps hurt Deville more than any other contestant, well, that could hardly be helped.

She gave a mighty tug. The ground clasped tightly one last time, then gave way. She tumbled backward, expecting to land on her rear, give a good laugh, and get on with things. Instead, firm arms banded around her breasts and effortlessly set her back on her feet.

She froze as the arms slid from around her. Swallowing, then pasting a smile on her face, she turned, hiding the stake behind her as she did so.

Sebastien Deville did not smile back.

Oh dear.

"Thank you for your help." She nodded and started to step backward along the path.

"Going so soon, Caroline?" He stalked her step for step until she bumped a tree.

"I need to change before the next game. Shouldn't you be resting, Mr. Deville?"

"I should." He rested a hand against the red maple looming over her. "But all of a sudden, I was gripped by an eager desire for another look at the obstacle course."

She waved her free hand. "I believe this is it. Good luck."

She tried to step away. He pushed against the stout trunk so that he was directly in front of her again. One hand ran down her arm, around her back, across her fingers, then slowly pulled the stake from her grasp.

"At first, I thought the pranks were a move to cheat through sabotage," he said, his lips a hair from hers as the stake came free. "Perfectly good thought as cheating is rampant. But no, everyone was affected equally in that first game. No competitor seized the advantage by riding directly to the rings. A good attempt by the perpetrator to hide his actions? Perhaps."

He pulled back and twirled the stake that had seemed so weighty to her. "But then I noticed that only those that were ahead in the standings seemed to be targeted, and me most of all. Who would do such a thing? Someone at the bottom of the list? Or perhaps someone who doesn't want the games to continue or certain people to win?"

Her lips remained stiff and unmoving.

"Perhaps someone with a stake in the outcome, forgive the pun?" He twirled the wood again. "Lady Sarah quite possibly?" He clucked his tongue. "What will the earl say?"

"What do you want?"

"Me?" He put his free hand to his chest in feigned ignorance, though anger flared in his eyes. "I'm much too much a gentleman to ask anything from a lady. I should go straight to the earl as an honorable, concerned man."

"Lady Sarah has nothing to do with the sabotage."

"She doesn't?"

"And what's more, you know it."

"I do?" He pulled the tip of the stake through the grass in a lazy pattern, only the hitch at the end showing his true feelings. "I must be exquisitely smart."

"Exquisitely." She took a deep breath. "You didn't just venture along this path. What gave it away?"

He considered her, contemplation mixing with anger. "You are trying to take all of the *fun* out of this."

"Good."

His eyes narrowed. "It was the protection aspect. You have the access. You have the motivation. You hate this competition. You have every reason to want to see the games crippled."

Her heart was beating so fast that her hands were shaking.

"And . . ." He drew out the word and moved forward, touching a loose curl of her hair. "You have every reason to target me, don't you, Caroline?"

She shook harder as his fingers curved around her nape, pulling her head back. His eyes fixed on her mouth. "Every reason to hope I fail."

"You think highly of yourself." Her breath hitched as his thumb pulled at her lower lip.

"I know I want to be high up in you."

Something strangled emerged from her throat as he pressed against her, connecting them. All heat in her body blazed southward.

"And bend you over my knee at the same time. Perhaps both of those actions in the same session."

His lips ghosted over her neck, then attached, sucking the skin hard and undoubtedly leaving a mark. "Or I could simply tell the earl about your actions," he whispered in her ear.

She squirmed away, panting. "You can't. You don't have any proof."

He shook the stake. "Proof?"

She drew herself up, forcing every emotion under ice. She tilted her head coolly. "How dare you sabotage the games for your own advantage by removing that stake, Mr. Deville."

"Touché, Mrs. Martin." He smiled darkly. His fingers pulled along the stake, and she fleetingly wondered if he would thrust it through her midsection. "I'm not sure a woman has ever kept my interest, nor irritation, piqued quite as much as you. If you push me, I can make our dealings much more unpleasant."

She swallowed. "That would be difficult. Now if we might go our separate ways?"

He laughed softly. "Oh, I don't think so, Caroline."

"You have no proof. It will be your word against mine."

"While my word is far from golden, I have alibis for my whereabouts during a number of the cases. And, quite frankly, I have been the express target of the pranks more than any other contender. Curious for the prankster to be so focused."

She swallowed at the way he said it. As if he knew a dark secret that she didn't know she possessed. "You could have easily had someone else perform the sabotage for you. Targeting yourself was a good way to avoid suspicion."

"I am indeed brilliant. But, no, all I need to do is plant the suspicion about you and I'll bet all kinds of incidents—servants seeing you, guests observing you—will suddenly come to light."

She knew it to be true. She had only been successful so far because she was under no suspicion. She didn't know if the servants would rat on her. Some probably would while others would not. But the guests? No, they would bend over backward to find the connections, just as they had done with the fake ghost story.

"You will rely on gossip?"

"Gossip has fueled my life."

If she weren't so shaky she might have snorted. "Are you saying all the things they say about you aren't true?"

"All vicious lies." She could almost picture the halo on his head as his beautiful aquamarine eyes widened.

"You have never taken advantage of a debutante?"

"Oh, I take frightful advantage of them." He flashed another shadowed smile.

"Then it seems those lies are true."

"Only sometimes."

She gripped her skirt. "What do you want, Mr. Deville?"

"I want you to call me by my given name."

"There are so many to choose from though. Rake, bastard, bloody—"

He put two fingers over her lips, and then slid them down, catching her bottom lip and rubbing it. "Clever girl, but not very cunning of you to irritate the man who can ruin you."

She pulled her face away, but his hand moved to grip her waist. "Ruin me? Hardly."

"No? Then you don't depend on Cheevers's goodwill to remain here? On the villagers' view of you?"

She batted at his hand. "I own my property."

"How fast that can change. A woman on her own, an earl with an agenda." He captured her hand against her waist and leaned into her, whispering in her ear. "The titled have all the power, haven't you learned that yet?"

She pulled away, and he let her. "What do you want?"

"Want? But for you to continue."

She stared at him, chest heaving as if she'd just run a race. "You're mad."

"No. Keep sabotaging the games, Caroline. Keep singling me out, *showing* me that which you are trying so hard to hide."

"There is nothing to hide."

"No?" He cocked a brow. "Is it that you do not want me to win because you want me for yourself?"

"You *are* mad."

He smiled. "Of course not. I'm simply an opportunist. For every game you sabotage, I demand a forfeit."

His lips brushed her ear as his cheek touched hers. "We'll hold our own tournament, shall we?" he whispered. "If you continue, I'll know that you want to owe me those forfeits. And believe me, they will be excruciating for someone as prim as you like to think yourself."

She pulled away. "That's blackmail."

"Is it?" He cocked his head, anger appearing again in his eyes. "You are trying to ruin my chances at victory. I think it's merely upping the stakes."

"I am trying to ruin *everyone's* chance at victory."

"I think that is up for debate, but what does what you do to everyone else matter to me? You are trying to ruin *my* chances, and I demand satisfaction."

"You are not a gentleman."

He touched a lock of hair and trailed his finger down the strand. "I believe we have long established that. And I think we have also established that you are not a lady." She stiffened. "What will it be? Should I tell everyone that you are the saboteur?"

Voices came from the path, heading in their direction. Deville twirled the stake in his other hand, eyebrow raised.

"What will it be, Caroline? I can tell them now . . . or . . ."

The voices drew nearer.

"Fine, fine." She grabbed the stake from him and turned to go. He whirled her back around, pulling a startled gasp from her as his body slid against hers, brushing in a shiver-inducing wave, connecting them together in a way that made her body strain to complete the interlocking puzzle.

He smiled languidly and let her go.

She stumbled into the brush, direction momentarily forgotten, the dirty stake clutched against her heart. She had thought herself in trouble before, but she hadn't known the true meaning of the word.

Chapter 10

It is a truth that anticipation is the ripest of emotional pleasures. That a good dose of nerves does wonders for the constitution. And in a venue so ripe with both, one wonders, Dear Reader, how the guests and participants at Meadowbrook are playing their cards and placing their bets...

Caroline waited like a bell awaiting its death toll. A knock on her door caused her arm to crash one cooking pot into another. She threw back her shoulders and opened the door.

"Caroline!"

Sarah hugged her and squeezed past. Caroline let out a whoosh of breath. "Sarah, what are you doing here?" She had expected Deville, dark and smirking, to be on the other side.

"I'm leaving for London and wanted to see you before I left."

"Leaving?" Anxiety spiked.

"Yes. Lady Tevon scheduled a bridal appointment with Madame Tardineau. Madame Tardineau! Can you imagine?" She whirled. "The best modiste in London is going to fit me for a trousseau. All of the younger women are joining us. We are to attend activities and a ball just for us tonight in London. They are treating me so well." She beamed.

Caroline swallowed. It was hard in the face of Sarah's radiance to feel anything but happiness in the farce of the games. And it seemed as if William's friendship was doing her personal good, if the color in her cheeks was anything to go by. Maybe she was doing the wrong thing by objecting to the contest? Sarah would be the toast of London. Her trip would be—

Her *trip*.

"Oh." Caroline's voice was a bit faint. Her mind switched from protecting her friend to protecting herself. With Sarah gone, Deville would have complete access to her.

Sarah breezed through the kitchen, popping a ripe strawberry into her mouth. "I have to leave, but I wanted to make sure that you knew and would be fine for a few days."

Caroline straightened. "Of course, silly. Have fun."

Sarah's smile dimmed. "I'm trying. I keep reminding myself that in a few months I won't have much of a choice. William has been helping. But what if the winner is someone wretched? Like Mr. Bateman?" She shuddered.

Caroline put Bateman firmly on her prime incapacitation list. He would be a pleasure to get rid of, especially now that she had to figure out another tactic to scuttle Deville—or forfeit all manner of things. She patted Sarah's hand. "Don't worry over it now. Enjoy your fitting with Madame Tardineau and have fun on your outings."

Sarah's smile returned, not quite as brilliant, but at least a good deal better than the sadness she'd carried weeks ago. "Thank you, Caro. Don't be lost without me," she said cheekily. "Until I return!"

She disappeared through the door.

Caroline slumped against the counter. The week was getting worse.

"Well now, that is hardly a position I enjoy seeing you in. Not happy to see me?"

She jerked up to see a smirking mouth and hot eyes surveying her from the open door. He leaned against the frame in a thoroughly indolent manner.

She crossed her arms. "Dreadfully unhappy."

He pushed forward, approaching her slowly. "Well, we will have to fix that."

She scooted around the table, hands out, eyes darting to the open door.

"Running away?"

"Yes," she said baldly.

She thought she saw a flash of real humor in his eyes before he reached her, fingers tipping her chin back. "Now, now, Caroline. I'm merely here to deliver an invitation for you to participate in some of the house games tonight."

"Sarah is leaving, along with all of the other young ladies. There is no reason for me to join the guests."

Perfect teeth flashed. "Maybe we just *desire* your company."

"Well, that is too bad."

Fingers smoothed down her throat to the area where skin met cloth. "Cheevers said you should come."

She stiffened. "And I suppose someone dropped it into his ear that I needed to attend."

"Perhaps." Fingers straightened the lace at her collar.

She batted his hand away. "Have you come to claim your blackmail price?"

"No, no, too easy."

She narrowed her eyes. "Are you mad?"

"Not last I checked, though you keep asking me that."

"Mrs. Martin?" Mary, her daymaid, called from outside.

Her heart skipped a beat as Sebastien raised a brow. "Just leave the stones next to the bench," she called back.

"Shall do. I'll return in five minutes!" Footsteps crunched away.

A card materialized in Deville's fingers, flipping so that the address faced her, sloped and mocking. "Your invitation."

She made to grip it, and he pulled her toward him. "Parlor games tonight now that the heiress is away."

"I'm not playing any parlor games." She futilely tugged the paper.

"Oh, I wouldn't be too sure of that, Caroline." He let the invitation go. "See you tonight." He slipped from the cottage on the same path Sarah had made, but with none of her bounce, the stealth of a predator in evidence instead.

She flipped open the invitation and swore.

Dinner had been pleasant enough, if filled with a strange sort of tension. A sort of primal, unreleased pressure. She had also gotten the sense that everyone was watching her. She slipped away to the retiring room after the meal to see if there was something caught in her teeth. Satisfied that her appearance was appropriate, she approached the large gaming room, observing the women enjoying cordials in small groups around the many tables. A lull in the conversation as she entered focused all attention on her. As swiftly as it had stopped, the conversation resumed as if never interrupted.

Harriet Noke sashayed over to her and clasped her arm, pulling her farther inside. "My dear Mrs. Martin, how wonderful that you decided to grace us with your presence. We have been atwitter to learn more about the estate and the mysterious spirit on the grounds. Lady Tevon mentioned that you have lived here most of your life and you'd be able to tell us more."

Harriet guided her to the middle of the elite group of gossipers. One of the ladies leaned in. "Yes, do tell us. What has it been like living in these parts with the marauding spirit?"

Caroline glanced around, wondering what to say. "It has been most educational. The spirits are strange—"

"Oh, assuredly. Why, I swear I heard him moan just the other night in the bedroom next to mine."

"That was the baron you heard, Samantha, as he brought himself off," Harriet said in her smoky voice.

The women laughed.

"As if you have been particularly quiet, Harriet. Moaning like a cat in heat. Too bad for you that your tiger has been enjoying plains other than yours."

"And how would you know, Liddy? Too concerned that Everly is tossing you over."

Liddy shot a quick glance at Caroline before turning angry eyes to Harriet. "You think yourself so clever, Harriet."

"Oh, I am," Harriet drawled.

It was like watching a female version of Deville, but without the benefits of base attraction. Caroline grimaced in distaste.

"Well, I swear I felt the ghost last night. Touched my thigh. Clammy." The woman shivered.

"That was Petrie's hand, Philla. Don't be a goose."

The women laughed again, and Caroline found the whole discussion nauseating. She could be doing a hundred and one other things right now. Making plans for the celebration, connecting with the village matrons, instructing the children on their dances, gazing stupidly into the fire. *Anything* but this.

"How about you, Mrs. Martin? Do you have a gentleman in your bower?"

All the women leaned in, and it was to her great relief that the men chose that moment to descend on the gathering en masse. They hadn't stayed long for brandy and cigars. Perhaps they had wanted to join the women again and begin the real games, or perhaps they couldn't stand being in one another's company for a second more. She wondered if both suppositions weren't a little true.

The men behaved much more freely with the unmarried ladies gone and spirits flowing so copiously. Conversation became raunchier, fondling more apparent. The restraints gone in a way that Caroline hadn't been privy to before, her only real brush with the cream of society coming at Sarah's side. This was more like a village soiree that had gone a bit naughty.

A few of the men headed straight for the gossipers, the group with the members who were the loveliest and most available.

Deville was unfortunately one of the men who sauntered over. She had to give him credit, though. He did it much better than the others. There was a sort of resistance in his gait, as if he didn't need any of them. After observing a number of increasingly covetous glances cast his way, she had to concede that his tactics worked superbly well.

"Shall we start with charades and cards first? We have plenty of people for both," one of the women said.

Timtree asked Deville something, and Deville's husky laughter shuddered over her in waves.

Harriet leaned into Caroline. "Does he visit as far as the cottage, Mrs. Martin? Has he visited your bedchamber as he has visited mine?" She smiled through heavy-lidded eyes. "The ghost, of course."

Caroline's eyes narrowed involuntarily. "Of course. And no, he hasn't, and he shall not."

"Pity," Harriet said, satisfaction brimming. She rose. "Sebastien dear, partner me?"

Caroline half expected him to look at her, but his eyes didn't so much as shift her way. "Of course, Harriet." He held out an arm.

Bastard. Tugging her every which way. Tossing skirts in every direction.

Card sets were forming while the rest gathered for charades. Caroline rose and started toward the forming group, resigned to an hour of gestures and sexual innuendos.

"Mrs. Martin?"

She turned to see Lord Benedict bowing to her.

"Yes, my lord?"

"Would you care to partner me in whist?"

She examined the partnerships for cards, then the charades group that was already making lewd gestures while forming teams. Besides, she rather enjoyed playing cards, and she was rarely able to indulge. "I do believe I would."

"Excellent." He smiled, and she thought how much nicer he looked with his features loosened up. The resemblance between Benedict and Deville was faint, but it was there, like rose stripes at the dawning of a day.

He held out an arm to her, and she hesitated for a moment before slipping hers inside.

"Lord Benedict. Mrs. Martin." Cheevers waved them over, barely paying her any mind. She wondered why he had even thought to include her in the night at all, actually. Must have been just the right words to get him to do so. Caroline studiously avoided looking in Deville's direction. Just because he was blackmailing her, it didn't mean he owned her.

Much.

Cheevers began pairing people off. And wasn't it just luck . . .

"Lord Benedict, Mrs. Martin, Mr. Deville, Mrs. Noke."

As Cheevers made his pronouncement, she saw William, a friendly face in the midst of the insanity, walking into the room and heading for the charades. She should have chosen that activity, obviously. She hadn't even realized William was still in attendance since he hadn't been present for dinner.

She worked up a smile for Benedict, trying to ignore Deville's dark look in their direction. Benedict was also shooting a dark look at the other two, and as he pulled out a chair for her, helping her into the seat with perhaps more care than was necessary, she wondered what she had accepted by playing.

Harriet's eyes narrowed on her. Deville and Benedict eyed each other with disdain and outright anger. Somehow she had found herself at a table with more cracking gouges than a Cornish rock face.

She fervently desired to be nowhere so much as in front of her cozy fire in the cottage, dreaming of better days.

"Highest card deals."

"See if you've learned anything about cards since the last time we played." Deville sipped his Madeira, casually taunting Benedict as if it required only half his effort.

Harriet was a fierce player, pouncing on tricks and scooping them gleefully. Benedict was a meticulous partner, weighing and examining each play, a kind of underlying desperation underpinning his actions. Deville, on the other hand, rarely unfolded himself from the back of his chair, letting Harriet collect all the tricks, lounging and appearing to lazily toss cards randomly from his hand. Only his eyes, tracking and piercing, said something different.

Deville made her the most nervous, and rightly so. Harriet, though a sharp player, gloated. If examined long enough it was easy to see which cards she held. Benedict also showed the strength of his hands.

Deville's face, rather than being the blank study excellent cardplayers mastered, was dark and predatory, languid and bored. There was *too* much at play in his face, though his main expression rarely changed. She couldn't guess from hand to hand what he had. It always seemed as if he had the best hand, and at the same time was bluffing. It was little wonder he drove everyone mad.

Harriet and Deville were up three games to one when Benedict said, "Shall we make a wager on the next?"

"Yes." Harriet's eyes were smoky and her cards skimmed back and forth across the prominent furrow displayed between her breasts. "Shall we start small, and then up the stakes?"

"Why not," Deville said, sounding bored. The look he sent her was anything but.

Caroline turned to her partner. "I don't particularly care for wagers, Lord Benedict, my apologies," she stated calmly.

"No?" Benedict's gaze drifted past her to Deville. "Pity, as there are others at the table much enamored of it."

An undercurrent sparked across the space.

She smiled determinedly. "Please, feel free to make a wager amongst yourselves, but not with me included."

"Oh, we would want to include you, Mrs. Martin," Benedict said, still looking at his half brother.

"Mrs. Martin, you are being quite the boor not to play along. A small wager. Surely you can spare your tight prudery for one night." Harriet tossed her head, a lock of hair drifting into her eyes in a seductive manner.

"Oh, I don't know." Deville shot Caroline a look that was edged and sensual. "I think she is quite interesting myself."

She was caught in that look, but she didn't miss the fury in the woman on her left.

"Tish tosh. Are you in or not? Even Benedict is willing to play, and everyone knows he never wins against Sebastien. Perhaps this is your lucky day."

Benedict's eyes turned dark, and there was something in his expression . . . The tumbler clicked. He *fancied* Harriet. He obviously had Caroline's proclivity for bad seeds and forbidden fruit. Harriet was the female coin flip of Sebastien Deville.

Caroline royally disliked her.

And had she just said in her own head that she desired Sebastien Deville? She was going to scrub that thought when she cleaned her cottage tomorrow. A few good floor scrubs to remove the bad elements.

" 'Benedict' wins most of his wagers," the man defended.

Harriet smirked. "Not against Sebastien you don't. Hard to live up to his prowess."

Caroline viewed her cards while Harriet and Benedict spat. Her cards were excellent. Wager worthy; more than half the win would be in her hands if she were to make an outrageous bet. She chewed her lip, then looked up to see Sebastien observing her. He raised a brow, smirked, then turned from her.

"So what should we wager?" Harriet's cards dipped into the valley of her breasts again, then scraped along the skin. Her heated look encompassed them all. "Should we all have a bit of fun together?"

Benedict's eyes shot to Deville, and he couldn't keep the distaste from his expression. Deville managed somewhat better, still watching Harriet. The tiny grimace in the lines of his lips gave him away, even as his expression smoothed back into boredom. "Really Harriet, must you tease Benedict so? He'll get his hopes up."

"Why you—"

Harriet's flowing laughter stopped Benedict, and he looked back to her, that covetous expression in his eyes. Lovely. "Oh, Lord Benedict, what would you suggest?"

"How about the winners choose? Anything they want at their disposal."

Caroline blinked. She didn't think that a good idea at all. Yet on second thought, Deville might choose Harriet. Harriet would assuredly choose him. Come to think of it, if Caroline lost, she wouldn't really lose, would she? She could simply rid herself of Deville for the night and slip out under the noses of the rest of the guests. And if Deville did win and chose her . . . well, she was in deep trouble with him anyway. She licked her lips nervously.

Harriet considered the wager, her sultry lips pursed. "Not very scandalous, but I do see the possibilities in getting rid of the chaff."

Obviously Harriet also thought she could rid herself of Caroline in the same manner Caroline wished to be rid.

"Mrs. Martin? Do you agree?" Benedict asked, something yearning and quite pitiful in his gaze.

Deville cocked an eye at her, challenge in his.

Caroline thought about her cards, winning cards, and the chance that she might be well rid of Deville or in his arms. Benedict's eyes pleaded . . .

"Very well," she said softly, already hating herself for her decision.

Patrick laughed uproariously somewhere in hell.

Harriet looked quite pleased and picked up her cards. Deville barely glanced at his. Benedict's gaze was a study in determination.

Caroline and Benedict won. Nearly every hand.

The shock on Harriet's face was priceless. The shock on Benedict's was almost as good. Deville curiously looked bored, as usual.

"We won," Benedict said, as if he couldn't quite believe it.

Caroline frowned. "It isn't as if this is a strange occurrence. Cards rely much on luck."

Benedict and Harriet looked at her with varying expressions of disbelief while Deville appeared fully amused.

Deville was already lighting a cheroot, blowing the smoke toward the ceiling as he reclined in his chair as far back as he could.

Benedict still looked as if he couldn't believe his fortune.

Harriet crossed her arms, obviously reading Benedict's signs aright. "There's nothing that says winners can't choose each other." She cast a critical glance toward Caroline. "Some men positively drool over the healthy-country-girl look."

Benedict gave Caroline a respectful glance, one that earned him more of her regard. "Mrs. Martin is quite beautiful." He suddenly paused, as if some thought had caught up to him, a queer look crossing his features, as he shot a furtive glance at Deville.

Deville froze, the cheroot at his lips, the undulating smoke obscuring his features for a second, before he took a drag, narrowed eyes on Benedict, and exhaled the smoke in his direction.

Benedict passed a hand in front of his face, anger lighting his eyes. He opened his mouth, then stopped, some sort of half-used discipline gripping him as he tore his gaze away from Deville, looked to her, piercing eyes that crinkled in agony, then smoothed too obviously as they shifted to Harriet.

"Shall we retire?" Benedict said to Harriet. Caroline had to hand it to him; he came off more smoothly than she'd thought he would.

Harriet's eyes narrowed on Benedict. "Very well," she said ungraciously. She gave Deville one last look, then gave Caroline a scathing glance. "Have a good night."

She stalked from the room, Benedict striding quickly behind her.

"Don't forget what goes where, Benny. I'm sure Harriet will help you, should you need assistance," Deville called out.

Benedict shot a look over his shoulder that promised death.

"That wasn't very kind of you," she said.

"No?" He shot her a dissolute look full of disregard. "Benedict is a bastard. Unfortunately not in the literal sense."

He smiled his patent dark smile before she could respond, exhaling upward. "I thought for a second Benedict was going to choose you to spite me. I would have murdered him, of course, had you accepted."

"You don't have any right to make such statements."

He leaned forward, stubbing out his cheroot. "No?"

"No, and furthermore, I don't see how Lord Benedict deserves such harsh vitriol."

"Benedict deserves everything he gets."

"Why? What has he done to you?"

Deville's smile was wide and not the least bit genuine as he tossed the stub into a copper bucket. "Not much Benny can do anymore. Especially after this tournament ends."

"And what do you expect to happen then?"

He lifted a brow. "I expect to win."

Tension coiled in her belly. "Sarah will never be happy with you."

"And you think she will be happy with Benedict? Everly?"

Her lips pinched.

"No," he said. "You keep sabotaging the games to protect your lamb from all the big bad wolves, and I'll keep collecting my due. And we will see who triumphs in the end."

The room was emptying as people were either pairing off or making their way to other rooms and entertainments.

He rose. "Come."

They walked down the hall behind a small group heading to the lake. Couples were already stripping off clothes as they stumbled and laughed. She'd be lucky if some of them didn't stumble the mile to her cottage and force their way inside in some drunken attempt at copulation.

She was examining the way one woman was vainly trying to remove her stays, mucking her ribbons royally in the process, when Deville turned and smoothly twirled her into a dark room and shut the door swiftly behind.

Enough moonlight shone through the full-length windows of the second parlor that she could make out his features and also see the first group of drunken revelers as they poured from the back door and out onto the lawn.

A key turned in the lock. He came toward her slowly, features shifting from moonlight to shadow and back. "I think it's time I started collecting."

She backed into the spine of a chair, heart racing. "But I'm the one who won the card game. Right from the first of the bet. And it was winner's choice. And I've decided to return home."

One hand curled around her waist. "Do you think I didn't know I would lose that first hand? I saw your face when you looked at your cards." She inhaled sharply as his lips grazed her neck.

"But that was only one hand. We won nearly every hand."

"I *may* have stacked the cards in your favor."

He sucked the pulse point at the side of her throat. "You cheated," she said in a strangled tone.

"For you." His lips brushed her skin everywhere as they moved. "Only in order to lose. I like to win on my own."

"But you *cheated*."

"Your shock is delicious." His lips moved along her jaw, and his other hand circled her waist, pulling her against him. "You should learn the skill—you have to know how to cheat in order to catch others at it. I'm surprised Harriet didn't catch on. She's a notorious cheater. You don't think her breasts brushed Benedict's sleeve that many times on accident, do you?"

Hands pulled up her rib cage and over the sides of her breasts, before returning to her waist. "We might have won if I hadn't helped you. Pity. I could have had you bucking under me tonight without using a forfeit at all." He lifted her hand, trapped against the chair, and pulled one of her fingers into his mouth, tongue swirling around it in a maddening, weak-kneed-inducing fashion.

"But why then?"

He smirked in the moonlight. The digit popped out of his mouth. "Because I can. Besides"—his fingers moved into her hair, tipping her head back— "Harriet would have made things messy. And I already have you. What is the win in getting you into bed tonight, for one night, when I can seduce and chain you there for good?"

He pulled back an inch and ran a thumb across her lips. "And I will, you can count on that. But tonight . . . tonight I seek merely a taste."

Lips finally covered hers, possessive and fierce. Demanding. Drugging. Claiming. Her back hit the wall, and in a flurry of skirts he was between her legs and she was arching into him in a more searing, intimate duplication of their actions at Roseford.

Chapter 11

A thief helping a poor flower girl on the street. A rogue not taking advantage of an innocent. Sometimes people surprise you, and sometimes they shock you square into a fog. It makes one wonder if it is all some wonderfully duplicitous plan.

Caroline tapped her finger against her chin, squinting against the bright sun. "Noah, let's go the other direction." The boy nodded and drew a box around another area of the grid, then looked up at her, waiting.

"Perfect. That is exactly the way to stage it, don't you think?"

His cheeks lit as only a sixteen-year-old boy's could. "Yes, Mrs. Martin."

"I think we need to ask Mrs. Francis where she wants the confections placed. Do you think you might inquire this afternoon?"

"Of course, Mrs. Martin." He jumped to his feet as she rolled the papers and set them aside on the bench. "I will also ask Mr. Reede and Mr. Wallace about the stands."

"Excellent. The committee members and I need to meet tomorrow. You make my life so much easier, Noah."

The blush intensified. "I don't do much, Mrs. Martin."

"Nonsense. Now give these to your mother and don't cause too much trouble for the village girls." She handed him a basket of sticky buns she'd placed near the twining tomato plants.

If his cheeks grew any redder, she wasn't sure what color palette they would enter. "I will. I won't. I mean, yes, Mrs. Martin."

Noah took off down the path, and she didn't have to stifle her smile. She remembered the easy affections of that age. The innocence. That Noah tripped over himself for her was beyond flattering. And would last, oh, a few more weeks, or months, before he was on to his next affection. Such was the way of sixteen-year-old boys.

Noah was a good lad. He would grow into a strong and true man. Not like Patrick, who had been a weak, unfaithful boy. She smoothed the creases on her forehead that had gathered there and turned.

As if called by the demon of all that was wicked and tempting, Sebastien Deville lounged against her door.

"Making conquests of the village boys, Caroline?"

She stayed where she was. Utter insanity to try and enter her cottage, as he would assuredly follow. After last night . . . no, not a good idea. "Nonsense. Noah will be back mooning after the village girls in no time."

"You think it so easy to get you out of the blood?"

"If I did, I would not share such with you." She crossed her arms.

He laughed lightly. "I see you made it safely home."

"You know I did, you wretch."

He put a hand to his heart. "You didn't allow me to enter—how was I to know whether you were spirited away by an evil villain lying in wait inside?"

"As if you didn't stare at the windows in a fawning fashion before leaving the grove."

A smile curved his lips. "So what did young Noah need from you?"

"He is helping with the arrangements for the midsummer celebration."

"I'll bet you invite Noah into your cottage."

"Actually we usually meet out here in the open. There are still proprieties to maintain, even when the boy is two-thirds my age."

"Older women are much a draw to men of his years."

"I'm sure you have experienced women of all ages." She tapped a foot. "Well, Mr. Deville, what brings you here?"

"Tea?"

"I unwisely brought you tea a few days ago, if you'll remember. You repaid my kindness with blackmail."

"I find myself disinclined to feel remorse under the circumstances. In fact, it might be that I wish to procure more than tea from you." His back arched as he pushed away from the door with his shoulders.

Shivers racked her as she stepped back in self-preservation. The spindly arms of the low maple poked her back, urging her forward.

His lips captured hers in the same confident way they had the night before, but where passion had been demanded last night, this was different. Strong, soft lips lightly stroked hers, opening her mouth, but not invading. Gentle strokes, soft pleadings, a yearning for a revered lover.

She tried not to respond, to stay lax in his grip. His hands rose to her cheeks, lightly framing them, lips tentatively tasting her, like a new lover extremely lucky in the ways of love. But she knew Deville was not a beginner. This was seduction at its finest.

And yet when his fingers stroked her lightly like the finest china and something in the back of his throat sounded like he was savoring the most delicious dessert, everything in her demanded response.

Her body leaned into his, her fingers clutched his shirt, and when a satisfied noise issued against her lips, she fought everything in her not to utter the same. Fingers worked into her hair, still gentle, still lovely and soft as the kiss.

Every debutante's dream kiss, and she couldn't even work up enough ire at that to push away. It simply felt too good. As his fingers gently threaded through the hair at her nape, the insidious thought that maybe giving in to his seduction would be a perfect idea threaded through her mind. As long as she kept her wits about her . . . as long as she didn't give him her heart . . .

"Thank you for your escort, Mr. Miller. I am quite able to find the rest of the way on my own, though," a strident voice intoned.

Caroline shoved away from Sebastien, her heart lodged in her throat as the voices drew closer.

"Yes, Mrs. Francis, I just—"

"Good afternoon, Mr. Miller," the older woman said, dismissing Noah.

Caroline looked around frantically, but the cottage was much too far away, and the opposite path looked a thousand paces off. Sebastien's brows rose, and his full mouth opened to say something likely either amusing or cutting. Footsteps came nearer on the path, and she did the only thing she could think of—she placed her hands on Sebastien's chest and shoved him over the bench and into the bushes. He toppled over the stone and disappeared into the brush beneath the overhanging tree.

She smoothed her fingers over her dress, patted her hair into place, and stepped forward with a bright smile as the town matron descended on her cottage garden in all her bright pink glory.

"Mrs. Francis, how lovely to see you." She held out both hands.

"Mrs. Martin. Mr. Miller said that you had plans for me to review? He stopped me on his way back to the village and nearly manhandled me into visiting right away." She looked down her long nose, shaded beneath a bonnet of apples and birds.

Caroline sent a gentle curse Noah's way and

pasted on a brighter smile. "My apologies, Mrs. Francis. Mr. Miller is a lovely boy and just trying to be helpful."

"As long as that is all it is." She cast a reproving look, then sat down on the stone bench beneath the tree.

Caroline tried to keep her smile firm and her eyes away from the boot half poking beneath the bench that gave credence to the statement that she might be less than wholesome. The boot disappeared, and she prayed that Deville wouldn't pop up to completely annihilate her reputation once and for all.

She reached for the sketches, relieved that they were still outside. The matron would surely look around were she to return to the cottage. A dissolute rake frolicking in her bushes was not exactly what she wanted the strict woman to discover.

Mrs. Francis nodded as she accepted the sketches for the village celebration. "Excellent. You have done well, Mrs. Martin."

She couldn't even preen a little under the infrequent praise, too concerned with the lock of brown hair and peek of aquamarine eyes she could see around the woman's voluminous pink skirts.

"Your mother would be proud."

Her throat closed for a second, and she swallowed the lump down. "Thank you, Mrs. Francis."

The woman patted her hand. "We weren't sure what would happen when you returned to the village after running off with *that man*. I'm happy to see you've realized your poor judgment and turned it around."

Caroline swallowed around an entirely different lump as the flash of a white shirt caught her attention.

"You are becoming a sterling member of the community and a fine example to the young girls on how to conduct themselves. Just like the good squire says, mistakes sometimes occur, but we learn and never repeat those errors."

Finally, acceptance by the strict matrons who had gradually been warming to her since the deaths of her parents, and she couldn't even enjoy it.

"You set a proper example for the young women. And Lady Sarah has been much helped by your good sense. I hear she is positively blooming now."

"Yes, Lady Sarah is lovely."

Long lonely nights stretched before her, as they had for so long. Trying to live up to the image she had set for herself. The image she had wanted so desperately. Maybe then— No. She shut down that line of thinking.

"Distasteful business the way they are running things at the house, and some of the goings-on . . ." She tutted. "The Londoners forget themselves sometimes."

Mrs. Francis was the strictest of the matrons. Most of the villagers were less prone to judgment —and the village parties could sometimes get a little wild. But Mrs. Francis was the woman whose regard Caroline had been coveting. If she had her regard, surely she would gain forgiveness from— No. She didn't need forgiveness! She didn't. She had done nothing wrong.

The constant pull of the insidious thoughts made her weary.

"I know you are forced to participate in order to help Lady Sarah. Do not worry, Mrs. Martin, that we are doubting you."

Caroline murmured her thanks, unable to say more through her frozen vocal cords.

Mrs. Francis looked at the sketch. "Yes, this is perfect. Everyone is looking very forward to the celebration." She nodded decisively. "I'll just turn this over to the council, and we will move ahead with the plans once you determine the location of the bonfire."

Mrs. Francis excused herself, and a minute later Caroline slumped against the closest tree. She didn't know why she always felt drained after a conversation with one of the matrons. If their acceptance was what she truly coveted, then shouldn't she be pleased?

The brush rattled and rustled and a booted foot clicked on stone, then clomped on the ground. "Don't tell me you buy that pile of manure?"

She couldn't even work up the energy to turn her head. She closed her eyes and leaned her head against the stone. "Go away."

" 'Do not worry that we are doubting you,' " he mimicked. "I see that I arrived at this estate just in time."

She pushed away from the stone and started walking back to the cottage.

Sebastien caught up with her on the third stride, a leaf stuck in his hair. "Do you honestly

buy into that claptrap? That you have to be good
to be accepted?"

"You do," she said tightly.

"Hogwash."

"Well then see how far it's gotten you."

She knew it was a direct hit from the way
his arms swung at his sides, more stilted and
clenched than before. He moved suddenly, and
she found her back pressed against the tree, Sebastien pressed to her front.

"I played their game once. It got me nowhere.
What is the use?" He dragged a finger down her
throat, making her heart speed. "Especially when
there are far better things to do."

She smacked his hand away. "Easy for you to
say. Your father is a duke."

"My father barely acknowledges me."

"Oh, please." She scooted under his arm. "Your
father's eyes rarely leave you. I feel more compas-
sion for your brother."

"I don't have a brother."

She snorted and started to walk away. He caught
her, clasping her back to him. "Do you really want
to be one of those starchy women who molder on
the sidelines?" he whispered in her ear. "Denying
yourself all the pleasure you could have?"

"Let me go."

"No." He spun her, and she glimpsed a wild
light in his eyes. His fingers pulled up the back of
her dress, over her spine. "Tell me that you don't
want this."

"I don't want this." Her voice was breathless.

"Liar."

His lips crushed hers, and her hands rose of their own volition, wrapping around his neck, fingers pulling the hair, long on his nape. Sin and forbidden desire stretched through her, curling claws into her skin.

She pushed away, looking around frantically once more. They were out in the open. If Mrs. Francis doubled back, she would see everything.

"Worried what those biddies think?" He stepped closer again, into her space. "I should take you in the midst of one of their gatherings. Give them a proper shock and release you from your inhibitions."

She backed up; he stepped forward. "No! Just stay there."

A regal brow rose. "Or what?"

She held out a hand against his chest. "I can't handle you on top of this."

Something flickered in his eyes. "There is nothing to handle."

"You drive me mad." She was aware enough to note the slightest tremor of anguish in her voice, but could do nothing to stop it.

His eyes held hers, and a hand stroked softly down her hair, loosening it and pulling her to him. "Then we will be mad together."

Teeth brushed her neck, softly pulling together to nip gently. She shuddered, her hands gripping his shirt to keep from falling—both physically and emotionally. Her hand brushed the crumpled edge of paper. The feel of it just like what she had imagined the ever-present parchment that stuck out of his pocket would feel like. She gripped it like a lifeline for her sanity, trying to think of anything but the way his lips felt against her skin, the way he made her body want to completely give in and physically be his for however long she could, and pulled.

Her breath hitched as he trailed his mouth back under her chin, and it took three attempts for her to shove the paper into her own hanging pocket. Her breathing was fast, the color in her cheeks high—she could feel the burn. He would discover her theft. He would demand something even further. Her soul perhaps.

But he simply smiled at her. A soft smile. One that she might fall prey to, if she didn't already know better. One that tugged at everything in her even though she *did* know better.

And she gave in. Just a bit. She curled a hand into his hair and pressed her lips to his, dragging them along his with the same damning slowness that he had mastered.

He pulled his fingers around her ear, along her jaw, to her chin, his lips pulling from hers with that soul-grasping slowness. "Just when I think there is something less than perfect about you, you stun me."

"You are full of pretty words." She tried to control the tremor in her voice.

"I prefer to think of them as cunning," he whispered against her skin, the waves skimming the hairs at her nape. "A good hunter uses everything at his disposal. And once he finds his prey, he never lets go."

Something in her objected to being prey, but something much larger and more insidious wanted nothing more than to have him catch her and never let go. To be the focus of all that dark, heady, uncontrollable passion.

Her heart constricted and she pushed away from him, unwilling to let the pattering beat convert to untold want. She swallowed. "Good afternoon, Mr. Deville."

He ran a finger beneath her chin. "I'll see you soon, Caroline."

He strode down the path, and her eyes followed his well-formed backside. Her fingers went unwillingly to her lips, then she jerked them away and hurried inside to the kitchen table. She wanted to see the paper before he realized she had taken it. She needed to see what he kept so hidden.

Caroline brushed her fingers over the crumpled paper, the image coming alive as her fingertips smoothed the surface, pulled the edges, softly flattening it. She caught her breath. Spider lines and spindle marks, a face etched in despair. As if the artist had understood exactly the emotions defined. The man in the picture *pleaded* with her. She ran fingers along the back of the paper. Dug into every line, like the sharpened chalk to the paper. The hope quenched. A wretched existence returning.

She recognized the face. The amazing likeness. The first man kicked out of the competition. The rules not allowing him another chance at the prize. The jeering from Bateman, the anger from his father, the despair.

Something deep inside her stirred, awakened,

strained at the chains she'd created. The picture, the curves, reached in and curled around the straight lines she had constructed.

She swallowed. Deville couldn't have drawn this. He must have acquired it from another source. Someone else must have dropped it in her garden, and he'd picked it up from the bushes.

Don't think about the improvements he made to the Roseford sketch.

She examined the emotion inherent in every line. Empathy and knowledge, a vulnerability that someone like Sebastien Deville could never possess. No, it had to be someone else who drew this. Deville must have stolen it from someone, then crammed it into his pocket. Evidence of his marauding ways, not his artistic talents. Not evidence of any depths.

Footsteps carried back along the stone path, and she frantically searched her kitchen. She couldn't crumple the paper. That Deville had done so once was criminal. She shoved the paper under a pot and hurried to the window. Peeking through the filmy covering, she could see him searching the area near the bench, a deep, intense look on his face.

A last look at the cottage had her pulling back. He was gone when she worked up the nerve to look back through.

He was the artist.

She jumped as a pot crashed in the kitchen. Her hand pressed against her chest, urging the erratic beat to slow.

Sebastien Deville was slowly driving her mad.

Chapter 12

In an estate the size of Meadowbrook, with the dazzling array of staff and diabolical excess, one can only think that some of the contestants who are hanging on to the fringe—and of them there are many!—do so in order to continue enjoying the largesse and notoriety. That every man with a stake in this competition is jockeying for that extra bit of advantage is assured. It is not only a competition in the physical and mental sense, but in the emotional as well. Only the strong will prevail, and even they may not escape unscathed.

"The last game before we break is a gentleman's quest. As this is a more subjective game, we have fifteen gentlemen scoring contestants on a variety of subjects. Three judges will sit at each of the five stations. Conversation, dress, deportment, strategy, and academia will be tested. Any of the judges may ask questions. The average of the three judges' scores will determine your total at each station."

Multiple adjudicators would limit some of the

bias involved. Though it was still a subjective game. A bloody pony show for sure. Sebastien smiled at Cheevers instead of baring his teeth in the manner he really wished.

Revenge.

He calmly drew a lot to determine order. A number of the ladies tittered and moved within range to overhear what was being discussed at the stations.

It wasn't until the conversation task, when he was chatting about politics and laws, that Sebastien noticed the rush of the tide. The ladies were twitching in their seats. Flashed ankles, dampened dresses, a slipped bodice revealing taut brown nipples. Everly, who was sitting with him at the station, completely dropped his train of thought halfway through a sentence.

"Mr. Everly? The Corn Laws?"

But Everly's face was transfixed.

"I think they need to be examined, of course," Sebastien answered smoothly, as Everly tried to tear his eyes away from a particularly ripe set of breasts. "Discussion and debate are the hallmarks of a gentleman."

And these men supported the laws to the utmost.

"Yes," Everly said, one last look at the deep slope. "Gentle swells . . . that is, gentlemen, swells that they are, know what is what."

Another man damned by woman.

The older men looked to each other, puzzled by his answer, then Baron Tewks cleared his throat. "Yes, well, what is your stance on—"

And the questions continued, boring and elementary. Sebastien kept half of his brain engaged—it would take intentional suicide at this point not to get good marks when compared with Everly. The other half idly searched the crowd during the intervals when he didn't need to maintain eye contact with the judges.

What had gotten into the women? The younger ladies, chaperones, and matrons were all sitting primly in their seats near the front. But the more available, scandalous women were in back, sitting up in their chairs flashing bits everywhere.

Men were going down around the room. Parley slipped off his chair, Petrie's jaw was permanently attached to the floor, Timtree looked amused, but his eyes were focused firmly on one of the widows, who was alternately veiling and then unveiling portions of her body to his view.

Bateman was in either heaven or hell as his eyes skittered around. Sloane was the only one who seemed somewhat composed, and even he was checking the crowds during breaks in his conversations and the interrogators' questions.

Some of the older men had started to notice. Old, decrepit Compton wasn't even pretending to ask questions anymore. Sebastien smirked. This was going to be simple.

It wasn't until the dress portion of the task that he was finally tested.

He was tying a waterfall when he spotted Caroline. She was staring straight at him, smiling as if there was something glorious about him that she had just discovered. Smiling in an almost *gentle* way, as if she *cared*. He nearly ripped the cravat, the tie coming unraveled.

"Tut, Mr. Deville. You were doing well on the first fifteen styles. I had thought you'd have this wrapped up."

Sebastien narrowed his eyes at the now empty place where she'd been standing, behind a jumble of large ferns. He picked up a new cravat and made the tie, eyes focused where they should be.

When his eyes found her again, she was chatting attentively with Benedict, all prim demeanor on display, unlike the other crazed women, who had either ceased their torment or had become more circumspect when the front rows began searching the audience for what was ailing the men. A dark icicle dripped down his spine as Caroline appeared fully engrossed with his half brother.

The entire game lasted throughout the afternoon and well into the evening. A trial that he placed securely at the feet of a crown of soft gold. He couldn't rid himself of the image of her smile.

"Supposedly Marjorie Widwell came up with the idea to pull the stunts this afternoon," Timtree whispered as they were assembling before going into dinner. "I thought Petrie was going to permanently injure himself considering the number of times he fell."

Marjorie Widwell was a vapid, giggling machine. Easily led and not very bright. There was little doubt to him who had slipped the suggestion in her ear to spread. And spread it had, like wildfire. Nearly a full third of the faster women had been involved. All in all, it had added to the heavy feeling in the air. Tension, hot and thick, permeated the space, the edges of the glasses, each droplet of wine.

Caroline sat down the table across from him. Just far enough to be safe. He swirled his brandy and thought about how lovely she would be splayed across the table, back arched and legs bent. The brandy caught the edge of a sconce's light, reflecting warm gold and hot browns.

Her eyes met his for a brief second, her cheeks heated to a luscious rose before she turned away.

The hunt. The anxiety and anticipation. Never had it been this strong. This worthy.

The duke caught his eye, raising a brow. Sebastien swirled his glass again. The duke assuredly knew about the bet, not that it mattered. The duke would think this game the same as the one Sebastien had played with the Plumley chit or one of the other countless twits he had enticed and played with but never bedded. The numbers exaggerated by the gossipmongers, but his attitude unchanged in each instance.

Yet there was something different about this one. Something under his skin that itched and tingled, writhed and begged. To his consternation, Caroline's likely inability to know how to take care of protecting herself against pregnancy mattered little to his addled urges. He had a fierce, uncontrollable need to possess her completely.

Not just to make her beg for the want of him, but to be the only thing she could think of morning, noon, and night. To be the first thing on her mind when she pulled her chemise against her bare waist, her stockings against shapely ankles, her necklace against the crest of firm breasts. The last thing she thought about as she stripped off the same.

Something had changed, an underlying impulse. The games ramping up the tension of the hunt. The girl being completely different from any other he had yet met. Country sweet and marriage hard. Strong and totally vulnerable. Easy to take advantage of, susceptible, but with a heart inured to seduction.

The hunt had never tasted sweeter. Never contained the shaky thrill of victory laced with the edges of defeat. Thrilling in the sheer need it invoked.

No longer a need to win a bet or bring a woman to her knees for entertainment. There was a much fiercer feeling behind the absolute want to have her.

Dinner continued on. Conversation flowing as freely as the wine. And Sebastian continued to strip each layer further from her, rose turning to scarlet, breasts rising from nervous lurch to deep heave.

He swirled his brandy and smiled darkly. Little did she realize that two weeks of torment stretched before her. He'd see that hidden smile on her face again soon, whether he had to use everything in his arsenal to bring it forth or not.

He wanted it—that little thrill, that shock, that warm trickle that made him feel nervous and alive.

* * *

A current of anticipation rode just beneath the surface of the final evening gathering before the two-week break. She recognized the current now for what it was, the dichotomy of the young set colliding with the mature, whereas before she'd just felt a vague itch, some feeling that was just beyond her reach.

She hadn't spotted Deville yet. That she was looking for him at all made her nervous.

Sarah was busy chatting with Everly and Lady Tevon. Sarah would probably welcome her interference with Lady Tevon, but Caroline felt sudden kinship with the woman's chaperonage in the face of a rake like Everly.

She spotted William in the corner, standing alone, watching the threesome, his eyes narrowed.

"That look on your face bodes ill, William," she said as she stepped next to him.

His face immediately wiped of all emotion. He turned to her. "Caroline. You look lovely this evening."

"Thank you." She dipped her head. "I must say I'm looking forward to a break in the competition."

"Yes, I think many need to relieve themselves of the stress. Head up to Town for a bit of gambling or other pursuits."

"Are you leaving?"

"Yes, I have to report to the King."

They both looked to Sarah and Everly again. "I will miss Sarah," she said. "Though not so much the other young women during the two-week break."

"They will have a different form of entertainment in London. It will be good for them to get back out and see things other than this tournament."

"Yes." She turned to William. "So, do you fancy Sarah, or do you dislike Everly?"

A forbidding look crossed his face, and then unexpectedly he dropped it. "I would take offense were I not to know your devotion to Lady Sarah."

"I'm pleased that you are not taking offense."

He ruefully smiled, then turned back to his observation. "Would it matter which it was? Nothing can stop this competition. Not even a little sabotage."

She froze.

"Or cheating, whichever."

Her heart started beating again. Between the shocks and Sebastien Deville, she wondered if the organ would ever return to normal. "Something must be able to stop the competition. You are the King's representative. Surely you can appeal to him? Sarah is his goddaughter."

He was already shaking his head before she finished. "And say what exactly? The King thinks she will make a good match. There is a lot of prestige riding on the winner of this tournament. Lady Sarah will be celebrated. It is why Lord Cheevers is so invested in the outcome."

"Cheevers cares nothing for Sarah."

"Oh, I wouldn't say that. He cares at least a little, don't you think?" He pointed to the earl, who was puffed up watching his daughter and the proceedings. His zeal revealed not a loving look, but a greedy one to her eyes.

"I do not. All I see is greed and the pride of ownership. Nothing softer."

"Caroline, don't you think you are being overly harsh?"

"No. I have seen his interaction with Sarah for years, where you have not."

"I will concede that. But I think he wants only the best for his daughter. He might just go about it in a poor manner. Society is not known for its best efforts in child rearing. But sometimes a parent can see what is best for his child."

Caroline thought of her parents. Of their loving gestures. Of how she had defied them to run off with Patrick. Fallen prey to his seductive words. How she'd had to have the earl clean up her mess.

She thought of the fathers here, most of whom seemed to care not a whit for their offspring past the possibility for an increase in their reputation.

"So you think marrying the winner will be best for Sarah? Cheevers doesn't even know who the winner will be."

William didn't respond right away. "Time will tell. Come, let's walk."

They walked around the edge of the room, making a circuit behind a few of the other pairs—both men and women.

"I wanted to warn you to be careful of Sebastien Deville."

She pulled away from him and stopped. "I don't know to what you refer."

He tilted his head, then tucked her hand into his arm and began walking once more. "I saw you leave with him the other night."

"I thought you were playing charades?"

"I was. For a bit. But you forget my mission here. I am a watcher, not a participant."

Caroline looked down at the floor.

"Do not mistake me, Caroline, I do not blame you for leaving on his arm. He is not Sarah's intended, not yet at any rate, and she does not fancy him any more than the other girls who fancy a streak of danger. I only urge you to use caution when dealing with him."

"He merely walked me back to the cottage, but I assure you he did not enter."

He smiled faintly. "No, you have no need to tell me. I am not your counselor. Just your friend, I hope."

"And I appreciate the advice. Though I think it only smart for anyone to use caution when dealing with a man like Deville."

He laughed softly. "Yes. Just as in dealing with a panther or a viper. Dangerous and unpredictable, always ready to spring."

"People can change and grow." She certainly had, and in fact, she seemed to still be in a state of transition even now. And his sketch hinted at possible self-acknowledgment brimming near the surface. Though she supposed artists were notorious for being unable to see within themselves that which they captured.

"It takes much for a man like Deville to change. Bitter and angry. Believing power and might to be what he truly wants and needs." There was something in William's gaze, some introspection. "I know what it is like. And that will temper eventually. Deville is nothing if not supremely clever. But will it be in time for you?"

She shifted beneath his gaze. "I don't seek to change anyone."

"Perhaps. Or perhaps you will be the catalyst to change him. But he is in this to win. There is a property on the line that Deville will do anything to possess."

She froze, remembering the look in Deville's eyes when he'd said that he knew why she was sketching Roseford.

"One of his mother's properties. The duke bought it from the lien holder after she died, and before Deville could pay the debt."

She couldn't imagine him *losing* the property. The rage he must have possessed—no wonder he hated the duke so.

"Can you envision what would happen should Lord Benedict win the tournament and win the one thing Deville has always wanted?"

No, no she couldn't. She bit her lip.

"Don't underestimate this competition, Caroline."

"I won't. I just don't want Sarah to be like . . ." She trailed off, not looking at William.

"I've heard about your first marriage." Sympathy laced his voice.

"You are well informed." She tried to keep the smile on her face as she looked at the backs of the couple fifteen paces in front of them.

"I see that I'm traversing into unwanted territory. I will end with repeating my caution on Deville. Guard your heart."

She smiled overly brightly. "I don't see that to be a problem. Perhaps we could head to the refreshment table for a spot of lemonade? I'm terribly parched."

William gave her a soft smile and led her that way. She didn't feel much better after one glass of wine. Or two.

People started drifting away from the party. Some retiring to their own rooms—others retiring to other's rooms. Caroline drifted around the edges, wondering why she had chosen to remain. Sarah had turned in thirty minutes past, a tightness to her eyes that hadn't been there at the beginning of the night. William's expression had also looked more strained, and he had slipped from the room a few minutes after Sarah. They had obviously exchanged words, and neither one, Sarah most frustratingly, was telling her a thing.

She remembered Sarah's strained smile after she had asked her if she was well.

"Yes. Do not worry about me. London should pick my spirits right up."

"Who has upset you? Everly?"

"No, not Everly. No one. Please, just let it be, Caro." She smiled brightly, a little too brightly. "My father says that I'm doing quite well."

Caroline had returned the overly bright smile, as false as the mirrored expression. She was well within her right to go home now that Sarah had retired. But yet here she was, aimlessly wandering with her jumbled thoughts.

Deville lounged in the corner, hot eyes on her. She held his eyes for a moment, then turned away and deliberately moved into a more crowded area.

"Mrs. Martin, isn't it?"

She looked to her right to see Mr. Bateman shadowing her in her circuit.

"John Bateman." He smiled, but despite his intent, she didn't find it at all charming.

She tipped her head and continued walking. She had seen him try his *charms* on more than one of the women. His reputation among them was not kind.

"I've noticed that you seem to have an in with the heiress."

"We are friends," she said in a clipped manner and attempted to increase her pace as a hint, the crowded space making it more difficult.

"That means you and I will be right cozy soon."

"I sincerely doubt that." Frost blew from her lips.

He just smiled in a more mocking manner. "I like spirited fillies. Much more fun to break."

Here was a man with the same background as Deville, and yet where Deville's mocking smile made him appear somewhat untouchable and the more appealing for it, Bateman just seemed . . . menacing. There was an inherent sense of danger about both men, but Deville's compelled, whereas Bateman's repelled. Maybe it was the overriding feel that Deville didn't need to use force to get what he desired.

That his prey would willingly surrender.

"Too bad there aren't any horses here for you then, Mr. Bateman. If you'll excuse me."

She caught sight of Deville again and decided that he was by far the better option and headed in his direction. He wore the same hot smile, but when his eyes skirted to the right of her, they turned frigid. She lost sight of him again in the shifting crowd.

"He's not going to win."

She gritted her teeth, but smiled at a passing widow who was amiably chatting with another guest. "I do not know of what you speak, Mr. Bateman."

"Deville. I saw you making eyes at each other."

She looked for an unattached guest that she might join, but all of a sudden everyone seemed paired off, with Bateman left as her match.

"Is that what it is called when you chance upon a person looking at you?"

"Hardly just looking. It is obvious to anyone with eyes that he has marked you."

"Marked me? You make it sound like an archery tournament, and I remember Mr. Deville not winning that portion of the competition." She brushed by another couple, trying to shake him off, but he determinedly stayed by her side. "And now that I think on it, I do not remember you doing well at it either."

Hardly a nice thing to say, but he was beyond the pale in rudeness, and she was safe enough inside the crowd.

She chanced a look over to see his eyes turn

cold. "So much fun to break. I see why Deville accepted the challenge. He's after you for one thing only. And when he gets it, you'll be left in the dust."

"Oh, and what is that? My witty repartee?"

"I can hardly reveal what he is after. The code denies me." Somehow from the slice of his smile she doubted the "code" would matter to someone like Bateman other than as a useful tool at times. "But be assured that Deville has little true desire for you. I, on the other hand, do not have such limits."

"How very fortunate for you."

"You should pick a winner, Mrs. Martin. It would be in your best interests."

"I hardly think you know my best interests. And I think you are confusing me with Mrs. Noke."

He laughed, a brittle sound that reminded her a bit of Deville's laugh when annoyed. She looked at Bateman, looking for any of the hidden depths that she had missed with Deville, but could see nothing.

"You seem a bit more circumspect than her ilk. But one bird is much like another."

"How clever." She steered in another direction, but he continued to shadow her. "I think perhaps we should pursue different walks now, Mr. Bateman."

"Deville is land hungry," he scoffed, completely ignoring her request. "Not something a clever woman would find attractive, as it completely ties up one's funds. I doubt he has a crown to his name, though he pretends otherwise."

"Your commentary makes little sense, Mr. Bateman." She switched paths again, only to find him still clinging like a creeping vine.

"If he has as much money as people say he does, he could buy any property, instead of that pitiful bit of land he wants."

"Hardly pitiful. Roseford Grange is quite attractive in many ways." She didn't know why she was defending him, but the beautiful lines of the sketch lingered in her memory. "And it's his family land—"

"Stupid. It's worthless property. And he's not the sentimental type. I'm sure he hasn't a groat."

She stopped, observing him with a tilt to her nose. "You sound jealous."

"Jealous of Deville?" He snorted. "The man doesn't have a thing I want. Thinks he is high and mighty because he is the son of a duke."

"Then I daresay you should spend less time thinking of him."

His gaze raked her. "I suppose he has *one* thing I want."

She stopped, her fists forming tight balls. "You are all alike. It's madness. But at least Deville has depth. Something beneath." She thought about the look on Deville's face when his last swing ejected that man from the competition. Then of Bateman's. "He may be arrogant and demanding and entirely frustrating to deal with, but at least he has a soul. What do you have?"

Bateman's mouth opened, and she turned to switch direction once again, this time bumping into a firm chest.

"My defender," Deville drawled.

She looked up and growled at his handsome face. His eyes briefly checked her over, as if she might have been scarred, and then turned to Bateman, cold and menacing.

Inexplicably enraged, she stomped on Deville's foot, her slipper doing little damage to his boot, and stormed out of the room with every intention of heading back home. She should have done so an hour past. She shouldn't have paid attention to the silly, lingering thoughts that William had planted.

Deville caught up to her halfway across the back courtyard. The moon was on the rise, half full and shining.

"Caroline," he called.

"Go away," she called back over her shoulder.

He stopped her with a hand on her arm. "At least you should have asked one of the footmen to accompany you home."

She should have, but she'd been too angry to ask. "I know the way to my own cottage. And there are hardly any rampaging Vikings waiting to spirit me away."

Amusement broke across his eyes. "That is good to know. There are a lot of drunken men though." His eyes turned serious. "Or men like Bateman."

"And you?"

"I have hardly had a thing to drink tonight," he said, completely ignoring the real thrust of her question.

"Well, you are hardly safe." She shook off his hand and continued toward the trees.

"Thank you."

She spun, hands on her hips. "What is the matter with all of you? Desperate for attention, or affection, I'm not sure which."

"Perhaps neither?"

She turned to continue walking and spun again, his natural grace the only thing saving them from a collision.

"And the arrogance! You fight tooth and nail for some prize, yet all of you seem to think yourselves derided."

He raised a silky brow. "I think you are throwing a tantrum."

She poked a finger against his chest. "I don't throw tantrums. I am dignified."

She threw back her shoulders and walked through the small forest to her cottage grove, her legs stretching to stay ahead of his.

"You attribute feelings to us that I'm not sure we possess."

"Feelings you do not possess? Like pain, loss, agony?"

He frowned. "What are you—"

"Like those men ejected from the competition? I know you empathized."

His eyes narrowed. The crickets chirped in the bushes surrounding her door as her chest heaved. "You found the sketch."

Something in her eyes must have given her away.

"You *took* the sketch." His assessing gaze shifted to her lips. "Tut, tut, Caroline. A saboteur *and* a thief. What lengths you will go to in order to win my regard."

"As if I need to win your regard. You strut like a peacock for me already."

"It must be working. Look at you."

She turned and opened her door with fumbling fingers. His hand covered hers on the knob.

"The sketch. Retrieve and return it to me."

Her breath met the oak of the door as he pressed against her. "I will return it if you promise to renounce your blackmail."

His hand dropped, though he didn't move otherwise. "A bargain?"

"Yes," she said firmly.

"No."

"No?" She turned, trapped between his body and the door. "But don't you want your sketch back?"

"There are others." The shadows shifted on his face, so close to hers.

She scrambled for purchase. "What if I tell the guests?"

"That I draw?" He lifted a brow. "It's part of a gentleman's routine. No one will care."

But that wasn't quite true. She could see it in his eyes. She narrowed hers. "You don't want anyone to see that sketch. It shows too much."

"Really. And what does it show?" His mouth moved toward hers.

"That you are vulnerable," she whispered. "That you want the prize too much."

He had the temerity to laugh, lips pulling to within a hairbreadth of hers. "That is what everyone feels and wants that is entered into this competition. Little harm that knowledge will do to me."

"The sketch shows a glimpse into you."

"Do you believe that?" He laughed, but the lines near his eyes and mouth creased downward. "Go ahead, show everyone the sketch. See what they say."

She watched him for a second. Mulled over calling his bluff. "No. Good night, Mr. Deville."

She reached behind her and turned the knob, but instead of falling into the cottage, she was pulled into warm arms . . .

"I don't believe I'm ready to call it a night." Smooth lips captured hers in a kiss of passion, of promise, hinting at something more, some unplumbed depths, just as his picture had. Sweet, gentle, heady, taking her completely off guard.

. . . he pushed her inside.

Chapter 13

What types of feat or scandal might be afoot to-night? The titillation as we head into the high heat of summer before the competition's respite has us tipped forward in our chairs.

Warm spice drifted around her limbs, curling and pulling.

Lips brushed her ear to the area where her hair met her neck.

He slid her hair to the side and attached lips there. Her breath hitched, the warmth invading her skin where his lips touched and then spreading in all directions. Down her throat, down her belly, down her legs, to her knees, which buckled.

"Shhh, Caro." The pet name that slipped from his lips, delivered in a different way from how others said it, the vowels softer, like the Italian pet form instead of a shortened version of her own name. Nothing like the friendly, familiar way Sarah said it. More like a husky refrain of a prayer to a lover.

"We can't—" Her breath caught as he nibbled.

"A lovely bite to claim you as mine? It won't

take much." The pressure of his lips built, pulled.

The drugging effect combined with terror and she pushed away. "No."

His eyes were heavy, as if he were the one passion drugged and not she. "How devastating."

She took a shaky breath and tried to calm the racing currents inside her. "Very well. Claim your kiss, your forfeit, and—"

A finger pulled along the exposed skin at the edge of her bodice. "You successfully make the others do your bidding—the women, the young boys, even that horrid hag Mrs. Francis. You have them all eating out of the palm of your lovely hand. I have to admit that it is a truly inviting hand and I'm tempted to sip from it, but too long have I pulled the strings myself. I will set the terms of your forfeits."

Outrage overtook her, swift and sure. "You dare—"

His finger dipped below her bodice and the edge of her rigid corset, and the tip of his finger brushed her nipple, strangling anything that might have emerged from her mouth.

"You are such a sweet, ripe plum. All outrage and defiance. High color and heaving breasts. Did you really think that I would demand a mere kiss in return?" His finger pulled back along the same path, tweaking her nipple again and causing the raging heat and outrage to convert into wildfire. "Do you know what I do when I think about you on your back, straining toward my hand, bucking against my cock? Wild and wanton and altogether delectable?"

She couldn't move, couldn't respond.

His lips moved near her ear. "Do you know how many times I've taken myself in hand, thinking it was you that was smiling up at me, you that I was entering, you that was swallowing every last bit?"

A strangled sound was the only thing that emerged.

"You might try and convince yourself that it isn't dreams of completion you are having night after night, but your body says something entirely different." A hand moved down her back and around her backside. She moved into him without conscious thought, fit around his leg like a snug wrapper.

His other hand joined the first, cupping her, pulling her against his thigh in slow strokes, making her hot and heavy. The entryway of her cottage vanished, and she didn't think she could even work up the outrage were one of the guests to open the door and peek inside. Everything coiled to the feel of his leg rubbing against her, to the heat and friction, the complete fire in his eyes.

"And that's why I know I will have you. All of you." His head dipped so that his cheek stroked hers. "And I cannot wait."

She felt the press of the wall against her back, the press of his leg against her, the relentless stroking and pressure. His lips moved along her jaw, down her neck, to her throat. Her head tipped back against the wall as he continued the assault. The ceiling blurred, and if asked to describe her own decor, she wouldn't have been able to give a single detail. She pushed against him on the tips of her toes, the feeling of orgasm pushing up on her, building. The strength of the one approaching made her breath catch.

"You won't let me outwardly brand you, but I think I can inwardly do so."

A tongue reached under the frilly material lining her bodice. A hand pushed her breast up and the tip brushed against her clothing, up and over, freed to his touch, to his lips. He sucked once, twice, ground his thigh into her, and she was convulsing against him, sounds escaping that she couldn't control. His lips covered hers, sucking the sounds greedily, just as he had done to another part of her a moment before. She shuddered and he slowly pulled his thigh away, let her gently drop to the floor, her feet finding purchase once more.

"You have played with more fire concerning me than you probably are aware of. And I have to admit"—he pulled a strand of hair around his first finger—"that it makes me want you even more, even though I know the games women play."

"I have never entered the game," she whispered, trying to calm her body and her mind.

"Which just makes you all the more sweet a fruit. I'll see you in the morning, Caroline," he whispered. "And then the morning after that, and each one following."

Chapter 14

Sometimes the heart works without the express permission of the mind, as surely a gadabout young miss is wont to tell. Such is the trouble with skirting out from under the strictures of our elders.

"That was an excellent resolution. Such a taciturn and stern man, Mr. Wallace is. I think he has the event well in hand," Mrs. Francis said.

Caroline nodded, wondering how they thought Mr. Wallace was in charge of anything, beyond ordering things done that were already in progress.

"The bonfire placement is of some consternation. If Mr. Wallace thinks that it should be under review again, of course it must."

Caroline nodded a little more sharply. "I am off to do so."

"Do bear in mind what Mr. Wallace said. He is such a good influence on your decisions."

Caroline held her breath, nodding again, her head bobbing on a continual axis of strained patience.

"I think he might have a care in your direction."

"As honored as I would be—"

"Yes, I think it a lovely match. I will send whispers to the right ears."

"I'd rather you didn't, Mrs. Francis. I am quite able to handle my own affairs." In every sense of the word. And she was feeling decidedly stubborn today.

Mrs. Francis's chin raised a notch. "Too proud for some good advice; for shame, Mrs. Martin."

Caroline swallowed, the rebellious thought that she didn't need this woman's goodwill springing forth. She quashed it. Deville's negative effect was worse than she'd thought. "Not too proud, Mrs. Francis, simply not ready. It is not good to rush into things, isn't that what you always say?"

The matron did not look pleased to have her own words used against her, but Caroline wasn't going to be a dormouse. "Indeed. But if you don't choose the good when it is in front of you, you may miss out completely. Good day, Mrs. Martin."

Caroline watched her stalk away, then pivoted and strode down the path.

She stopped in her tracks as the path split, seeing *him* leaning against a tree, smoking, that lazy disregard that he excelled at practically stripping the bark from the trunk of the tree. "Are you ever anywhere other than near me?"

"Not if I can help it," he said, dragging the cheroot from his lips, a smile curving his mouth.

"I'm not pleased with you at the moment. You are a bad influence."

"I'm pleased to hear it."

"You shouldn't be. I quite possibly will be avoiding you indefinitely."

He lifted an indolent brow and tapped his thigh. "I don't think I shall allow that. Who will relieve the tedium?"

"I don't much care. I told you to leave during the break. That you'd be irreparably bored—ye of so little entertainment. Unfortunately, Mr. Deville, I have no time at present to be your entertainment. I'm in a hurry."

"Am I still Mr. Deville? How unfortunate indeed," he drawled.

She stalked past him, assured in her new resolution to keep him firmly in check and to reassert herself as the capable, stern woman that she knew she could be.

He pushed off the tree and strode next to her, his strides eating up the distance in no time. "Where are we off to?"

"The council can't decide where they want the booths and staging. *I* am off to sketch multiple options so that they can decide."

"Are you serious?"

"Quite." She ground her teeth against the disbelief in his voice. That she had to do this again for Mr. Wallace was almost more irritating than Deville.

"You seem delighted."

"I'm not."

"Well, then I must help you. Far be it from me to leave a lady in the lurch."

She turned from the path, marching across the open expanse of the valley. "No, thank you."

She reached the spot, visualizing the place-
ments. Why Mr. Wallace couldn't just accept her
assurance . . .

Deville stepped next to her. "This looks
familiar."

She pursed her lips and tried to shift things
around in her mind. If the table went there, and
the first set of chairs there, just like her design . . .

"What are you doing?"

"Thinking."

If the bonfire were placed just so, and the—

"About what?"

She glared at him. "If you are going to pester
me, you may as well help."

The next fifteen minutes consisted of her issu-
ing commands and an increasingly fidgety rake
following them.

She tapped her lips. "Put that one over there."
She pointed toward a pillar, and Deville moved
the rock she was using as a tool to visualize the
result. "And the next one there."

He dutifully moved the other into place, though
it was more like he languidly hefted it; everything
he did had some sensual movement, a glance or
wicked smile.

"Perfect." She nodded sharply and examined
the placement. "Much easier to visualize this
way."

"What are you attempting to do? I've been a
good boy this whole time as your brood stallion,
not asking questions."

"Brood stallion?" She snorted. "More my hearty
donkey."

An eyebrow lifted. "Caroline, what are you trying to do?"

"I need a good place for a bonfire. Somewhere not in the way, but in the midst all the same. The problem is that the rocks will make it more difficult to dance."

"A bonfire?" he asked evenly.

"Well, it's hardly a problem of epic proportions, but we need one," she defended.

He looked around the space for a maximum of two seconds and then pointed. "There."

"There? How can you say that? You've hardly looked."

He gave her a look. "Put your fire there."

She chewed her lip. "I'm not sure."

He dropped the rock he was holding with a thump, and drew out a crumpled piece of paper from somewhere and a chunk of black chalk. A few quick swipes with the chalk, then his finger, the paper bending over his palm as he sketched, and he shoved the paper in her direction.

She gripped the piece, the lines uneven and flowing, movement already on the page as the lined figures danced around the flames, the tables and chairs where she had wanted them, everything in a place that *worked*. He had solved her problem in two minutes.

"How did . . ."

He folded his arms. "Can we leave now?"

She continued to examine the paper, the emotion that she didn't think he knew he revealed—that he would most likely be aghast if he ever discovered. The unrelenting glimpses of a man behind the masks. She carefully folded the page and stuck it into her bag. "Would you care to enjoy a repast with me?"

Horror overtook her as soon as the blurted question left her mouth. If anyone stopped by her cottage while he was there . . . but something else ran through her as she saw his narrowed eyes, then the pleased expression cross his face.

"Lead the way."

She was slightly surprised when he helped her arrange a tray of cheese, fruit, and sausage, cutting or peeling as needed. Mary was visiting a neighboring town to help her sick mother, so she was on her own for at least a week.

"Why did you stay?" She nibbled an apple slice as they put the tray on the table and sat down, wondering why he had participated in helping her with the layout.

"Isn't it obvious why I stayed?" He drew a finger along the table, then tossed a piece of cheese into his mouth.

"You want another boon?"

"What if simply being by your side is my boon?"

She stared at him, then picked up another slice, nibbling.

"Are you always so careful about how you eat?" he asked.

"What, instead of popping them down my gullet like you do?"

"You eat that like a squirrel. Not with any intent to savor the flavor, but merely as a way to stay on top of the nut."

"I enjoy them slowly, carefully, in order to savor the essence."

"Do you?"

She picked up a strawberry, her favorite fruit, and bit the end, the burst of sweet flavor encasing her tongue. "It's lovely this way. Makes the experience last."

"You can simply take another." He popped an entire berry.

She looked at him from under her lashes as she took another. "That is the difference between us. You see endless supplies of berries. One as good as the next. While I try to hold on to and enjoy the ones I have."

His eyes narrowed. "I assure you, I enjoy them to the utmost."

"Oh, I don't doubt you enjoy them for the few seconds they take to consume. But then you are on to the next fruit." She pointed at a pear. "Or the next platter."

"Do I sense a thread of jealousy?"

"Simply observation and good sense."

"And I think that is where you go wrong, Caroline."

"Is it, *Sebastien*?"

His eyes darkened in pleasure at her use of his name. "You rely too much on your good sense, instead of simply accepting the pleasure in front of you."

"That is because I know where the pleasure goes. And how it ends."

He tipped a pear slice back and forth along its

curved back. "I've heard that your husband wasn't much of a man."

She stiffened. "Oh, he was plenty much of a *man*. He just wasn't much of a husband." Not much of one at all.

"And you judge all men by his standard."

"Only the ones that shift in his footprints."

He raised a brow. "You are attracted to rogues. Don't you think that says something about your spirit?"

"That I am fond of painful relationships?"

"That you are a rogue yourself."

She laughed; she couldn't stop herself. "You are certainly creative. I suppose that comes with your artistic abilities."

"Some kind of abilities." His hand brushed hers as he selected another slice. "Your husband didn't even maintain a steady income, is that correct? Had no position of power?"

"Little does it matter what position a man has. It is what is inside that counts."

"You don't truly believe that fairy wash, do you?"

"I do," she said quietly. Patrick was a terrible example, but her papa had been a wonderful one. The earl had a plethora of power and a kingdom of coin, but Papa had trumped him in every other way. "Why wouldn't you?"

"No one believes that it is what is inside that counts. Ask any of the women at the house."

"I have no need to ask anyone else. I know what I believe, Mr. Deville."

"You only *think* you believe that. It is a noble sentiment, but foolish. A man is what he has in this world. What he represents."

"Then it shows poorly on the commoners, does it not?"

"Absolutely. You don't see them triumphing over the nobility, do you? They who have nothing . . . truly have nothing."

"That is ridiculous. And what an unhappy thought to live with."

"Better to know the truth than to delude oneself."

"So you are saying that only someone below your station would be willing to marry you?"

"Of course."

"Then you know some poor characters."

"Ask any of the women at the house."

"I repeat that I do not need to." She crossed her arms. "I ran off with a man who had nothing because I thought he had something inside."

"And you were wrong."

"In that instance, I was," she said as calmly as she could manage. "But it does not negate the fact that he had less than I did and I ran with him anyway."

"And you were miserable."

"I was miserable because of the circumstances, not because that was a faulty judgment to have. But to judge all men by that—"

"You can't tell me you do *not* judge all men by your husband." She tensed. "You hold all men to his standard, or nonstandard as it were."

*   *   *

Sebastien watched the way she tensed up. The way she tried to defend herself. He smiled thinly, suspicions confirmed.

"I loved Patrick, Mr. Deville. There was once a time when I thought the world rose on his smile," she said softly.

Sebastien's smile dropped, his eyes narrowed. "And?"

"And . . ." She rolled her mug between her hands. "He decided that wasn't quite enough."

"He took a mistress?"

"There were a string of women, not just one. And he steadily drank more, gambled more. Ran away. It turned rather unpleasant."

"So your test did not quite pan out."

"My *test*? My *life*. Why am I even telling you this?" She stood and abruptly jerked the dishes from the table, taking them to the sink.

Something unidentifiable tweaked within him. "You seem to be doing well now."

She vigorously scrubbed one dish, her back to him.

He rose and removed the dish from her hands, setting it on the counter. He nudged her to the side with his thigh, turning her just enough toward him that he could smooth the hair wisps at her temple that were always coming loose, straining to be free. "Why don't you just let go, Caroline?"

"And do what? Do you know how hard I've worked to put that bad decision behind me?"

"It was one bad decision. That doesn't mean you will make the same mistake again."

"Won't I?" She gave him an ironic look, to which he smiled winningly.

"Never." He brushed a kiss to her temple, replacing his fingertips in smoothing the hair there. He felt her shudder against him, and for a second the thought that maybe he shouldn't continue this course of action—perhaps he should leave her alone and mostly whole—unnerved him. But when she pressed into him, accepting the comfort, her lovely body molding to his—the promise of fully connecting with her, of completing two pieces of a puzzle—he crushed the uncertainty.

Besides, he was doing her a favor by unlocking the side of her she had restrained for so long. She would thank him eventually.

The strange, uncomfortable feeling returned, and he ruthlessly pushed it aside, rubbing a hand down her back and pulling her closer, nearly meshing them together in a perfect fit. Almost. His body strained to complete the fit. But years of practice reading women told him not yet. *Not yet*.

His fingertips pulled along the back of her dress, smoothing the material beneath, edging down her spine. He jerked his hand back up and into her nape, his fingers wanting to curl around her backside and bring her closer, his body completely ignoring his brain's commands.

She pulled away. Slowly. As if she'd rather stay pressed against him.

Perfect. It wouldn't take until nightfall for her to fall into his arms in perfect surrender.

"I need to go into the village and deliver the sketch and then help the children learn their new dance." She nudged him aside and washed the other dish. "I will be gone the rest of the day, so I'm sure you'll want to return to the manor to find other pleasures."

Not perfect. "I thought that you were done with the dreaded village tasks?"

"No."

"Stay here." He smiled his best smile, the one that always worked. "I'll be good."

There was a softening of her expression, just for a second, then steel as her head cocked to the side. "No. Don't push me, Sebastien, or all your tactics will be for naught."

Shock and pleasure ran through him in equal measures. The combination of innocence and steel was like sharp fingernails raking his back, followed by a cup of warm honey that dripped straight to his groin.

"Then I'll just have to accompany you."

She gave him a doubtful look. "I didn't ask you, first of all. Secondly, they are children. Somehow I don't see you . . . or them . . . surviving."

"I love children."

Naggy little bastards. Snot-nosed and demanding.

"Right. Well"—she wiped her hands—"I'm due for some comedy. And you know how to dance. We'll see how long you last."

It was a standoff. Caroline hid a smile. Sebastien stood, one eyebrow cocked as the children stood in a line, staring at him with various expressions on their faces. Some mirrored his slightly nauseated look, others were curious, and some of the little girls already looked enamored. Caroline decided not to do a thing as she cleared the area for practice.

"What's he doing here?" Phillip, one of the oldest boys present, and a bit of a bully, thumbed toward Sebastien.

"He's going to help us learn the dance."

The boy crossed his arm. "We don't need him."

Sebastien leaned against a tree; blasted man always seemed to have one at hand. "Let's see you dance then."

"I don't know the steps yet."

"Then seems as if you need a teacher, loggerhead."

Phillip's color went red. "Loggerhead? A cit dandy calling someone a loggerhead?"

"Seems that way. Don't you know a good cut of cloth when you see one?" He flicked his collar.

Phillip flicked his own collar. "Mrs. Martin says it is the man beneath the clothing. Don't see why she is keeping with the likes of you." The statement was somewhat ironic, as Phillip was always dressed well. As the son of one of the wealthier villagers, he lorded it over the others. She had uttered the statement for his benefit as much as for sweet Noah's.

"That's enough, Phillip," she said.

Phillip's eyes narrowed further on Sebastien, and she decided to watch him in case he took it upon himself to bully the younger ones as a way of relieving his pique.

One of the smallest girls, Polly, tugged on the bottom edge of Sebastien's coat. "I like you," she said, in a manner that only a six year old could.

He dropped to his knees. "And what good taste you have."

Caroline rolled her eyes and clapped her hands. "Let's pair up."

The younger boys reluctantly paired with the younger girls, while the older ones were much quicker to grab the girl of their choice.

"Let's start with the boys. Girls, you will be doing the opposite. Right foot front. Yes. Left side step. Correct."

She kept calling directions, the children stumbling or gliding as they alternately found or lost their footing. They made it through one round of the eight-minute dance.

"Let's try it ag—"

Arms swept her around. The first step would have been a stumble if her feet had even touched the ground. He set her down in the right position, easily pushing her into the next form, leading her around, twirling her, being gentle when he needed to be, firm when required.

The children's eyes were wide when they were finished. New respect shone in the boys' eyes, though Noah looked irritated. The girls were all moon-eyed.

Caroline smoothed her hair and tried to calm her racing heart. "Let's switch partners. The person in the couple to your right should be fine."

They continued to switch, Sebastien surprising her by dancing with the smaller girls intermittently. She would have expected him to dance with the older ones, the ones near Sarah's age who were perfect for a flirtation. But he left them to the older boys, which seemed to gain him an ounce more respect with that group.

They took a break, and a tentative salvo by one of the older boys had the rest clamoring around Sebastien asking questions. Even Noah clung to the edge of the group. More surprising was the way that Sebastien seemed to consider each question seriously before answering it. She neared the cluster.

". . . you don't want to be seen in that light," Sebastien said. One of the boys saw her and nudged the boy next to him; the nudge rippled through the crowd. "It will not help your hunt if—" A boy at the front did some complicated hand motion.

"—if you do not have your hunting equipment and dogs." He turned to her. "Mrs. Martin, is there something I can help you with?"

She was sure that "hunting equipment and dogs" was not what he had been about to say. "I was curious about what you were discussing."

"Merely hunting tactics."

"You should be discussing dancing."

"And how hunting relates to dancing, of course. You would be surprised how well they relate."

"Do enlighten me."

He raised that infernal brow. "I think not. You have your areas of expertise, and I have mine." He waved a hand toward the girls, who were practicing with each other. "We will rejoin you in a minute."

She narrowed her eyes, but the pleading expressions on the boys' faces, even Noah's, made her sigh and turn back.

"Mr. Deville, how do you attract the prey away from the herd though?"

She closed her eyes and decided that she had not just heard that.

Ten minutes later the groups were back together and the older children were practicing the steps with each other, the boys considerably better than they had been. He hadn't shown them a single step, but their movements were more purposeful, even when wrong, their leading and motions making the girls' eyes go wide.

Sebastien moved among the younger ones while she helped the individual dancers. She neared him sometime later surrounded by a group of girls of all ages.

"Now, if one of the boys pulls you too close, you step on his foot just like this." He stomped on a stubby branch. His eyes caught Caroline's. "Mrs. Martin can tell you its usefulness as a way to keep the boys in line. You try."

Each girl did a little stomp; Polly actually jumped up and down on the twig, shouting, "You stay away, boy!"

"Good going, Polly, but temper your stomping to the offense. If it's only a little close, you should just press lightly."

She stomped again with two feet, then looked up at him hopefully. He paused a moment and shrugged. "Well, you'll make an impact at the very least."

Caroline clapped her hands. "It's nearing time for you all to be getting back to your regular tasks. One last go. Everyone," she said over the crowd.

A number of groans were heard, and wasn't that the odd thing. Some of the boys actually looked disappointed.

"Yes, everyone. Line up. Boys, right foot," Sebastien said.

He swept her into the dance again, but this time she was ready. Every once in a while he would call out a cue, the other boys calling cues as well. The world whirled around, colors shifting and becoming brighter as she moved against him, and he against her.

Everything felt so right.

He pulled her close, leaning over her, putting a dip in her back in the last move.

"Mrs. Martin! Stomp on his foot!"

Polly's shout sent the children into giggles and loosened the tension that had taken hold of the space.

They walked along the path, a companionable silence enveloping them, unlike what Sebastien was used to in the presence of previous women. They usually needed to talk or be complimented. Not that they were all that way, but most of the women of his acquaintance, the women of the *ton*, were.

"You were good with the children."

"Is that surprise I hear in your voice?"

"I have to admit that it is. I didn't think you would even tolerate them, no less help as much as you did. What did you say to the boys?"

"I merely reminded them what dancing is for."

"Dancing is for merriment."

He looked at her, unsure if her matter-of-fact tone was sarcastic or truly meant. She looked earnestly back.

"You do not honestly believe that, do you?"

"I do. Dancing is lovely. Moving to the music. The body fairly sings along with the instruments."

Another glimpse of that passion in her face, humming beneath her skin. His body thrummed. "Dancing is a mating ritual."

She snorted. "Why am I not surprised that you think so?"

He abruptly twirled her, dipping her back, his face inches from hers, his gaze switching from her eyes to her mouth and back again in a slow perusal. "Don't you?"

"No." But her voice was too husky.

He reluctantly let her up. "Do not make light of the power of a dance. The ability to touch and lead, to learn about your partner."

"You make it sound like a conversation."

"Isn't it? It is the body's way to communicate without the interference of the mouth." He smiled slowly. "Not that I would want to limit the communications between mouths."

"You are a terrible wretch."

But there was no irritated heat in her statement. It seemed almost . . . fond. She was in a surprisingly mellow mood. The interaction with the children had softened her up, which had been his intention. The little jackanapes had turned out to be entertaining in their own right. He had not needed to interact with children after leaving childhood behind, and therefore had expected a bunch of screaming hoydens.

Not that they hadn't been screaming hoydens. But entertaining screaming hoydens all the same.

"Dancing is a mating ritual," he reaffirmed.

"I will grudgingly concede that dancing allows men and women to further matches."

"In order to make one's *ideal* match."

She shook her head. "Many a couple do not dance well together who are perfectly happy."

"Did you dance well with Patrick?"

"He was a charming dancer. He danced well with everyone." A note of sarcasm worked its way into her voice. "So, if that is true, I suppose that if a man dances well with all women, then he is the perfect mate to all of them?"

He smiled in a way designed to make her steam, but there wasn't any true ire in her expression as they continued to argue and talk—as he fell into the most comfortable chat with a woman that he'd ever had. He still wanted to do unspeakable things to her, but there was something very satisfying about watching her cook, trading glances with her over dinner, keeping her entertained with stories of London while she worked on the tournament banners in front of the hearth.

Sebastien watched her eyes close. Her breathing evened. He knew the seduction was going well. But that she was comfortable enough with him to fall asleep in his presence, while he was inside her cottage, surprised him. As did the feeling of peace that encompassed him sitting in the ratty, comfortable chair, in front of the red, waning fire, watching her sleep a few paces away.

He considered leaving and going back to the manor house. A log popped, the warm coziness keeping him firmly in his chair. He withdrew a piece of parchment and the chalk he kept in his sewn pouch. He had irreparably damaged a string of trousers with the black substance long ago before sewing himself the answer.

Starting with her face, he made quick lines of her features, her form, the gentle curve of her chin, the planes of her cheeks. He wiped a thumb along her neck, blending the lines into the hitched curve of a bodice. Pulled a finger along her hairline, wisping the hair there out in a cloudy halo around her face, the rest of her wavy blonde hair spread out on the pillow, clinging to the back of the sofa.

She was beautiful; there was no denying that. But it was the hand under her chin, the way one foot tucked under her shin that captivated him. The peaceful look on her face, lashes gently brushing cheeks he itched to feel beneath the pads of his bare fingers. Yet at the same time he wished to stain the fabric of her dress with charcoal black, to push away and run back to the stately manor with its pristine, glossy surface and promise of treasures beyond belief.

The picture took form, the details added and arranged, smoothed and indented. She sighed, and his eyes drew back to her sleeping form, then to the paper.

Finally, a finished sketch. It was a good likeness, a true reflection of some feeling, like peace or comfort. There was something he hadn't been able to capture about her fully awake. Hadn't been able to duplicate in her eyes yet in the half-finished sketches of her he had made. Something that was uniquely Caroline that he hadn't been able to wrangle onto the page.

He pulled out his cloth and wiped his fingers, staining the fabric.

He uncurled and slipped his arms beneath her knees. Her arms sleepily curved around his neck, and he felt a twinge. That feeling he was trying to capture slid past him once more.

He carried her into her bedroom and stopped to look around, keeping her close as he did so.

The bedroom was decorated in cream and gold, speckles of colors in the objects and paintings in the space. He pulled back the bedcovers and set her gently on the bed. The top laces of her dress easily came free beneath his fingertips, the worn muslin soft and downy, provoking feelings of comfort and need. He slipped it off one arm, then the other, lightly moving her to accomplish the task.

The need to wake her and show her all the things a boon could be was strong, but the softened contours of her face, the wispy wings of hair, made him continue to undress her in the same manner he had started.

The dress shimmied down her legs, rolling off perfect limbs. A locket, heavy and gold, hung to the side, straining, pulling. He had long wondered what it contained. He picked it up, turning it over in his hand. His fingers clenched around the edges, the clasp taunting him to flick it open. The tantalizing pull of the gold vying with his abject resentment of the color and all it represented. He tucked it closer to her, resisting the urge to remove it along with everything else.

The press of the gold in the room pushed in on him. Her hair, golden and fine; the glow of the gilt in the lamplight; the linens threaded and shimmering. It made him want to push back. To ravish the pristine environment, to make her beg and scream, her head thrashing from pleasure, the gold wild, streaming through his hands, under his complete control.

The bedspread, instead of her chemise, bunched in his fists. The hard-won control that had turned his rage into resentment, his loss into bitter strength, forced him not to touch her. Not to give up the control, to fall to someone else's spell. She stirred, one hand tucked against his thigh. So easy to take what would be so willingly offered once he started. They all fell before him if he desired it.

He had never been so tempted before. Or so sure of his own demise.

He pulled the covers up to her chin, tucking them around her shoulders, brushing the gold strands away from her face, spreading them over the pillow. A fairy who cared for others first. Who felt something for other people that wasn't just desire or hate. Who didn't judge everyone based on his usefulness. Who possibly could distinguish love from desire.

Her cheek moved into his fingers, and he stroked the smooth skin.

No, love was just a softer form of desire. A desire for companionship, or parental feelings, or understanding. Love stopped when a person turned less useful—became less of a companion, less of an achiever, less of a prize. When those feelings faded, what was left of love?

He stood and looked around the room in the diminishing candlelight, at the softening of the edges, of the gold. He blew out the candle and strode from the room. He would continue his quest, because at the moment he couldn't consider doing anything else.

Chapter 15

~~~⚬~~~

London is alight with the contestants who have chosen to return to her bower for the fortnight. One wonders why all the guests haven't traveled to her hearth for the break in the games.

A beautiful, dusky pink rose blinked at her from the pillow next to hers. She smiled, turned, closed her eyes, then froze.

Every sense went on alert. A leftover thread of spice and warmth stated that Sebastien had been in the room, but not for many hours. Her chemise and stays were still on, tangled about her. There was no indentation anywhere else on the bed. No soreness of her limbs. The sounds of birds chirping and squirrels nattering were the only noises that met her ears.

She turned back to the delicate flower. She didn't remember falling asleep. She doubly didn't remember being tucked in. And the bloom? He had to have returned to lay it there.

She picked it up, bringing it closer to her nose. The sweet fragrance claimed it as one from her own garden. She unwillingly smiled again.

The man was a menace as intoxicating as the rose, as dangerous as the thorns he had shaved from the stem. Alternately thoughtful and rude. Something like a disreputable pet—the one who wets on the floor when everyone is looking and lifts an eyebrow as if to say, *Yes?*

She smiled at the image and pulled the rose against her chest. She had to be cautious, yes, but life was more than the sum of her fears, founded or not.

Images of Patrick unfolded. Of daring eyes and hands, of promises that were always broken. Of a troth that had led to mussed sheets and heartbreak, wandering eyes and dissatisfaction. Of a marriage that would not have taken place without the earl's interference—her name changed with the exchange of a few pounds of coin and pride.

She looked at the rose. The earl wouldn't clean up two mistakes like that, but for once she didn't feel the dread of the earl's wrath. It was her choice to make. And Sebastien wasn't making promises. She knew where he stood.

It was the broken promises and betrayal that hurt the most. As long as she kept her heart strong, she could wave farewell when the tournament came to an end.

She had to believe that.

The festivities were in full swing by the time Sebastien sauntered to the edges of the ruins. His eyes immediately sought Caroline, finding her in the midst, nodding and pointing to the others, the general at the head of her troops.

Her soft crown of gold glittered against the lanterns and firelight. Three men surrounded her on the side facing him, dressed in their backcountry finery; even the gentry males hardly held a candle to the lowest of the *ton*'s ware. He didn't like the looks in their eyes—the appreciative and considering stares. Even from here he could see the rusted wheels working in their heads as they surveyed her or asked a question, watching her throat move as she talked, the tilt of her head.

He flipped his tinderbox and exhaled a stream of smoke. Easy enough to pick off the "best" of them. In Town it wouldn't even have registered as something he needed to do, but here, with her, a barely restrained urge to throttle someone gripped him.

The man in blue would go first. Jelly-filled and weepy-eyed, he'd either bluster or cry. The man in green—

He felt a tug and looked down to see huge glassy eyes staring up.

"Mr. Deville, I've lost the steps," Polly whispered in a tone that was anything but quiet.

Her grubby little hand gripped his expensive coat, watery eyes blinked. Appalling little creatures, children. He should remove his perfectly cut coat from her fingers, in order to salvage as much of the material as he could. The firelight caught her eyes, making them shine blue-gray, much like Caroline's. A bitty angel in disguise.

He knelt down, which allowed her to grip another part of his coat, infecting it as well. "You've forgotten the steps to the dance?" He stubbed the cheroot on the ground, his eyes staying focused on the color of hers, so like another perfect pair.

"Yes." Her head bowed.

"Well, that won't do." He lifted her chin. "Have you asked one of the other girls to help?"

She grimaced. "They said they are too busy. But all they do is giggle after the boys."

"What about the boys? Have you asked Noah?"

She shook her head miserably. "Too busy giggling after the girls."

Amusement ran through him. "Only thing for it then." He stood and offered his hand. "Right, back, left."

They danced just outside the first ring of columns. Just far enough that no one near the bonfire would see.

Polly stepped on his foot an average of two out of every five steps, so he started to simply spin her around, to her laughing delight. When he finally put her down, she was breathing hard and her color was high.

"I must show Mama before I lose them again."

"Off with you then."

She waved and took off down the gentle slope.

A slow clapping brought his attention to the left, a sense telling him who it was before he saw her. Caroline leaned against one of the columns in a mockery of one of his own well-worn poses. "Really, Mr. Deville, a little young for you, isn't she?"

"How utterly common of you, Caroline, to suggest such a thing. I'm shocked." He sauntered over and leaned into her, pressing into the same column. He kept his hands in his pockets, using only his shoulders to bring himself nearer to her position. He watched with satisfaction as her eyes darkened and her lips moistened. She darted a glance around, no doubt to check if they were being observed.

The moonlight and firelight glinted and reflected off the columns, pulling and dispelling the shadows in turn.

She tilted her head. "Little can shock you, I think."

"Much can shock me, just not the types of things that normally shock others."

"Mmmm. Well, I can't say the same in this instance. I can't believe you chose to come." She looked at him skeptically, then cast the look over the joyously ratty entourage below.

"No?" He touched a curl. "Do you not know that I would do anything for you?"

She gave him a deadpan look. "You will behave if you attend."

"I will be nothing but the most charming gentleman I can be." He smiled winningly.

She bit her lip. "I don't know . . ."

"Come now, Caroline, where is your sense of comedy now? Didn't you fancy a scene with the children earlier? Think of what awaits with me in the midst of a mass of dreadful commoners."

She hesitated.

"Mrs. Martin!" Noah burst into the clearing. "The group dance is set to begin! It's a good thing I saw the edge of your dress!" He hustled around her, then stopped when he saw Sebastien.

"Oh, good evening, sir."

Sebastien tilted his head.

"Are you to attend the festivities?"

"I do believe I shall, thank you, Mr. Miller. Shall we see what waits below?"

He strode forth down the hill with Noah, allowing Caroline to nervously catch up.

"Noah, you will help Mr. Deville, won't you? Introduce him to some of the men?" She tossed Sebastien a warning look edged with challenge before walking toward the matrons and leaving him behind.

Noah looked uncertain, but then motioned toward the fire, to the glowing shapes and happy faces. Hands covered mouths and eyes darted toward Sebastien as the mass of the hoi polloi whispered and ogled. He pulled forth his most disarming smile and began to chat with the more stringent-looking women and men. He could play the game if he so chose, and the only way to get Caroline was to play it tonight. She would little thank him if he threatened her reputation.

No, he thought, as her erstwhile suitors shook his hand, he didn't think that he would let anyone else discover what she tried so hard to hide beneath her magnificently competent facade. He smiled charmingly and joined in a discussion on crops, all the while watching her work her magic.

She handled the children. She handled the bullies. She handled the matrons and the upright prigs. She handled the men who had tipped the bottle a little too heavily and were apt to grope a little in their quest for the physical support of a helping shoulder. More than a few sported bruised ribs after being "handled" by her, he was sure.

She had never elbowed him in the ribs, not even when he had been his most annoying. Not that he ever expected to be elbowed, but now he wondered at the lack. She was obviously quite capable.

"Mr. Deville, is it?"

A severely dressed man stood in front of him, brown hair lightening to silver at the temples. His back straight as if the pole up his backside had been in place since birth.

"Yes. I don't believe I've had the *pleasure*." Eh. He only needed to make a good impression on most of them. For some reason this one raised his hackles.

"Mr. Wallace."

Ah, so this was the man who sought Caroline's hand and whom the matrons were pushing her toward. He looked the man over more fully. No, he wouldn't do at all.

He was trying to decide whether to simply ignore him or to break the man when Wallace spoke first.

"How do you know Mrs. Martin?"

Sebastien considered the man. "We met at the manor. She is helping with the games."

"So you are a competitor?" He said it in the same vein one would define a cockroach.

"No, I am *the* competitor."

The man's back snapped even more rigid. Not dim-witted, then, this one. He understood exactly what Sebastien was saying.

"The games will be over in a few weeks and you will be naught but a distant memory, Mr. Deville. I wouldn't presume anything."

That strange twinge gripped him again, but he shoved it aside. He might one day be a distant memory, but this rigid man would snuff out the last carefree light in a pair of beautiful blue eyes, were he able. And that, Sebastien wasn't going to let happen.

"But you presume, don't you?" He smiled and rolled an unlit cheroot between his fingers. "Hasn't gotten you very far, and I daresay that it won't get you further in the future. Perhaps you should take the hint from the lady herself? Look to less fair pastures that encourage your attentions?"

The man's color went high and his mouth opened, but a tug on Sebastien's sleeve had him looking down.

"Will you dance with me again?"

Sebastien smirked at Wallace, then extended a low arm to Polly. "Of course, sweet girl."

They left the man fuming in their wake.

The music filled and surrounded her as she watched Sebastien dance with Polly, and Noah dance with a pretty villager whom he had been making cow eyes at all night. Everyone paired together and enjoying themselves. Even Mr. Wallace was leaving her alone for once. She hadn't seen him in a good ten minutes, and he was usually relied upon to hover at her side and chide all manner of her decisions. The matrons had even loosened up a bit under the wild midsummer moon. Free to show some affect in the midst of the festivities.

She wanted to move, to be free too. To feel the music and passion, the release. But she couldn't afford to do so yet. She had just gained the matron's respect. She needed a place . . .

The perfect spot blinked in the moonlight, and she felt the pull. Breaking away from curious eyes and reminders of bad choices past, she disappeared into the night, the itch needing fulfillment, her body needing to be free.

He had seen her tapping on the sidelines, trying to ignore the music and dancing. Trying to stay aloof and restrained. He had danced with Polly, and when he had turned she had disappeared.

He excused himself from the group and headed toward the edges of the festivities, hoping that everyone would think he was simply going to relieve himself.

Skirting around the edges, he kept eyes focused on finding her. She wouldn't have left yet. Not her celebration. Not after the preparations and effort. She was the hostess, the queen, the general of the assembled troops. Not able to share in the celebration because of her need to maintain dignity in public at all times.

He surveyed the grounds. Where would she go?

His eyes went to the ruins, and he instinctively headed toward the columns, the broken hall perched along the slope. They were shadowed and dark, haunted if one believed the tales Caroline spun.

He heard a soft swish as he rounded the path into the still-standing entry room of what was once a great hall. He could almost believe in spirits as he watched her move.

She swayed in the shadows, dancing, her body bending and twirling, hidden from the view of the celebration, yet close enough to hear the music, the laughter, the people singing. The atmosphere was alive between the cold stones, the vibrations clinking within, the sound echoing in an eerie, hypnotic way, wrapping around limbs and pulling to the melody and beat. She swayed like some earthen fairy, unable to come out during the day, only caught at night by the diligent or lucky man who fell upon her path.

Sebastien felt himself pulled toward her across the turned stones and moon-shadowed path. And when she made a gentle turn into his arms, they both froze, the laughter from outside washing over them, the voices and fiddles, the chatter and merrymaking, seeping in and around with the strike of the perfect moment and the triviality of the banal.

He slowly lifted her hand, pressed his lips to her knuckles, eyes never leaving hers, lips straying across perfect skin, fingers wrapping together. He twirled her and she gasped, her eyes bright in the moonlight, startled, then heavy with some emotion that went beyond want and into pure need. Erotic, wanting and sure, her eyes held his, only breaking as he spun her again, then reconnected, the deep need within sending pure heat straight down his spine.

He twirled her into his chest, and her fingers rose to curl into his hair, her breath heavy against his throat, lips gasping against his chin as he led them in some strange dance he had never done. Never attempted. A writhing need, expressed to music that beat in his blood rather than whispered in his ears. Caught up in some spell she had cast, had become ensnared in herself in the midst of a temple of ancient stone.

Forbidden longing to bind himself to the siren's song rose within him, and he turned them in a writhing circle, pushing her against one broken wall, grinding into her and capturing her lips as she tried to climb him, to seat herself on him and fulfill the spell. Desperate movements, mewing whimpers, forbidden promises.

Something about completing the ritual in the stone said that it would be forever, and he resisted the pull, the longing that rose in him for home and desire-struck love and Caroline. He tugged the hair at her nape, bending her back, and captured her breast between his lips, fingers sliding up her thigh, smoothing glossy curls aside, reaching into honeyed depths. He cupped her in his hand, seating her on his fingers, his thumb free to rub the prize nestled within. Her fingers gripped the back of his hair more fiercely, and it only made him pull harder at the perfect nipple, delve more deeply and stroke more firmly.

She shuddered against him, arching farther into him, pulling harder at his hair, and kneading the back of his neck. "Sebastien." His name was a breath on her lips and he pressed against her, all of a sudden out of control with want and need and desire.

He tugged the buttons on his trousers, freeing himself. The whispers of the stone circle taunting him to give in. He pulled hard against her nipple, causing her to give a cry. He pulled her head forward and captured her lips, kissing her as wildly as she was kissing him back, feeling the threads of the spell winding and writhing around and between them. He gripped himself and pulled, one, two, three times, releasing at the same time she moaned uncontrollably into his mouth, her shudders and clenching making him more determined to be inside her.

The threads of the spell slid down, the cries of distant peacocks echoing through the merrymaking, the sounds of which pushed back into his consciousness with a bang.

He gently removed his hand and stepped away, righting himself. Her hair was a riotous mass, her lips swollen and delectable, her eyes heavy and beautiful. Blue-gray eyes grew wide, and a hand reached to smooth her hair, the other trying the same motion on her dress.

The music curled around the stones again, and she froze, mid-smooth. He touched her hand, wrapping their fingers together, and pulled her into an easy dance, swaying to the music, holding her close. "Why do you not dance in the clearing with the others?"

He didn't think she was going to answer for a moment. The hitch in her shoulders loosened as she swayed with him. "I get lost in the music."

A riotous mass of cheering rose in the distance. "There were plenty of people lost in the music earlier. There still are if the shouts are any indication."

"And did you not observe the looks they were given?"

"Envious looks. Were you to dance like you were when I found you, no one would be able to focus on anything else. Wild and free."

Her expression disappeared from view as her head tipped down. "Most people prefer domesticated and tamed."

He smoothed a finger down her cheek and lifted her chin so she was looking back up at him. His finger continued its circuit down her neck, over her bodice. Her heart beat erratically beneath her skin, writhing and alive. The flush on her cheeks and across her chest and throat was the loveliest thing he had seen.

"Tame is boring. Wildness speaks of life."

The wistful lines of her face deepened. "It speaks of a complete lack of discipline."

His fingers moved beneath hers, lifting her hand and grazing her pulse point. "It speaks of passion."

"Passion leads to sorrow."

"Sorrow is a state without passion."

"But one that first bespeaks deeper emotion. You seek passion without deeper emotion."

He pulled her hand to his lips. "There are plenty of profound emotions in passion."

She peered up at him, her eyes more open than usual. "Don't you wish, just once, to have the promise of something richer? Something that surrounds you, that crushes you at the same time it sets you free?"

A violent twinge clenched his stomach, and he shoved the tendrils of emotion twining up, threatening to cling to his throat beneath the glass barrier. He continued to kiss her fingers, her wrist, shielding himself from view. "You speak from experience, yet the experience wasn't a happy one."

Her head tipped down again, shadows shifting over her eyes as they lowered. "No, but I have been running for so long from fear of repeating my mistake. Letting that dictate my actions. There was something missing with Patrick. Something that I thought was there, but with hindsight I can see only a gaping hole. I did love him. But it was the love of a silly girl overcome by circumstance."

"And now? You want to experience a deep love?" He thought about how easy it would be to escape from the stone structure, which was getting smaller and smaller by the second.

She smiled somewhat sadly. "No, I just don't want to be scared anymore. Of my own judgment, of men like you."

The relief mixed with something else. "I think I should be feeling affront."

"Men like you don't feel affront." Her tone was almost affectionate. He wasn't sure which irritated him more—that he was lumped into a group or that she accepted his rakish status so totally as to be amused by it.

He could picture her face, younger, but still lovely and wanting, excited and glowing, as she looked upon the faceless Patrick. Tender and full of crazy ideas and overwhelming emotions. He had seen that expression on each new crop of debutantes when their eyes met his. The picture of Caroline mooning over some faceless man irritated him more than he was willing to admit.

Shadows shifted over her eyes again as she pulled away from the darkness and stepped into the moonlight, a glow illuminating her skin and hair. A wild night fairy who had just garnered her wings.

A smile tugged her lips, and a heavy lidded promise lit her eyes. She took his hand and walked backward a few steps before dropping his hand, turning, and running from the stone-columned room, laughter trailing behind her.

She was transformed into a different person, pulling stunned villagers into the dancing circle, sharing her light and mirth. No, that wasn't right, he thought, as he was tugged into moving with the crowd. She was the same person; this was another side of the real Caroline.

It was late when the festivities wound down, everyone looked pleased as they stumbled from the clearing. Even the matrons had been seduced into joining the swaying crowds, as Caroline had encouraged the children to pull them into the dancing. They too had gotten caught in the grip of the night's spell.

All in all, she had to consider the night an unqualified success. In every way, she thought, still light and breathless.

Sebastien walked her to the door and she fumbled with the lock for a second, her hands uncharacteristically shaking. He took the key from her, fit it into the slot, and smoothly turned it.

"Would you like a cup of tea?" she blurted, staring at his fingers as they fell from the key. Silence greeted her, and it wasn't until she gripped the knob and opened the door that she dared to look up.

"No, I don't want tea." He prowled the last few steps to her, edging her inside and locking the door behind him. "I want you."

His voice was low and tinged with a gruffness that was unusual. She backed up unwittingly like the chased prey she often felt like in his presence. Chills skittered over the top of the immense heat pressing out from every pore.

All of a sudden, the wall was at her back, a picture digging into her skin at odds with the warm, sliding mouth on hers and the gentle pressure of fingers demanding her surrender.

The moment was upon her—high passion and questionable judgment. Raging sensations and emotions in a package that was undeniably dangerous. Not safe. Not secure. Not wrapped up in a neat little bow for her to hide behind.

A finger quested along the skin revealed above her bodice, questioning. She kissed him back in answer.

He peeled the top of her dress from her in a few smooth motions, and a hot mouth captured her lips, her neck, her breasts as he moved her backward through the hall passage to her room.

Somehow he managed to divest them both of their clothing as he feasted and she pulled his hair, seeking his mouth more firmly against her.

He turned, pulling her forward, and they fell to the bed, limbs and clothing remnants entangling, mouths and hands searching.

She ran a hand down his chest and gripped him, fingers wrapping and pulling, his searching and curving, the emotions from the celebration still running high. Her body responding as if made for him.

He smoothed a hand down her side, down her waist and around her backside, gripping her, flipping her, and pulling her hips up—sliding into her with little effort other than the delicious fullness. She shuddered and dug her fingers into his shoulders. Surely nothing had ever felt quite so good, so perfect.

The last bit of internal resistance melted as he joined their bodies together.

His head dropped to her shoulder, heavy breaths ghosting her skin. He lifted himself and met her eyes. He made a slow circle, then very deliberately pulled back. She arched up, seeking renewed contact, but he held himself still.

His face was a picture of intense concentration and anticipatory delight. His eyes glowed as he leaned on one hand and reached his other forward, pulling fingers down her bare chest, between her breasts and around, pulling one nipple into a hard peak.

Her breath caught and he smiled. He flicked his thumb over the tip of her breast and she arched.

But this time when she arched, he drove straight into her, hard and deep, thrusting her up the sheets and pinning her to the mattress, setting her cheeks on fire and her body into a frenzy.

She curled a hand around his neck, pulling him against her, bringing his lips to hers, each kiss echoing the movements below as he quickly repeated the motions, branding her everywhere. She found herself reaching for the peak that had sometimes eluded her in the past. But here it was, brilliant, seductively taunting her to take hold. She reached for it and found herself rolled, suddenly looking down, instead of up.

"I've waited to be in you for too long to have this end so early."

He pulled her more firmly on top of him, languidly stretching his body as she slid down, seating him in her more deeply. She arched back, gaining the extra bit, feeling him so far in her that her eyes closed involuntarily. Hands gripped her hips and pulled down, and the extra little bit became an extra little bit more. Heat licked straight up, and every part of her body from her toes to the roots of her hair felt delicious and heavy, an even fuller sensation. The peak glowed more hotly. More brightly.

He arched up and pulled down on her hips slowly, an excruciating hairbreadth at a time, making the heat lick again, a dull throbbing starting somewhere in her middle as he touched a spot deep within, then brushed past, surging into a fist of wild need.

She lifted her hips and sank back down just as

slowly, his groan joining hers. She repeated the motion, but it became more jagged as his eyes tightened and his chest heaved, his fingers digging into her hips, forcing her to take all of him and to beg for more of the same.

Hurried motions to connect them more closely became more frantic, and soon she was stuttering her movements, riding him with her hands above his shoulders, her head thrown back, her breasts brushing his chest back and forth in a heavy pendulum of need.

"You can't even begin"—his eyes tightened and his breath caught—"to understand what you look like right now."

Despite his taunt of slowing down, the peak galloped wildly toward her, or her to it, spurred by everything about him—the look in his eyes, his words, his hands on her, and movements within her. All their actions had done was to intensify the feelings, slow and throbbing within her as she sank more wildly upon him just in front of the beautiful wave.

Up, up, up, she reached for it, and suddenly found herself again on her back facing the ceiling as she crested and he drove into her relentlessly, over and over again, the waves spreading as she opened her mouth in a silent scream. He shuddered into her, and she felt another peak, the longest orgasm of her life continuing on and on as she wrapped her legs around him, and he shook the foundation of her cottage, of her soul.

Chapter 16

❧⟨✦⟩❧

Jealousy is a force that can drive one to the ex-
treme. We have seen more than its fair share of
drive these last few weeks at Meadowbrook,
but surely during the break, the sentiment has
taken a well-deserved respite.

She woke, stretching and smiling—pleasantly
sore, invigorated, and free. She turned to see
a piece of paper on the empty pillow next to hers.
His scent still lingered in the soft cloth. She lifted
the paper and turned it toward her. A sketch of her
sleeping peacefully graced the page—all gentle
lines and curves. She lightly touched a softly
curved arm thrown back, spiky lashes drawn on
a cheek, the blanket wrapped around her legs.

She smiled and hugged the picture to her.

On Thursday he left a bouquet of flowers, wild
and sweet. On Friday he left a gorgeous sketch of
her cottage, homey and comforting. On Saturday
he left a fairy ring, delicate and fine.

She touched the ring with her fingertips and
smiled giddily. It would be smart to be more careful of her mood—to stay watchful and safe, but

she just couldn't work up the negative emotions involved. It felt too good to be free. She hadn't allowed herself to be free in so long.

As the clock struck noon, she turned to see him leaning against the frame of the door. Hair falling in his eyes, looking devilish and delicious. She didn't know what he did each morning. Just that he was in her bed when she fell asleep each night, and was gone when she woke, a present in his place instead.

"Ready?"

"Where are we going today?" she asked.

"I'm challenging you to a game of quoits."

"Quoits?"

"A game where you toss circular discs at pins." He traced the shape in the air.

She whacked him on the arm. "Hush. Why quoits is what I meant."

"I can have my wicked way with you after I win." He leaned forward on the frame. "Perhaps right there in the bushes if you are really bad."

Her skin grew warm as she thought about a similar incident two days ago.

"More people are returning. There are only a few days left."

He shrugged, but his aquamarine eyes darkened at the reminder. "So? We won't allow them to play should they ask. I'll just have you smack them if they try. You do it so well. One of these days I'm going to take you over my lap and return the favor, but to other parts of your body."

One hand brushed her backside, squeezing. She leaned into the hand involuntarily, and he pulled her against him, sliding her against his heat. "Or we could simply spend the afternoon here."

She shivered and thought that sounded like a fine idea. No one would miss—

Drat. "Noah's coming by to prune the plants. We can't."

"When is he coming?"

"An hour."

"Mmmm, plenty of time."

It wasn't until two in the afternoon, after giggling and avoiding Noah, who kept peering toward the cottage strangely, that they finally made it to the quoits courts.

She was an adequate thrower, having played with Patrick before. She let a piece of her past go as she stepped onto the court with Sebastien. Not Patrick. No living in the past.

They started play, Sebastien as fiercely competitive in this as he seemed to be in everything. But he was smiling more than he ever had before the tournament break. Smiling more today than all the previous weeks of the competition combined.

Something cold lifted her dress, rubbing her leg as she tried to throw her first disc in the new game. She squeaked and the toss went wide, his quoit touching between her thighs before she jumped away.

She couldn't contain a laugh. "What are you doing?"

"I'm cheating. That should be obvious." He cocked a brow, but the edges of his smile were pure grin. "What are you doing?"

"*I* am playing by the rules." She moved to side-step him as he reached for her.

"We can't have that." He stretched, grabbing her waist and pulling her to him. She wiggled and squealed and he swung her around, the second disc arcing from her hand. His foot got caught in her skirts and they went tumbling to the ground, laughing. She giggled and turned on his supine chest.

Her giggles became a full-fledged guffaw to see him spread beneath her, spitting out mouthfuls of fabric, her skirt having lifted just enough to cover a portion of their faces. His hand lazily tangled into the hair at her nape, tugging her closer. The look on his face sent whimpers of sensation through her. She leaned into him and was about to succumb to the invitation in his eyes when a booted foot moved into view.

Caroline followed the leg up to crossed arms and the disapproving frown of Lord Cheevers. Mortification and terror mixed in an unpleasant cocktail. She scrambled to sit up. Sebastien let her go, though his fingers lingered in a caress along her neck as she moved away.

"My lord," Caroline said.

"Mrs. Martin. Mr. Deville. I see that you are . . . enjoying . . . the afternoon weather."

Sebastien leaned back on one hand, one knee bent, the other hand loosely picking clumps of grass from the lawn. "It's a fine afternoon."

"Indeed." Cheevers looked sterner than she had seen him in some time.

"Mrs. Martin, if you would accompany me inside, I wish to speak with you."

She turned to Sebastien, whose eyes shuttered. His expression was that of the man she'd known weeks ago. He waved her away, grass blades falling from his hand. "Thank you for the game, Mrs. Martin. I look forward to seeing you at supper." There was a lazy emphasis on her full name, one he hadn't used in a while. She was grateful he had decided to use it in front of Cheevers though.

"Thank you, Mr. Deville. I—I will see you at supper then." She hadn't planned on taking a meal at the house, but now she would have to unless she wanted Cheevers to think they were having a rendezvous or tryst in her cottage.

The earl tapped a foot in irritation, then turned on his heel. Caroline followed him to his study with trepidation. He slammed the door as soon as she was inside.

"What is this insanity?"

She calmed herself. "We were playing a game is all."

"A game. A game? One that involves you sating Deville?" There was an unusual screech to his normally steely voice. "Do you have any idea what that man's reputation is? Do you have any idea who his father is? Do you have any idea what is at stake here?"

"I'm quite familiar with the answers to all of those questions, my lord."

"Then you know that he runs through women like a beggar through prayers?"

"That seems a mite harsh, my—"

"I can't believe you, *you*, of all people are falling for his twaddle. What the devil is going through the female head these days?"

"The females that fall for a line and some money, you mean?" she asked coolly.

His eyes narrowed on her. "I expected the competition to involve most or all of the contestants making use of the available mature female guests. I didn't expect you to be one of them."

"I'm quite old enough to decide of what *use* I can be."

"Yes, we all know how well your decision-making process is."

"That is hardly fair. I'm no longer green."

"Even worse! You broke your mother's heart when you ran off with that penniless whoreson."

"I broke Papa's too. He died shortly thereafter," she said bitterly, watching the earl's eyes go cold. "But I'm hardly going to repeat that mistake."

"Just dabbling with Deville is repeating your mistake."

"You don't know—"

"If Deville wins this competition he will be very powerful. The *ton*'s memory is selective, and he is a man that can easily make them forget his sins with the right incentive. He knows that. We all do. He won't give that up for anything." The earl stopped abruptly and pinned her with his worst stare. "And whoever he is married to will share in that power. There is only one person he can marry in order to gain that influence."

She stiffened, her heart suddenly pounding in her ears. "There are twelve men left vying for the prize. Deville hardly is running away with the competition. And Sarah's eyes are firmly on other cont—"

"Foolish girl. The games left all favor Deville. All he had to do was stay in the top half of the field for the first half of the games. He more than did that. He's tied for first! He will undoubtedly win. And you are out there romping with him. With your"—his lips tightened—"your cousin's future husband."

She found it difficult to breathe. Breathe in. Breathe out. She inhaled a stuttered breath. "I can't believe you."

"What is there to believe? You think Sarah won't bend to the marriage clause? You think Deville will give up this competition for you?" He gave an ugly laugh. "Marry you? He would truly be ostracized then. The duke would drop even the minimal support he has given. Deville would gain nothing from the match. The prize has everything he's ever wanted. The Duke of Grandien made sure of that."

"You make it sound like this competition already has his name penned as the winner. What about the duke's other son?"

"Lord Benedict? Deville would throw himself from Blackfriars before letting him win."

"Sloane then? You make it sound as if none of the others has a chance. Everly, Parley—"

"They all have a *chance*. The competition was a joint project between us, and every son's strengths were taken into consideration. But only the strongest, the most cunning, the ones who want it most will prevail to the end. Only one will win. And in our diabolical need to make the prize as seductive as we could, we have entrusted too much to the winner. You haven't read the contract. The winner will have power beyond all of us if used properly. The other fathers can believe their spawn will win, but mark my words, Deville will be standing in front of the contract in the end. And he'll sign."

Her heart seemed to beat in every part of her body—her ears, her legs, her stomach.

"Sarah doesn't want to marry him. It would be disastrous for both of them."

"Disastrous? Power, undeniable power, and wealth? A new title?"

"Sarah—"

Cheevers suddenly made a sharp motion. "Go. I can't stand the sight of you. Play with Deville. See where it gets you." He walked to the door and yanked it open. "But don't come crying to me"—he hissed as she walked past—"when Lady Sarah marries him and you are left in that little cottage. Alone."

The door slammed behind her. Caroline strode through the manor, angry and upset. She wondered if Sebastien was still sitting in the grass, destroying a small patch of green, or if he'd wandered off to different pursuits. He could have wandered off to another woman. There were still a handful at the house. Harriet Noke had surprisingly left, but there were a number of women remaining who would grasp the opportunity to strike up an affair with him.

The earl's words ran through her head. Sarah and Sebastien? The idea made her nauseous, not only for the fact that she was currently involved with him, but also because she knew Sarah would be miserable with him. Sarah had a quiet strength buried deep, if only she would trust herself enough to bring it forth, but she'd never handle someone as wild as—

A hand spun her into a chest, pressed against a small indentation in the wall. No servants were in the hall, a small miracle.

It was immediately identifiable who held her by both his grip on her and the erotic scent. His hands clasped her waist as he nuzzled her neck. "Were you Cheevers's mistress?"

"What? No!" she barely choked out, shock mixing with horror as she turned in his arms. All her thoughts jumbled together in a chaotic mixture. Cheevers's words, her doubts, the way her body reacted to Sebastien's, the slight pining that she felt in his presence, terrifying in its existence.

He cocked his head, studying her. "You are actually quite his type. And you live on the estate."

She couldn't even gurgle an answer.

"It is fine if you were. I have to admit the idea makes me want to strangle him, but far be it from me to deny you a partner before. I can still be the one to untame you."

"No, not his mistress. Definitely not." The horror was the defining element, completely overcoming the shock, until she thought about his statement. "You are jealous?"

"Terribly. I am horribly possessive when I have something I've wanted." He tipped her head back and sucked her pulse point hard enough to leave a bruise. "I've never been possessive over a woman before though," he whispered against her neck. "I wonder what spell you cast?"

Her lingering horror and chaotic confusion was replaced by pleasure and a small spike of reassurance that maybe the earl was wrong. He'd been wrong before. Plenty of times. And the thought that maybe there was something more here was too seductive to lose. There would be plenty of time for second guessing and recriminations when the tournament restarted. Right now she just wanted to bask in the freedom and heedless pleasure Sebastien had awakened.

She met his eyes. "A closely guarded fae spell to make you fall madly in love." She had meant it to be lighthearted and teasing, but it emerged far more seriously than she'd intended.

"Mmmm." Something twitched in his eyes. The same mask that had dropped at Roseford those many phases of the moon ago, when he had talked about the lonely peak, dropped now. "I think I will have to punish you for it."

"Your forfeits have been collected."

His lips dropped to her neck again. "Oh now, Caro, are you really going to hold me to that? Not until the competition restarts, I don't think."

He opened the door behind him, one that led to an old study that the earl used to use. It had been mostly empty the last time she'd been in the room.

Hands ensnared her, and his scent surrounded her once again as he pulled her to him, pulling her inside. The falling sun shone through the partially covered windows, but the grounds were in view between the opened fabric. Something jangled, and he turned from her to inspect the door he was trying to lock.

He turned back to her, pulling her close, branding her with his lips, his hands. "No key, Caro. You are going to have to be very, very quiet."

"What?" she asked, a little dazed.

"You are going to have to be quiet, because I'm about to have my wicked way with you right under the earl's nose. Under the other guests' noses. In this room with no lock."

"I don't think—"

Fingers stretched into her hair, and she melted into him like oil on a master's canvas. He tilted her back, pulling the fingers down, down, down, then gliding around her throat and down her chest. She saw his eyes search the room as his fingers circled her. Her head tipped back enough to see the sparse furniture. The only thing in the room that didn't look like it would break upon impact was an ornate wooden desk covered in burgundy leather.

Sense returned as she realized what was about to happen, right underneath the earl's nose, as he'd said.

"Oh no, I'm not—"

He pulled her head back up and devoured her lips. "I wouldn't hurt your pretty back on that," he said against her mouth.

She relaxed infinitesimally. "Just a kiss then?"

"I don't think so." He eyed her, and there was something about the way he was closing the physical gap between them, his mouth stalking her by inches, that made her heart pick up speed and beat wildly against his chest. His lips curved.

He let her go and she backed up a step, putting space between them.

Her nerves increased rather than lessening. She laughed unsteadily. "Shall we simply meet again at dinner then?"

"Oh, why don't we." His eyes said anything but, as he began to advance on her.

She backed up until she hit the table. She moved to skirt it, but he captured her wrist. He slowly brought it to his lips and kissed, licked, pulled at the pulse point.

He moved two steps forward until he had her in the vee of his legs against the desk, bending her slightly back. There was little use arguing, not when her heart was racing and her body ached for his.

"I thought you said you wouldn't hurt my pretty back on the desk?" Her voice was a mere whisper under his hot gaze, which branded her as he had branded her neck minutes before.

"I won't." He leaned forward and whispered in her ear, "But I never said anything about your front."

Heat raced through her alongside panic as his words registered. She had thought surely that in broad daylight, even on the sun's downward path, he would not truly go through with it. Anyone passing by the windows on the grounds would be able to see them if he looked hard enough.

She scrabbled to get away, half of her fighting against him, the other half fighting herself as they brushed together repeatedly with her movements. "Sebastien, let me go."

He nipped her ear. "No."

"Sebast—"

He spun her around so fast that she would have tripped on her skirts if he hadn't been in control of her motions.

"Sebastien, this is foolish. The earl is already angry and we were barely even caught in a compromising—"

He pushed her down on the desk, and she roughly grabbed for purchase. "It's hardly a good idea to talk about another man when I'm about to brand you mine, Caro."

His free hand unerringly worked up her skirts, fingers curling around her, discovering easily, to her mortification, how aroused she already was.

"I told you he—"

His hand pressed harder into her back, not enough to hurt, but just enough to push her breasts further into the leather. "I'm going to have you so hard that you won't remember your own name when I'm done, no less your tatty husband's name or anyone in between."

Panic spiked again along with a fierce longing.

"Let me go," she whispered, but her breath was too heavy, her voice too aroused.

"Never," he whispered back.

And then he pulled her back against him, lifted

her skirts, and pushed her down again, causing the bunched cloth to collect underneath her stomach, lifting her. A smooth, rounded knob on the desk rubbed against her, and her words got caught in her throat as he paused for a second, then deliberately pushed her against the knob again.

A finger trailed around her heat and found its way exquisitely inside, crooking exactly where it should, stroking the perfect trail of fire. Her heavy breaths ghosted over the surface of the desk, and her fingers scrabbled for something to grip as her world tilted on end. She pushed against him, trying to push away from the desk, toward him, away from him—desires colliding into madness.

One hand nestled in the small of her back, continuing to hold her down. She heard the sounds of his trousers opening. Anyone could enter the room at any time and see them—almost full daylight, her bent over the desk, skirts everywhere, about to get tupped to kingdom come, Sebastien behind her, poised and ready.

Shock mixed with desire and understanding.

"Sebastien—"

He surged within her, and her plea turned into an animalistic sound at the sheer impact of him filling her so swiftly and at such an angle.

Footsteps pounded down the hall. Caroline stiffened, every muscle in her tensing, and his head dropped to her shoulder blades while he emitted some sort of breathy moan as she clenched around him.

His breath ghosted over her ear. "Mine." Another deep thrust slid her exposed front over the knob on the desk, setting nerves on the outside and inside into chaos, his statement pulling some sort of violent mating response from her.

"Tell me you are mine, Caroline." He stroked into her, deeper still, and another sound ripped from her throat.

"There it is again," a voice said.

She clenched in crazed warning, and he shuddered against her. "Seb—" Fabric tore and long fingers shoved something, some wad of cloth into her mouth. Then he was thrusting into her again, clearly not caring that there were people on the other side of the door and they were in imminent fear of discovery.

He pulled almost all the way out and slid back inside her in such a long, smooth motion that she bucked over the knob and it slowly slid against her in a manner that made her shudder harder and her fingers scrape furrows in the desktop. She bit into the material as hard as she could. He slid into her again, pushing all the way up, and her breasts spilled from her dress as they moved forward, dragging across the patterned leather, tracing every valley. She sobbed from the overstimulation.

"Sounds like a cat. Probably in heat. Maybe that ghost the women keep bantering about is true. Come on, you owe me that billiards game before dinner."

Sebastien withdrew a few inches for a second as the footsteps pattered down the hall, then tilted her hips and drove into her so hard, hitting something deep within her, that she saw spots. The need to push back into him and yell his name was nearly making her delirious.

He would own her then and she couldn't allow that, not after the earl's warnings or her own deep fears still seeded within. She dug her fingernails into the surface, knowing that even doing everything in her power to restrain herself, he would still pull whatever reaction from her body that he desired.

He paused for a moment, and soft kisses trailed up her backbone, to her nape, her hair carefully brushed to the side, his hands smoothing along the planes of her back, pulling heat up and out as he pushed them along her shoulders, along her arms which had gone lax under his ministrations, fingers trailing on the soft underside of her elbow, up her forearms and entangling with her fingers, pulling them against the leather surface of the top.

His lips maintained a steady rhythm.

"Say you are mine, Caroline." He used their clenched hands to pull her back against him. The gentleness was gone once again, and savage need returned to its place. He rocked his hips into her, hitting places she couldn't name. Making dancing stars appear in the leather and causing gouges to mar its surface. She could feel the intensity of his movements change, and it caused the buildup inside her to coil and ascend.

His hands moved to her waist, gripping her hips as he pounded into her, the knob, the leather, his claiming thrusts causing her to babble phrases into the cloth that she didn't know the meaning of. And from the muffled sounds above and behind her, he must have stuffed something into his own mouth as well.

All of a sudden he stopped, poised at the edge, and she strained back for him. "Say it."

She shook her head, nearly delirious. She wouldn't give him that power.

"Say it, Caro."

He tore the fabric from her mouth and pulled his hands down to grip her breasts firmly in both hands, still edging into her in small stabs, but not enough to sate the overwhelming pressure. He rolled her nipples between his fingers and thrust into her, tearing a sob from her throat that formed the word. "Yes."

The muffled shout accompanying the surge of him as deeply as he could go pushed her over the edge and she clawed the desk, clenching him into her over and over again, meeting every stroke until she was too weak to move and his forehead rested in the curve of her back. He slipped out of her, a twinge of loss, and gathered her, laying her on top of the desk, fixing her clothes and cleaning up, a slightly wild look in his once-jaded eyes.

"I told you, you were mine, Caroline."

Chapter 17

Secrets long kept rarely stay secret in a society so keen on rumor and innuendo, betrayal and pride. Be careful what you reveal in a game with consequences so far-reaching and wide.

A log snapped in the glowing hearth. Chalk scratched over paper. She poked another hole in the needlepoint and pulled the thread through, enjoying the intimate atmosphere. She positioned the needle and nearly poked her thumb when fingers curled around her necklace, down the chain and over the heavy gold. She met his eyes, deep and questioning—his gaze full of curiosity and focus. She had hardly seen the jade edge to his aquamarine eyes in weeks, now that she thought on it.

He seemed to be seeking her permission. She cocked her head. One finger flipped open the locket.

"Who were they?"

She didn't have to look down to know what he saw. "Mama and Papa." She touched the edge. The miniature had been in there so long.

"You take after your mother."

"Yes."

"You look nothing like your father."

"Oh, I do if you look closely enough."

She watched him examine the portrait, light fingers caressing the gold. "In the cheeks, perhaps."

"An old family trait." She pulled the chain from him, examining the miniature.

"You haven't a picture to put on the other side?"

"No." She had once wanted one with fiery features and a reckless expression. Those fiery features had faded to a dull memory.

"Ah."

He fingered a pastel with something like satisfaction in his gaze.

They went back to their tasks. He to his drawing, she to her needlepoint. It was soothing. In, out with the needle. No care except for executing the perfect stitch over and again. Her toes curled under him and he leaned into her. A lovely humming, a distant sound of music played by crickets and night birds filled the air.

The morning would bring the return of the guests and with them the competition. It would likely be awkward, at least for her. Sebastien rarely seemed to understand the concept of awkward.

She finished her last stitch and looked up to see him watching her, his supplies spread to the side of him. She set down her completed piece and held out a hand. Uncurling from his large cat sprawl, he lifted her easily and set her on her feet. Warm bare hands framed her cheeks. The energy drew into a lazy circle of need as he brushed her skin with his thumbs, then pulled her closer, a gentle kiss that turned into heated embers of the fire.

He pulled her into the bedroom, and with a tangle of clothes and tumbled bodies he was stroking her inside and out, easily moving against and into her. A glorious feeling combined with the look on his face above her, an expression she couldn't read as she arched back, he slid into her one final time, and she touched the stars.

She woke to the gentle light streaming in through the window and the sounds of her recently returned maid puttering in the kitchen. Nothing was on the pillow next to her. A stab of disappointment swept her, even as she called herself a ninny for expecting something to be there— rich brown hair attached to a breathtaking body, most desirably. Or a flower, a curiosity, a lovely sketch . . .

Nothing.

She bit her lip. Ninny she might be, but he'd never failed to leave her something—small personal gifts that delighted or amused her.

On Sunday he had left her a set of the finest pastels. On Monday he had left sketching paper that likely cost more than her yearly stock of food. On Tuesday he had left a beautiful, unsigned note that had caused her to kiss him immediately upon his arrival.

She closed her eyes. But the games were to begin again, and she was merely a delightful amusement herself. She couldn't forget that in the midst of all the feelings he conjured.

She sat up, her locket heavy against her neck as it slipped to the side. She pulled it to lie in the middle of her chest. A smudge of chalk on the gleaming surface had her twisting it in her grip. She popped the latch.

Her breath caught.

A tiny sketch of a blonde fairy dancing, arms free, body flowing, nestled inside the once bare side.

Sebastien walked away from the cottage and across the grounds. He had fallen deeper into the abyss. Repulsed and attracted, envious and desperate. Being near her was like an addiction he couldn't quit.

A carriage pulled into the drive, a distant dot from where he walked. He could see a few of the men already up and about the grounds, looking at the terrain for the next game, strategizing, possibly figuring out ways to cripple other contestants.

Benedict's moppish brown head disappeared into the garden maze off to the left, Everly and Parley following behind—he could see Parley's distinctly uptight walk and Everly's red hair. Likely setting up some mischief or a malicious prank against one or all of the remaining bastards.

It had been a seductive notion to forget . . . to forget why he was here and why he needed to win. He wasn't just winning for himself, though he would reap the rewards.

And a pleasant enough bride.

When he had set out at the beginning, Lady Sarah, *anyone* as the bride really, had been a footnote, a codicil. The least important piece of the document. She was wellborn, pliable, quiet, could run a household. Nothing outstanding about her, but she would make a fine, respectable wife who would be forgotten as soon as the documents were signed and a few *legitimate* children produced. His lip curled. The games one had to play.

He still wouldn't care even now if he thought for a moment that he could carry on his affair with Caroline and keep the status quo once he won. Though relying on the status quo was a rocky proposition. Rarely did it stay as it was supposed to.

What if she got with child? Doomed to repeat his father's mistakes and inflict them on a woman for whom he actually cared? No.

And even so, if there was one woman in England who would not have an affair with a man married to her beloved cousin . . . well, he'd gone and started an affair with that woman.

There was time still available to push the subject aside. He'd put off thinking about it until he had to.

"Deville!"

He turned to see Sloane and Timtree motioning him over. He sauntered their way, amused to see Timtree's eyes narrowed on the maze.

"Worried about the three wretches?"

"You saw them too?" Timtree's mouth pulled into a tight line. He was in the middle of the leaderboard, and Parley and Everly had been running their mouths.

"I did."

"We're going after them."

Sebastien snagged his sleeve before he could take another step. "Timtree, use your brain. They want someone to follow them. They were too obvious. Send a maid to find out what they are up to, or the widow you've been pushing against every flat surface of the house."

Timtree's color went high for a moment.

"And we'll go up and look at them through the second-floor windows in the west wing. One of the windows looks straight down into the maze."

Timtree's color rose again, and Sebastien had the distinct impression that Timtree and his widow had made use of the maze over the past weeks—was it six now?

"Awfully fond of her, are you?"

Sloane stayed quiet, though his amusement was apparent as they walked through the high doors into the gilded back hall.

"As if you have any room to make judgments, Deville. Hardly strayed from the side of that blonde piece, if what I hear is correct," Timtree said.

"Can't expect me to give up a woman that delicious, can you?"

Timtree cast him a glance that held the slightest bit of serious regard. "I think you ought to be careful, Deville. Either that or let one of us have your place at the top. We'll make sure those three are beaten."

Sloane made a sound in the back of his throat that sounded like he was going to argue. He was in contention for first place, so Sebastien could appreciate his irritation.

"Timtree, dear fellow, you are mad."

The hook-nosed man shrugged. "You realize it is only a matter of time before Benedict repeats the terms of your bet to her, don't you?"

Sebastien froze mid-step, then forced himself to continue forward. "Of course."

Bloody . . . no. He'd put the bet from his mind. Of course Benedict would blurt it out, and at the worst possible moment.

They climbed the stairs, and he nodded to whatever the other two were saying. He needed something on Benedict.

The second-floor west wing was mostly empty of guests. Servants, barely noticeable, walked in and out of the doors and down the halls, completing their tasks and keeping themselves out of the way. He contemplated a man dusting the relics atop posts in the hall. This was Benedict's wing. That man probably had to clean near here every day.

He hummed to himself. He usually let his valet handle the information-gathering aspect, not wanting to dirty his own hands in the business, determined to win on his own and show them . . . something.

Sebastien shook his head to dislodge the cobwebs that had suddenly gathered. The hall came back into view, and he led the other two to the small alcove with the window. Grousett was excellent in ferreting out locations where either a liaison could take place or others could be caught in a liaison—whichever was needed. He had discovered this alcove overlooking the maze during the first week. Sebastien had studiously avoided the maze since.

Another servant passed by with a dust cloth, but this man didn't look at all like an upstairs servant. There was something entirely too shifty about him. Sebastien would think he was a thief, but for the way the other servants barely spared him a glance. They knew him.

The man had been heading right for the alcove, only shifting direction when he spotted them standing there. He dusted a bust that the other servant had already brought to a shine.

Ah. So Cheevers had finally started watching. Was he waiting in the wings to influence the game, if he found someone he didn't want to win? Or just keeping tabs on things? Watching for future favors?

They gathered in the alcove and watched through the window. The threesome was doing something in the center of the maze. From the angle, it was hard to see exactly what they were doing, but it looked like they were setting up something inside one of the ledges.

Sebastien kept an eye on the servant who was absently dusting the wallpaper and trying not to be too obvious as he watched them. Even if they couldn't pinpoint exactly what the three were doing in the maze, this spying venture had turned things well in Sebastien's favor—just in a way he hadn't expected.

"They are leaving. We could catch them. Let's follow and see," Timtree said.

Sloane and Timtree strode away, talking about

what they could do with the information and how they could trap the men. Sebastien waited until they were far enough away, then approached the servant with a smile on his face and a hand in his pocket.

Sebastien lounged in the sitting room and smiled in satisfaction when he heard the door open, then close.

Benedict walked in and immediately spotted him. "What are you doing in my rooms? Finney? Finney?" he called out, eyes never leaving Sebastien.

"Your valet is . . . out for the afternoon. No worse for the wear than what you did to mine, never fear."

Benedict's eyes narrowed as he stepped forward, casting suspicious glances around the space. "What do you want?"

"An exchange."

"What do you have?"

"One of Cheevers's servants saw you in the maze, going into my room and sending your valet with a 'suspicious' substance to the kitchens. Tut, tut, Benedict, I didn't think you had been responsible for the more heinous attacks, but even pulling a schoolboy prank—will others believe that you had nothing to do with the actual poisonings?"

Benedict turned white.

Sebastien rubbed his thumb along the fabric on the arm of the chair. "He can tell the earl his findings at any time, no need for me to say a thing."

Benedict's chest pushed farther out on every breath. "And?" He crossed his arms tightly.

Sebastien lifted a brow. "And?"

"You are bloody well here to bargain, Deville; stop taunting me."

"Ah, no one likes to play these games anymore. I have offered Cheevers's servant an . . . incentive to keep the information to himself."

He didn't have to tell Benedict that another servant would likely tell Cheevers anyway. He didn't think Cheevers was going to kick Benedict out without further provocation.

"Why? Why wouldn't you want me out of the competition completely?" Every line of Benedict's face drew taut in disbelief.

Yes, why was he not putting Benedict up for ejection? He could simply confirm to Cheevers exactly what had happened, let Cheevers know he knew, and the earl would likely be forced to act. The question made him shift in his seat.

"Because I don't need to."

Benedict snorted, sinking into a chair, obviously waiting for his demand. "Well?"

"Our bet on Mrs. Martin. It's dissolved and it never existed. Do you understand?"

Benedict's eyes went wide, then narrowed, considering. "A well-made bet, wasn't it? I *knew* it."

"You knew, you *know*, nothing."

Dark humor appeared in his eyes. "You are in deep trouble, my dear illegitimate brother. I still plan to beat you, but all I really need to do is come in second, if you are first, don't I? You won't be able to sign."

"I will be able to sign, and what's more, I will do it with your face in mind."

Benedict uncrossed his arms and tapped a finger on the chair. "We weren't alone when we made that bet. How do you propose to keep the rest of them from telling her? Think you can blackmail everyone?"

"That is your job. Tell them whatever you need to in order to silence those who know of it."

Benedict's mouth turned down. "Mrs. Martin seems a good enough sort. Too good for you really. But then most are."

"Yes, cry, cry, whinge, whinge. Is it a deal?"

Benedict traced the pattern in the chair. "Yes."

He knew he was giving Benedict a weapon, but he would deal with the consequences. He knew how Caroline would react to finding out about the bet, even if it hadn't ruled their interactions for weeks. With only a week to go, he didn't want to kill their affair before it needed to be over.

Chapter 18

⎯⎯⎯⎯∽◯◯∽⎯⎯⎯⎯

Oh, Meadowbrook, that you will fill our ink-wells and hasten our pens! What deeds are afoot that you might titillate us once more? No secret will stay safe in your bower.

Parlor tricks, parties, cards, and amusements. The past days of the resumed competition had been full of games and jockeying. Caroline had barely seen Sebastien except at night when he'd sneak over to the cottage. Sarah had been sending her odd looks during the day—puzzled, probing looks. But then she too had been frazzled, her attention always following William.

When the competition adjourned to London tonight, they would need to sit down and chat. Most of the guests were following the competition to the city, so she and Sarah would be left to their own devices.

Cheevers clapped his hands together. The earl must have gone through two scores of gloves by now. "Today we have a special event planned. Not part of the competition, which will begin again tomorrow in London, but instead, an ancillary game in which we can all participate before the carriages leave."

The ladies tittered as he shot them a waggled brow.

"A treasure hunt, with a three-stone ruby necklace as the prize."

The ladies stopped giggling and now looked as interested as the men, if not more so.

"We will draw for partners."

Caroline sighed, knowing that her name was assuredly in the folly.

Names began to be drawn from the basket and teams started to form. Motley teams consisting of different makeups of contestants, women, fathers, and sons not competing. Sarah was picked for a team that included Everly, William, and Timtree. Caroline just hoped that William kept her out of the crosshairs of the other two.

The Duke of Grandien was chosen as the head of the next team to form. He reached in to pick slips for his team. Seated where she was, she could see him unconcernedly watching the crowd as he withdrew a slip.

"Sebastien."

She kept her mouth smooth, her brows from creasing. Caroline wondered if she was the only one who saw Sebastien's shoulders clench, his body stiffen. Not a second later he was lazily unfolding from his chair and walking toward his father.

The duke's hand slipped back into the basket. "Benedict."

Benedict stiffly walked forward as well, and the

murmurs grew before the duke's cold gaze stifled them. He reached forward once more.

"Caroline Martin."

She froze. Only Sarah's wide eyes and subtle motion across the crowd forced her from her cold seat.

"Mrs. Martin." The duke greeted her, his gaze direct and dissecting.

He handed the basket back to Cheevers, and she saw the slips fall from the duke's fingers back into the basket. Crafty man. She would bet her last bonnet that their names hadn't been placed in the basket to begin with.

That meant the earl was in on this plan, whatever it was, as well. Nervous energy tripped through her.

She stood next to them as the other teams formed. Her imagination ran wild as many of the male contestants kept eyeing her, not in a particularly coy way, but more watchful. It was unnerving. Harriet Noke regarded her through cool eyes but tilted her head in a vaguely companionable way, much to Caroline's surprise and increasing unease.

As soon as all the teams had formed, Cheevers handed each team captain a packet of papers. The duke rifled through them, sorting them. Sebastien had already removed a cheroot and lit it. She had become entirely too used to it being just the two of them, and he had rarely smoked in her presence when they were alone. She found it jarring to see him do so now.

The duke handed a paper to Sebastien without

looking his way. He lazily grabbed it, exhaling as he did so. He might have seen Benedict's wrath at being passed over, but for once he didn't gloat. "Maps of the grounds. They look as if produced from a once-familiar hand—one which is thankfully unfamiliar now."

She leaned over to see that they were the maps she had drawn before the competition began. Before she had sketched Roseford. Before she had met Sebastien Deville.

The uninspired maps had markings on them that weren't hers though. Lines and dashes and a big starburst. A key told how many paces each dash was and what the other symbols meant.

The earl cleared his throat. "Every map is different so that teams can't just follow one another, but there are intersections between each map, so you will have to beat different opponents to each spot. All teams start at the maze."

The earl and his gaggle of solicitors had obviously learned a lesson from the horse hunt.

Caroline saw Timtree and Everly arguing while Sarah nervously chewed her lip. Sarah wouldn't say anything to override the men, even if she knew the estate backward and forward. William finally stepped between them and grabbed the papers from Everly, who did *not* look pleased. Everly might not be aware that William had the support of the King, but Timtree seemed to as he smirked and motioned for Sarah to go ahead.

"You should give Mrs. Martin the map," Sebastien said, dangling it between two fingers.

Benedict held a hand out. "Figures that you

would try and weasel out of this, Deville. I'll find our way around." He moved to take the papers, but the duke barely acknowledged him as he made a cutting motion.

"Give the map to Mrs. Martin then. We'll see what a woman can do. She must be incredibly good at something to garner this level of support."

Foul man. She wanted to borrow Sebastien's tinderbox to set the map on fire.

Sebastien handed her the map, a wink hidden behind a screen of smoke. Benedict couldn't see it, and good thing too as he already had a petulant set to his face. She knew they disliked each other. Intensely. But she felt for the moppish man who always seemed to be on the lesser end of his father's stick.

She couldn't help herself when they entered the maze. She whispered to Benedict, "You shouldn't let the duke bother you. He thrives on it. Take away his entertainment."

Benedict cast a surprised glance her way, pinched his lips together, and continued on without answering.

They stepped to the edge of the maze, where the other teams were gathered as well, a large contingent of people milling about, excited and fierce.

"This is a race. Collect all of the items on the list and cross the line first to win." Cheevers held up the necklace so that it sparkled in the sun. "Good luck. You may begin."

A few teams took off in various directions, while others examined their maps, noses buried in the folds and creases.

The duke raised a brow at her. The first marking said fifteen paces inside the maze and look right. She repeated the directions, and they were off. The three men walked briskly forward, each counting as he went, not trusting the others.

They found the approximate spot and immediately spotted a small ring inside a hedge. Rings from the first competition were being reused, and something inside her felt a strange thrill from it, the games coming around full circle.

They collected the first three tokens easily. The duke and Sebastien immediately strode in the direction of the next one. Caroline stepped after them, turning to see Benedict absently touching a wildflower near where they had found the third ring. There was a wistful expression on his face. He obviously thought he was unobserved, and she felt a twinge.

"We will not run like unmannerly children, but do keep up, Benedict," the duke said stridently over his shoulder.

He said nothing in response, frame tight. It was the fourth such casual insult. Even maintaining the pace of the duke and Sebastien, Benedict had been derided for the number of steps to his stride—"ungainly," the duke had said.

They continued collecting, a sort of chilly, tense grip in every quip and response.

The duke had not uttered a single negative comment about Sebastien's role, but his eyes tracked him. The cock of Grandien's head questioning whether Sebastien was going to trip up and disappoint. And the way Sebastien held himself in return said he was well aware and used to this look. He shot Benedict a sneer as the other made a less than wise suggestion.

Caroline had a sudden moment of clarity. Each son thought the father favored the other more. Benedict would never believe Sebastien's hardships, and Sebastien would never acknowledge the duke's shabby treatment of Benedict. Sebastien chose to give the duke a flash of his bare backside with his responses, whereas Benedict was forever trying to curry his favor.

She stumbled into Sebastien's back, too caught up in her epiphany.

Sebastien whirled and caught her as she pitched backward. His hands comfortably secured about her waist, as hers grabbed for his arms, scrambling up and around his neck. He paused for a second. She looked up at him in shock, and the urge to giggle rose at the absurdity of the whole game. She laughed, and his eyes reflected humor, before turning into something more intense. He lifted her, and her fingers curled farther around his neck, bringing them closer.

"If you would let Mrs. Martin go, we can get on with the hunt."

Sebastien didn't look at Benedict, but he did smile lazily at Caroline before lifting her so that she could stand on her own. She ran a flustered hand over her dress, having forgotten for a second that there was anyone else there besides the two of them.

Benedict's lips were tight, but he nodded at her before moving forward along the path. The duke's eyes were narrowed upon her, before he too resumed walking. She wondered at the picture they had made.

"Don't mind them. Benedict has always been fussy and priggish. And the duke—little does his opinion matter."

She thought about her own dealings with the earl and how much power he had. No, she didn't believe that the duke's opinion meant so little to Sebastien. But she was also sure that he would never let the duke's opinion sway him, unlike Benedict.

They collected the last ring and strode toward the finish line, winning with time to spare. For all that the three might not like one another, they worked remarkably well together—if one didn't pay attention to the underlying tension and dislike.

Cheevers handed the necklace box and other prizes to the duke. "Congratulations to the duke and his team!" He turned to address the rest of the guests. "You may continue gaming outside or retire within. The first fleet of carriages will be called after dinner, for those of you desiring to travel together."

The duke opened the box and inspected the necklace within. "I think we should award the prize to Mrs. Martin, for putting up with the rest of us." Narrowed eyes that unnerved her took in the two younger men. "Wouldn't you agree, boys?"

Sebastien raised a brow at the address and tapped an unlit cheroot against his leg. Benedict watched his father, his gaze untrusting.

"After all, she helped Sebastien win his bet, did she not? I think it only fair since you boys made a bet on her that she also reap a reward."

Benedict's face turned white, his eyes panicked as he looked at Sebastien. She turned to Sebastien, who was looking at the duke with eyes flat and cold. Deadly.

"What bet?" a voice asked that sounded unfamiliar coming from her mouth.

The duke looked at her in amusement. "I believe the bet was about bedding you at first, but turned into something about making you fall in love with Sebastien. Since it is well-known that Sebastien doesn't believe in love and Benedict has silly notions about the state, I must claim myself the arbiter, and I believe the bet has been resolved. I took the liberty of securing the item which was bet from Benedict's room. Timely. The look on your face after you stumbled and Sebastien caught you can hardly be faked."

He lifted a pocket watch and held it out to Sebastien, who pivoted and walked away without a word. The duke slipped the watch back into his waistcoat, smiling. Benedict looked unnaturally alarmed as his eyes switched from his brother's retreating back to the duke, then Caroline. He took off after Sebastien.

"Manners obviously do not run in the family, but other ill traits do, alas." The duke's outline went blurry, even as his mouth kept moving. He tapped the box. "You have earned this, Mrs. Martin. Good day to you."

She numbly took the box that was thrust into

her hands. The duke smiled and walked away, following the path of his sons.

The earl appeared in her view. "Mrs. Martin? Mrs. Martin, I need you to run a few tasks for me."

She swallowed and nodded. Just because Sebastien had looked as if he wanted nothing more than to kill the duke, it did not mean the bet was not true, and Benedict's strange reaction indicated there was some truth to the duke's words as well.

"Good. First I need you to go into the village, then to the Wallace house to drop off a piece of correspondence. Then—"

Clarity took hold. She held up her hand. "Why would you send me on these tasks? You have plenty of servants, and I am hardly one." Her spine snapped rigid. Something she could control in front of her.

"Everyone is busy helping the guests pack. Besides, you can get Mr. Wallace to cede twice the negotiated rate. I've received more than one word that he is going to offer for you."

She smiled bitterly, seeing the earl's influence in more than just this. "Just hand me what you will. I find I don't care at the moment." She'd find out from Sebastien what the bet was about, though from her knowledge of him over the past six weeks or so, the bet made sense, if the feelings behind it did not. If he chose not to come to her, that would be an answer in and of itself.

She went on the tasks, and by the time she returned, it was after dinner and nearly every guest was gone. Most noticeably, the one guest she'd inquired after. The watching eyes of the other men as they'd begun the treasure hunt made sense the more she thought on it. They probably all knew about the bet. No wonder Cheevers had tried to warn her off. Why hadn't he just told her instead of playing the duke's game?

She handed the wrapped box she had been carrying around all day to a messenger who was leaving for the city. "Deliver this to Mr. Sebastien Deville's residence." She gave him the address she had found after going through the earl's study. "Tell him he's earned it."

As the boy disappeared down the drive she felt a wave of pettiness from the action, but she straightened her shoulders.

She trudged back to her cottage after pleading a headache to Sarah. The reasons for telling Sarah everything had become jumbled and confused, and she needed to think first.

She opened her locket, irritated by the need to remove the sketch mixed with the desire to keep it forever. She removed the locket instead and set it on the side table. She tried not to think of rich brown hair and warm aquamarine eyes turned mocking and sneering.

She never saw the flower or the note that was snatched from her pillow by foreign hands before she made it home.

Chapter 19

◦─◦◦─◦

A return to London for the tournament to-night! Invitations have been served, servants have been installed, and the games will be merry and fierce. Who are those lucky enough to have a front-row seat? Only the very cream of society—those who look to welcome a new star to their fold.

The box arrived as Sebastien was tiredly fumbling for a button. The night had been hell. He'd pictured her face over and over again, stunned, betrayal just starting to surface along the edges of her expression as the duke watched, smirking. He'd had to leave abruptly, to say nothing in response to the duke's words. He would have committed murder. His fingers had itched to wrap around the duke's neck and squeeze, squeeze, squeeze until there was nothing left between his hands.

It had taken everything in him to walk away from the urge. Everything.

Benedict had completely gone to pieces, sure that he was going to extract vengeance in the way he had threatened before. But his chest was so full of hate for the duke that there was little room left for Benedict. He'd simply turned and walked away from him as well.

He examined the wrapped box, not wanting to open it. His butler had told him that the only message that accompanied it was, "You earned it."

He pushed the last button into place. He'd left Caroline a note explaining, probably poorly, the circumstances. Depending on how the message was read, it could be a positive—that he earned it, as in her heart—which frankly made him shake a bit. Or a sarcastic negative depending on what was inside.

He pushed aside the twine and opened the box to see . . . the ruby necklace. Something tightened in his chest. Sarcasm then. She hadn't forgiven him even after reading his note. Not that he had expected it. Things rarely worked out the way he wanted them to.

He closed the lid and tossed the box onto the nearest table. The expensive bauble inside thumped as it hit the wood with jarring finality.

He stepped into his closed carriage, a ridiculously expensive purchase that he had made after seeing Benedict look enviously at a similar model one night. He grimaced in the dark over his show of immaturity.

The streets passed by and the wheels of the carriage clicked along the stones, rotating and ongoing, an echo of his life. Alone, but forever moving forward.

The vehicle stopped at a prospering section of

town. A new, tasteful gaming establishment had been rented for the night, all the facilities in place for an evening full of monetary debauchery. He resolutely stepped down and looked up to see the lights brightly flaring in all the windows. No sleep for the wicked tonight. He walked up the stairs.

"Mr. Deville." The man at the front bowed. "You'll find them gathered in the back salon."

He exchanged a handshake and a palmed note with the man and headed for the indicated room. In the gambling world it was rare not to know or at least be aware of the major players and the managers at each establishment.

The others were hunkered around the room in the back. Timtree raised his glass, and Sloane gave him a smile. William Manning nodded without judgment. The rest didn't look nearly so friendly, which was fine with him.

The duke and the rest of the older gentlemen, minus Cheevers, who was conspicuously absent, were seated around the area with drinks in hand, or cigars in mouth. Sebastien steadily avoided looking at the duke, his fingernails curling into his palms. There were another ten or so anonymous-looking men standing at the far edge of the room.

The last man entered the area, and Viscount Dullesfield stood. "Very good. The rules are very simple. Each of you will receive one thousand pounds tonight to play, and the person with the most money at the end of the night will be declared the winner."

And they claimed to be worried about cheating. It would be like a feast for starving men where all the dishes were laid out at once before they were told to have at it.

"You will each be shadowed in order to keep play fairly aboveboard. You cannot bribe these men as we've already ensured that they cannot be bought."

He thought that highly unlikely. Anyone could be bought. Isn't that what they were counting on with this tournament?

"Your shadows will rotate on a previously arranged basis. Just pretend they aren't there, and play well."

"What games should we play?" Everly asked.

"Do I look like your nursemaid, Mr. Everly? Play whatever you wish, and with whomever you wish. There are plenty of outsiders here tonight who wish to play against the contestants of this tournament. It is only the amount of your purse that will matter in the end." He pointed to a few men standing near the entrance. "Empty your pockets and give the contents to these men. They will return your items to you at the end of the night."

One night of gambling? More bets. Apathy overtook Sebastien as he surrendered his pocket money to a keeper. They were each given their hefty packet of one thousand pounds. He looked at the denominations, then at the faces of some of the other men. Stakes would be high tonight. He was used to such things, but some of the men present never left their fluffy boudoirs.

As they made their way into the main room, he tossed around the idea of just sitting at the edges with his thousand pounds in hand. At least half of the contestants would gamble it all away. Another quarter would lose most of it before the night was out. If he just kept his thousand pounds, he'd likely be near the top and the others would be aghast at him not playing.

He mulled it over, then threw himself into a chair at the hazard table. He tossed fifty pounds onto the table. Self-destruction at its finest.

"Deville."

He looked up to see the Marquess of Edsfield address him before sitting down.

Sebastien's curiosity overcame his malaise for a moment. "My lord."

"Call me Edsfield, Deville."

As if they were on the same social level. Curiouser and curiouser. The Marquess of Edsfield had never given him a moment's notice before.

Sebastien nodded and made another bet. He toyed with an unlit cheroot while Edsfield made his bet, far more conservative in nature.

"I hear congratulations are in order."

Sebastien watched the dice. "For what?"

"For the competition."

He indicated the pile of money. "It isn't over yet. I'm hardly the only one at the top."

"Ah." Edsfield smiled. "But there are but a few games left and in some of your favorite pastimes, yes?"

He stopped fiddling and lit his cheroot. "Perhaps."

"Then I can but give early congratulations— hedging a bet, if you will."

He exhaled and watched the marquess place another bet.

"What are your thoughts on the Corn Laws, Deville?"

Sebastien placed his next bet, trying not to betray his surprise. Half of him was sick with the whole thing, and the other half was eyeing the power already being laid before him if he but reached out to take it.

"Edsfield, what are you up to, my good man." Baron Lockwood approached from his other side. "Not troubling Mr. Deville with any of your twaddle, surely."

The marquess looked like he was going to object, but then he leaned back. "Not at all. Join us, Lockwood."

Lockwood took the seat, reaching over to shake his hand. "Deville, good to see you back in London."

The world had gone mad. Irrevocably mad. "Likewise."

"Been reading about the competition in the papers for weeks, and the wife is ready to murder someone to get an invitation for the final days. Wouldn't miss tonight's events for anything."

Sebastien gave a cursory look around the hell, half expecting the madness to produce the baroness and a dozen of her closest twittering confidantes.

"Gads man, of course I didn't bring her. Can you imagine? I hear the widow Noke has been trying to get into one of the clubs for years though. A lovely pair on that one. Enough to tempt any man to want to gain her subscription. Prime property."

Harriet had once promised him unimaginable

pleasures if he'd sneak her into a gaming hell. The thought of both the woman and the activity left him completely uninspired now.

"On that note, there's some prime property up near the border of Thurston Place, Deville," the marquess said, idly fingering the sides of his glass. "I can probably find a good bargain on it for the right sort, should you know of someone."

Thurston Place was on some of the most prime land in the country. Any bordering land would be valuable. He had been looking to purchase land near that area for years.

The offer would be good only as long as he won though. That was very apparent. If he lost, the land would be off the market or offered to the winner.

The game swirled around him, both the one he was currently competing in and the greater one that beckoned him forth. These were men who wouldn't normally approach or even acknowledge him, and here they were tentatively bidding for his favor.

He tossed in another bet and continued to play the game and win.

"Caro?"

Caroline stopped her forward progress at Sarah's call. She turned and let her catch up.

Sarah gripped her sleeve. "I've been looking for you all afternoon."

"I was doing some tasks for the earl; I'm sorry I didn't send a note." She was sorry for a lot of things.

"Do you have time to talk?"

She took the other girl's arm in hers, guilt, a now-familiar companion, rearing its dark head. "Of course. How are you?" she said as they made the turn into the west wing, toward Sarah's room.

Sarah bit her lip and shook her head. Caroline nodded and waited until they were out of the hall and away from the servants' ears. Sarah dismissed her maid, who curtsied to them before leaving.

"I'm doing terribly," she uttered as soon as the door had closed. She flopped into her dressing chair, and Caroline sank into the maid's chair to the side, a reflection of her existence.

"What has happened?"

"Everything, everything about this tournament has happened."

"I don't understand."

"William tells me I'm being irrational about the whole affair."

Caroline blinked at her from the fog. "You've confided in William?"

"Yes." She picked at her skirt. "You haven't been around as much, and I've also been busy with fittings and things, and he is always near. He has a ready ear, and I have been making use of it."

"Oh." She felt the need to apologize again and readied herself to make a good one.

"I kissed him," Sarah blurted.

Caroline felt her eyes widen impossibly. "You kissed William?"

"Yes." She cringed. "He rebuffed me very nicely, but I made quite the fool of myself."

Caroline remembered the looks she had seen

William give Sarah and thought that maybe she hadn't made as much a fool of herself as she thought.

Sarah rose and paced around the room. "I knew before this competition started the contestants weren't playing for my hand. That I was merely the bride price, but I hoped, Caro, deep inside that one of them would be my knight."

She stopped pacing and closed her eyes. "Father tells me over and over what a great match this will be and how proud he is of my conduct. I am ecstatic to please him, I am. But other than a few gruff words he barely speaks to me. I'm like a costly statue that needs to be taken off its shelf and dusted every once in a while. But then I go right back on the shelf. He talks to you more than he does to me, and you aren't even his daughter."

Caroline's heart stopped, her breath caught in her chest, lodged like a hot air balloon in a tree. "I—"

"I'm going to be just like Mother, aren't I, Caro?"

"Of course n—"

"I thought perhaps Mr. Everly was interested in me, really me, but then he went and had that vulgar Marjorie Widwell out in the maze. I saw them rutting against the cupid. I'm amazed the stone didn't tumble to the ground."

Caroline's mouth dropped before she could stop it.

"And I realized I had just been trying so hard to put on a brave face, to try and get someone to see me that I was willing to overlook any flaws." She slumped into her seat as far as her stays allowed. "I want to please Father, but the more I get to know William, the more I dread the outcome."

"Perhaps if you said something to the earl—"

Sarah closed her eyes. "I can't. I can't. There is only one more week. Can you imagine the scandal? I would be ostracized completely. Father would toss me on my ear."

"William—"

"Doesn't want me." She chuckled humorlessly. "He said it wasn't to be."

"But—"

"He's illegitimate and landless. I only found out by hearing Mr. Deville make a comment on it, including him in their ranks."

All manners of things clicked in her mind. Why William looked familiar, his mission, his diplomatic status, to whom he reported.

"But I don't care. I don't need him to be those things. I would listen to my heart for once, Caro, just like you."

"That didn't get me anywhere good, Sarah," she said, somewhat lamely.

"But you took the chance." She took an audible breath. "You keep taking the chance."

Caroline looked at her sharply. Sarah turned her head to the side, studying the tapestry on the wall. "I—I saw Sebastien Deville leaving your cottage one night."

The balloon ripped and Caroline plummeted through the branches. "Oh."

"I'm not angry with you. Why would I be? I

hardly have a tendre for Deville. Besides, William explained the circumstances to me, and I hope for the best for you."

"He did?" How could he explain something she could not?

"Yes. And everyone has noticed the changes in Mr. Deville. How could one not?" She swallowed. "But he is in the lead. And—and Father says he will surely win."

"He is not so bad, Sarah." She smiled forcefully. "When he is not making bets. I daresay he will keep you in style should you marry."

Sarah shook her head, a tear falling down her cheek. "I want to run away now, Caro. To India or France. Somewhere on your list."

Caroline sat down next to her and pulled her head against her shoulder. "I know," she whispered.

And both of them knew that wasn't going to happen.

Sebastien idly peered at his facedown card as the deal continued. A smart gambler knew when his luck turned. It was the defining characteristic between a man who won or lost little, and one who lost it all.

His luck had turned almost immediately after his third drink and the addition of his seductive new shadow.

A graceful hand attached to a curvy little blonde piece touched his shoulder. She had followed him around the club for the last hour, and he had let her. The lights caught her hair in just the right way every few minutes. For a second it would shine a rich gold, but then any movement would turn it back to straw. Wrong. Irritatingly wrong.

Ever since she had attached herself to him he had played poorly. He'd gone from écarté to speculation to vingt-et-un and left a trail of money behind. And yet he hadn't turned her out. He kept seeing blue-gray eyes shining in betrayal and a bloody necklace in a boxed cage in his bedroom.

If he couldn't have the real thing . . .

A three flipped to the top of his facedown card. Lovely.

"That sweet little property from the documentation. I went by to see it during the break," Everly said.

His shoulders tightened, and the blonde's hands immediately tried to loosen them.

Benedict froze across from him at Everly's words, then continued counting his pot. "Interesting."

"It's a beauty, isn't it?" Parley said. "I think I'll put up a lovely little plaque with my name on it, should I win."

"Lord Benedict said he'd tear it down at the beginning of the competition." Everly looked to Benedict, who pretended not to hear, concentrating on his cards. Everly's brows creased before he turned back. "That would be a shame though. I'd like to inhabit the current structure. Make it *mine*."

Sebastien let his fingers curl around his cards, letting his rage show in a way that he usually didn't when playing. Everly smirked in a satisfied manner.

"What about you, Deville?"

He hadn't been planning on doing anything rash with his hand, apathy having swirled too far down his throat, though the destructive element within whispered to keep asking for cards until he reached the limit. A hot breath of emotion swept up his spine at Everly touching Roseford, at any of them trying to take something else from him. Sebastien shoved his remaining money forward. "Five hundred pounds."

The crease between Everly's brows deepened, then smoothed. "Gaming suicide, Deville? Didn't think you'd kick it in so early. So melancholy and defeated." His hand hovered over his pot for a moment, but he was looking at a king and a high card hidden underneath—his face said as much. He pushed the matched bet in. "But I'll happily finish you off."

Parley looked as if he was about to fold his cards, but a sharp glance from Everly had him reluctantly pushing in five hundred as well.

Benedict threw his cards in. "I'm out."

Everly examined him, displeased. "I'm surprised at you, Benedict. You've always wanted a chance to beat him. Here it is." Benedict didn't look up. He just lifted his money and pushed away from the table and through the crowd. There was a moment of silence before Everly turned back to him.

"Well, I suppose it will just be Parley, me, and this lovely little crowd to enjoy your defeat, Deville." He tossed his king and a ten onto the table, about what Sebastien had guessed he'd have.

Parley made a little moue of disappointment. A

pair of nines. Idiot. He should have known Everly would beat him if he'd made him play the hand.

Sebastien allowed his hate to fully show and Everly's smirk increased, interpreting the look exactly as he'd intended. Everly reached forward to scoop the pot.

"Getting a little ahead of yourself, Everly?"

He motioned to the dealer, who flipped a card. The queen of hearts landed on top of his other two cards to form a jagged fence.

He leaned back and looked at Everly. "Your bet. Do you wish to continue?"

Everly's face had lost most of its color, as he must have started to guess what Sebastien's hidden card contained. Sebastien flipped it and the eight landed on top of the queen, suffocating her below.

The crowd immediately started exclaiming. Sebastien leaned forward so that only Everly could hear him. "Best hope we don't meet outside of the crowds tonight, Everly. *Best hope.*"

He pulled the winnings back and lifted them from the table. The blonde chattered something in his ear. He headed toward the faro table with fifteen hundred pounds. He had a game to win.

Caroline directed the last servant under her watch. She had to admit that Lady Tevon was very capable at running an estate. She had helped with all the domestic concerns of the penultimate and final games. Sarah had a pod of servants too, and they were running like an efficient machine. They had another day left before the men and the influx of guests, old and new, descended.

She idly scanned the servants running to and fro, the crofters, villagers, and hired hands. No one was paying particular mind to her position. She dropped her handkerchief near the constructed bench. Crouching, she pulled the rope she had secured in her skirts. She knotted and arranged the twining fibers into a noose. She'd attach the other part later, but this would do the trick for now.

She stood with her handkerchief, putting it conspicuously in her pocket in case anyone was watching. She had realized how deceptively simple sabotaging the last game would be weeks ago when she'd begun the sketches. A minor thing that would affect everyone, yet really only affect those she especially wanted. She could end Sebastien Deville's victory with one stroke, if she chose.

She looked at the army of servants, the droves of minions constructing the theater around her in which the final acts of the tournament would take place in front of the eyes of society. Power came in many forms. The ability to create, the ability to lead, the ability to destroy.

People so often underestimated the last.

He was up five thousand pounds two hours later. A wise man knew when it was time to stop. A destructive man didn't. He grappled the destruction in hand for a second, stood, and waved his handler over, letting the person count the money and make a note. He also recorded it with another handler, Valpage, and with the duke, just in case.

The blonde who had been pursuing him the

entire time followed him into the hall, perhaps hoping to make use of one of the rooms farther back. He let the destruction free.

"Mr. Deville, I have a proposition for—"

He turned and swiftly swung her against the wall. Not harshly, but enough to make one of the paintings hanging farther down fall to the floor with a thwack. The quick intake of breath and arch against his body let him know she was completely willing to play rough.

He connected their hips and she arched back farther, her eyes smoky and green. Wrong, wrong. Fingers wrapped around his neck and lips came toward his. He turned his head at the last second and moved into her throat instead.

She smelled of rosewater and lavender. Wrong, all wrong. Her skin was soft, but there was just something incredibly wrong about it. One of her hands traveled down his chest. An oily, strange feeling trickled down his spine at the same speed. He caught her wrist at his stomach, the unpleasant feeling coiling there, waiting. She panted in his ear, straining to connect them. He stared at the wall an inch from his nose. The paint and putty not able to hide all the cracks beneath.

He released her wrist and pushed away from her, striding down the hall, not caring that he left her standing there, ready and willing to do anything he desired.

"Come back!"

He didn't so much as look behind him.

Chapter 20

⌒⟋⟍⌒

*When one asks for forgiveness—does one seek
it from another or from oneself? Sometimes it
seems that the asker doesn't even know what
he seeks forgiveness from.*

Most of the guests would be back in a few
hours. She had exhausted herself speaking
with Sarah again. They'd had so many conversations in the last few days, especially concerning
the seductive thought of running mixed with the
practical aspects of such an undertaking. Two
women on the run with barely a useful nonsocial
skill between them? They had decided to see what
happened over the next few days, the last of the
games. To put off the decision as long as possible,
for neither could see a perfect outcome, or an easy
choice.

She thought of the rope under the stands. One
on which to hang herself or someone else.

She made another stitch in her embroidery. It
usually allowed her to free her mind, but she just
kept making mistakes and then having to undo
them. Her elbow knocked into her bed stand, and

the locket clanged to the floor. She looked at it for a few seconds before setting her embroidery aside and kneeling to pick it up. There was a whisper of sound, and she froze in her crouch. Slowly she looked up, a part of her knowing who was there before she saw him.

He stood just inside the door, in the shadows, hunched against the wall with his arms crossed and his features shuttered. She clutched the locket and set it on the coverlet, her hand resting on the soft fabric to keep it from shaking. "Sebastien."

He didn't move for a second, but then he stepped farther into the light, his features heavy and hard to read. "Caroline."

She fiddled with the heavy gold without looking away from him. "You are back early."

"I left London before the other guests."

"Oh." She didn't know what to say. She wanted to ask him why he was here, why he had made the bet, why he had left without a word. She simply watched him and waited instead.

"I won. Both London games."

"I'm not surprised."

"Because one involved gambling?" His voice held an aggressive note.

"Yes, and because both involved you."

Where normally she would have expected him to prowl toward her, closing the door to trap her inside, instead he fell back against the wall, leaving the door open. She had never seen this Sebastien, less than completely certain and capable.

"I didn't expect to see you here," she said.

"No?"

"No. Are you going to come inside, or just stand there brooding?"

He took a half a step before freezing. His posture was defensive, like that of a feral animal caught in a poacher's trap tentatively reaching out to someone seeking to free him.

She pushed the locket between her hands, and pushed up to kneel with the bed between them, a safer position than standing. A penitent woman who didn't know for what she was asking. "Why did you make the bet?"

His shoulders tightened; she could see by the shift in his coat. "Benedict made the bet at the first party. After we danced. It was stupid."

"And did you win?"

He watched her, blue-green eyes heavy. "I don't know."

She half expected him to ask her if she loved him, but then realized that this Sebastien, this serious, half-feral incarnation, wouldn't ask. He'd be afraid of the answer, possibly either answer she might give. The previous Sebastien would have demanded the answer, seduced it from her, never truly believing in the question. That thought gave her pause and a spot of courage.

Her knees creaked as she shifted. She rose and walked around the bed. He stiffened as she neared him. "Sebastien, I'm still angry with you."

"Yes."

"You should have told me about the bet instead of letting the duke make the announcement."

"I know."

She looked away. "I know it doesn't matter in

the scheme of things. You will likely win this tournament or go on to great acclaim in society, but it did hurt."

"I know."

She thought of her conversation with Cheevers. That even in the unlikely event that Sebastien didn't win, he wouldn't marry her. To secure a position in society and continue his aspirations, he would need to marry someone for power. She had none.

She touched his sleeve, and his entire body shuddered.

"You sent me the necklace," he said.

"A fit of pique on my part. I told you I was still angry."

"I tried to explain in my note."

She frowned. "What note?"

"The one I left on your pillow with the rose."

She cast a glance to her bed. "There was nothing there. I even checked my—" She cleared her throat, cheeks heating as she nearly gave away that she had looked everywhere in a desperate attempt to find something that did not exist.

A shadow swirled in his eyes. "That damn—" He closed his eyes and reopened them a moment later. "It doesn't matter."

He reached out a hand, and when she didn't move he curved fingers around her forearm slowly, as if afraid she'd dart away.

He drew her toward him, and his eyes slid shut as he inhaled. "Cinnamon and wild spice." One hand reached up and curled into her hair. "There was a woman last night, at the game." She froze in his arms. "Blonde hair, lithe, willing."

Eyes caressed her face. "But the eyes were wrong, the color, the shape. Her scent."

"Did you—" She swallowed. "Did you kiss her?" She couldn't ask if he'd done more.

"No, I couldn't." His thumb ran over her bottom lip. "Her lips were completely wrong. How could I?"

Her breath caught as his eyes held hers. "Oh." And something inside her, some devil, prompted her to add, "And mine?"

"Perfect."

He pulled her the rest of the way toward him and her lips met his. Like a spark of flint, his hands lit a path of fire as they trailed gently downward, curving around her waist. As he pulled her against him, locking them together in a perfect fit.

There was a languid reconnection of lovers reunited, combined with the urgency that this might be the last time they would be together. Fierce, wild, lovely, caring touches. Untamed passion vying with forbidden love.

Chapter 21

◦◦◦

Oh to be a guest at Meadowbrook today!
Would there be any finer privilege? Every con-
testant knows what is at stake, and the stakes
grow ever higher with the most Special Guest
in attendance.

Sebastien walked away from the cottage, warm
and cozy. The morning air contained a chill
as he strode toward the towering manor, stately
and cold.

He passed the perfect manor gardens, constricted and constrained. The stones of the house
gleamed, the one strand of ivy near the bottom,
viselike in its grip, trying to keep a tenacious hold
under the master gardener's ever watchful prun-
ing eye.

Servants moved out of his way, already up and
polishing glittering gold accents. Heavy, dripping,
slithering gold. A dark, heavy style after seeing
the warm tones of Caroline and her bedroom.

If he won the next two games, he would win the
tournament. With the points the way they were, it
was a given. If he placed second in the next two

games, he would likely win also, depending on who won each. If he did poorly in one of them, it was anyone's game at the top. Benedict had done well in London. And had remained surprisingly quiet. Even with Everly and Parley spurring him on, trying to get him to taunt Timtree, who hadn't done as well, and Sloane, who was still doing well, but had been beaten by Benedict, Benedict had simply completed his tasks and retired. It was altogether unsettling. Something about Benedict had changed.

As he neared his room, a flurry of servants flew down the hall, nearly flattening him.

"Can't believe it!"

"—King—"

"—here!"

Further cries were swallowed as they sprinted around the bend in the hall. He stood where he was, the walls pressing in. The King was coming. Hardly a surprise, and yet it was as if any last hope was extinguished. Of what, he hardly wanted to consider.

The remaining ten contestants gathered in the "arena" that had been constructed for the final two games. Astonishing that they had constructed the set in the few days the contestants had been gone. In reality it was little more than raised benches, chairs, and a track, but the design was creatively executed in that it looked like so much more. Made you believe in it.

He could see Caroline's hand in the design, in the streaming banners. He even recognized them from pieces she had sewed or brought back from the village. She had never told him what they were, even when coaxed with strong incentive.

This work wasn't by the hand of the woman whom he had first met at Roseford, but by the skillful design of a woman who had grown into her own passion.

The King loved pageants and medieval lore, and the area looked like a strange cross between a medieval tourney and something straight out of ancient Rome. Earlier he had wondered why they had decided to hold games in London, but obviously it had been to get the men and guests off the estate.

Guests flooded the area, winding into the stands. Society's best, waiting for a chance to herald the winner who would grace their halls with a sparkling new title, wealth, and power. To get a firsthand peek at the games they had been rabidly reading about in the papers the past seven weeks.

Harriet Noke sashayed toward the stands, casting glances at the competitors, a smoky but rote one his way, a more considering one at Benedict. Interesting. That is, if he was interested in caring about such a thing at this point.

King George the Fourth made his entrance with much fanfare, pomp, and circumstance. Trumpets blew, and he smiled hugely, in obvious delight. The King wound his way through the contestants, shaking hands and exchanging words, a small contingent of men, women, and children following behind.

The King greeted him heartily. "I have heard you have been dominating the competition. Your father is quite pleased. Quite pleased."

Sebastien bowed and inclined his head. "He seems to take it in stride, yes."

The King leaned forward. "Going to be writing your name down on those letters-patent before the week is out?"

"Perhaps."

He chortled and patted Sebastien on the back. "Should be interesting to see what you do in Parliament. Shake them up a bit. Change things for the better maybe. Lot of people counting on you."

Sebastien knew exactly what he meant. The illegitimate children in the land would all be watching this tournament's final days. A victory for them if he were to win.

"Good luck to you, Mr. Deville."

The King and his entourage set off for the large box decorated with streaming banners that proclaimed the coat of arms of the royal house and George.

Sebastien concentrated on Herakles as the horse was brought to him by the stable hand.

It was a blur of colors and cheering, flags waving and wild screams as they positioned themselves at the start. The pistol sounded, and every piece of the track pulled into detailed view, crystalline and clear, as Herakles's muscles bunched beneath his.

Two sharp turns, then three. Horseflesh jostled and riders fell behind or surged ahead. He kept a tight grip on Herakles, not letting him have his head, not yet. One more turn . . .

They took the turn, and energy rushed through him as they pulled ahead and he let Herakles loose. He was out in front with the best horseflesh and a steady hand, the finish line near enough to taste. He couldn't lose. The metallic ting of his victory was already proclaimed and absolute.

A bright blue ball rolled out onto the track ahead, right into his narrowed crystal view, and a tiny figure of pink and gold rushed after it. Time slowed. The figure reminded him of Polly, a little Caroline angel.

The tiny Caroline reached the center of the track before she caught the ball. She picked it up, then seeming to realize where she was—from either the stomping of the hooves beating on the dirt, or the wild sounds of the crowd—she looked straight up. He couldn't see her eyes, but all he could picture was wide blue-gray.

She'd never make it off the track. He glanced over his shoulder. The riders on his right veered, causing them to lose a stride of ground, but the ones in the middle didn't so much as pull the reins. It was only a split second, but it was enough.

He jerked the reins right and Herakles responded instantly. As if she were a big gold ring, he leaned over and snatched her from the track by the back of her dress. He swung her wide as Herakles continued the tight arc. The blue ball shot out. Air whipped him as the other riders passed, snatching his coat and sending it in an arc swirling around him as well. The riders in the middle never broke stride.

Herakles stopped at the end of the circle,

chest heaving. Sebastien's heartbeat echoed his mount's.

He stared at the pack of riders as they crossed the finish line without him, then to the pink-clothed miniature hanging from his fist. A small girl of indeterminate age—he never could tell how old the little toe rags were—stared wide-eyed back, her eyes starting to fill.

"Don't cry," he said uncertainly, as he pulled her into a more comfortable position against him and dismounted.

The little girl's arms wrapped around his neck as the crowd pushed in from the emptying stands, each person clamoring for attention. He couldn't pick out the distraught face of a woman or man to indicate parents.

"Who is your father?" he asked the poppet.

"Just Mama." She stared up at him solemnly, finger twirling a curl. "She said I would meet Papa someday."

He returned her stare. Time ticked the years back. His fingers tightened around her.

"My baby!" A blonde woman pushed through the crowd and came rushing forward, a terrified look on her face. He held the girl out and the woman snatched her to her chest, burying her face in golden curls.

He stood there awkwardly for a second, before turning to push through the onlookers. He could see the contestants by the finish line circling and looking back. He remounted Herakles in a maneuver that was occasionally difficult, but at the moment was effortless; he was so filled with rage.

Herakles cantered past the finish line, and Sebastien patted the horse and dismounted, throwing the reins to a groom.

He stalked toward his prey.

"Deville, what the devil, man, are you hurt?" Sloane asked. He had been in the twosome with Benedict on the left, well away from the girl.

"I'm fine." He found the man who had been at the head of the middle pack and pushed him against the wall. "You weren't going to stop, were you, Everly?" He pushed him again, holding him against the wall. "I saw you and Parley; you didn't give it a second thought. Didn't even veer."

"You're cracked, Deville. As if you would have stopped had you been in your right mind. What's gotten into you?"

"What's gotten into me?" He shoved him again. "A child, Everly. You were going to trample some woman's daughter."

"Some woman's? Some little bastard no one would miss?"

Blood seeped from Everly's mouth before Sebastien even realized he'd hit him.

"You'll pay for that, Deville." He wiped his mouth and narrowed eyes on him. "When I win this tournament, you will pay for that in spades."

"I'm shaking in my linens, Everly. You disgust me."

"I disgust you? There was a time not so long ago where you would have done the same thing. You didn't care a thing about anyone but yourself; it was the one strength you possessed. And now you suddenly have a care for women and children?" He laughed unpleasantly. "Have at your disgust. I feel the same way about you. Weak. You don't deserve to win."

Everly turned to walk away and Sebastien couldn't help himself; he swept his leg out and Everly tumbled facedown into the dirt.

Sebastien pivoted and pushed through the gathered crowd, every ear and wide eye focused on the spectacle.

Timtree and Bateman were farther down the line. Bateman gave him a mocking look and slipped off. Good thing for him too, as he'd been right there with Everly and Parley.

Sebastien narrowed eyes upon Timtree.

Timtree looked back coolly. "I wouldn't have hit her, so you can stop looking at me that way."

"You didn't stop."

Narrowed eyes looked back. "And you did, though you didn't need to. It wouldn't have been you hitting her. Everly's right. Where has this whinging selflessness come from?"

Strange emotions filtered through a surprisingly clear head for once. "You are all completely despicable," he said with a small bit of wonder.

"There was a time not too long ago you were exactly the same, *friend*. And now you might have cost yourself, *us*, the win. You'll have no points for the race." Timtree's lips pressed together.

"Fine.

"Fine?" Mottled red worked up Timtree's neck, then into his face. "You're going to let Benedict or Everly win?" Timtree shoved him. "Fine."

He looked like he was going to shove Sebastien again, but Timtree simply stomped forward, knocking his shoulder into Sebastien's as he passed.

Sloane gave him an apologetic look and opened his mouth. He shut it abruptly as the hair on the back of Sebastien's neck lifted.

"Mr. Sloane, leave us."

For a moment Sloane looked as if he might defy the duke and stay, and Sebastien felt a warmth for the man that he rarely had for any of the members of his acquaintance. He inclined his head, and Sloane returned the gesture before walking away.

"Sebastien. Lovely little stunt with the waif."

He turned toward the duke, who was resplendent in his London finery, gilded walking stick ticking an irritated beat against the grass.

"I thought you might admire my finesse."

"I didn't." The duke's tones were clipped. "You're a fool. You don't know that anyone would have run her over. You hardly needed to hurt your own standing for someone who could do nothing for you."

"I didn't realize someone had to do something for me in order to be saved." But that wasn't entirely true either. He knew how society worked and had long played the same.

"The cloying country air has done you little good, has it? I start to think that perhaps Benedict might be worth something after all."

And you not at all. It didn't even need to be said in order to accomplish the same thing as a shout.

The cold yaw of darkness opened up inside

him. It was so like the duke to remind him of a part of him he hadn't missed. The cold pool had been there at the edges waiting, but warm gold mist had been keeping it at bay.

"I've started to think that as well, Your Grace. Especially the further and further I see him falling from the tree. Lord Benedict has been a credit to the line of Grandien in the last week. Can you say the same?"

He pushed past the duke, who had gone stock-still at the grave insult.

He saw Benedict standing to the side, watching, eyes wide, mouth slightly ajar.

"Close your mouth," he said beneath his breath as he passed. "Or I shall take back every word."

Benedict's mouth snapped shut, but Sebastien didn't turn to see any further reaction.

All he wanted to do was go upstairs and have Grousett draw him a bath. Soak his tight muscles away. Perhaps he'd drown himself while he was at it.

A scarlet-robed figure stepped into his path. He readied a scathing curse before swallowing it when he realized who was blocking his retreat.

"Your Majesty."

"Mr. Deville. I must say that you didn't leave us without entertainment today."

"My apologies, Your Majesty."

"On the contrary. Though I don't think you much helped your standing, you made quite the spectacle."

It took everything in Sebastien to swallow the retort that leaped to his lips. "Yes, Your Majesty."

"And I'm sure the child's parents are pleased and would see you rewarded." A number of people crowded around, trying to hear the monarch's every word. A reporter hovered near the edge.

"There is no such need." He just wanted to hide in his room. Was that too much to ask?

"Ah. But there is one more day, is there not? Perhaps you will delight us tomorrow as well?"

"Perhaps." Usually he watched for every expression and nonverbal sign from the King or from those of high stature. He thrived on knowing when to hold his cards and when to toss them in a flurry of showmanship. But at the moment he couldn't read a thing, not because it wasn't there to be read, George obviously wanted something, but Sebastien was just too worn out to read it. The King was likely disappointed as well. Wasn't everyone?

"Good, good. Good day to you, Mr. Deville."

Sebastien bowed as the King walked away, his entourage trailing. Something tickled at his senses, but it wasn't full enough to realize, and he pushed it aside, the open pathway to freedom splayed before him.

The reporter stepped into his path as he walked forward, but he simply skirted the man and continued. Another man walked up to him, and another, a bevy of guests of all stripes, colors, and sizes got in line. It was a long time before he got that bath.

She didn't know what to think of Sebastien's actions. He had saved that little girl. Put his standing in jeopardy. Done something purely selfless for another.

She watched from the earl's study as he continued to fend off the crowds, then picked up the document the earl wanted and skirted the desk to return downstairs. Her progress was abruptly stopped in the middle of the room as the Duke of Grandien strolled inside.

"Your Grace."

"Ah, Mrs. Martin." One hand held a walking stick, while the other turned and shut the door, sealing them inside.

"I must be leaving Your Grace, if you would excuse me."

"I do not." He tapped the cane against his palm. "I came here expressly to speak with you."

She shifted nervously, wishing he had left the door open. "Perhaps we can discuss whatever you need on the way back downstairs? The earl would like this document right away." She held it up.

"Cheevers knows I'm here." He cast a glance left, then right, before strolling a few steps forward. "I come with a proposition for you, Mrs. Martin, and I'm not going to mince words or be coy about it."

"A proposition?" Her heart started pounding in her chest.

"A swap if you will. Or a trade up, if I do say so myself." He smiled the vaguely smarmy smile that seemed to make all the women melt at his feet.

She watched him for a moment, not believing her ears. "Are you—are you asking me to discard Sebastien and take up with you?"

He raised a brow, so like Sebastien's. "For all your plain speaking, you sound far more appalled than I would have thought. We look alike, Mrs. Martin, or hadn't you noticed? And I possess far more wealth than Sebastien ever will, and I say that knowing the type of wealth Sebastien will likely acquire. But there is no beating the sheer amount of fortune that a legacy can amass. Most people find it easy to substitute us one for the other."

The way he said it . . . she could barely work up any anger above her shock. She had a feeling she wasn't the first person the duke had approached in this way either. She wondered if Sebastien knew, then chastised herself. He definitely knew. That amount of bile wasn't spawned from nothing.

She examined the duke critically, trying to figure out what it was about the man that was so different from Sebastien, for all that they looked alike. They possessed the same eyes, the same build, the same lock of hair that didn't want to stay back. High cheekbones, strong chin, full lips.

But the little things were all different. The aquamarine might be the exact shade, but the way the duke's eyes moved was different, the way his mouth curved, the stern control he exuded versus the wildness of his natural son. The duke's lips seemed to be perpetually pressed together, thinning them, while Sebastien's were quick to pull into a smile or smirk, whether the feeling was genuine or dark.

"You wouldn't be alone, as you so often are, isn't that true, Mrs. Martin?"

Someone like the duke would *never* leave personal gifts on someone's pillow. He would buy ruby necklaces and expensive, showy, meaningless items. He would crush a person into submission or seek to buy her affection.

"Sebastien is still young," he continued. "There are years of experience that he lacks. And his drive is singular."

The man in front of her would never understand what drove someone like Sebastien, not really. He might correctly estimate his actions and responses; he might even give the right *answers* about what drove him. But he would never understand. This man was tight control and firm arrogance. And while his son carried those traits as well, he was rebellious and resentful and wild.

He pulled his cane through his fingers. "Sebastien will leave you. Do you know his reputation? No mistresses, no long-term relationships of any type. He never stays."

And she was going to lose him to this tournament. Sarah was going to marry him, and Caroline would have to stay away from both of them.

"Why are you doing this? Why do you want Sebastien to win so badly as to do this?"

He watched her from heavily lidded eyes and twirled his walking stick. "Are you so blind as not to see the obvious advantages of choosing me?"

He had avoided the question. Sudden clarity pierced her. "You bet on him to win, didn't you?"

His cocked head was her answer.

"How much did you bet?"

"That matters little. There is more riding on this than a paltry twenty or fifty thousand pounds. How many men can claim multiple sons in the aristocracy? We are talking about dynasty. I always knew he had it in him. He just needed the right incentive, the right opportunity. Denying him all these years has made him hungry, fierce. And you come by and undo all of my work in a few months? I think not."

Her mind had started to whirl under the amounts of money he was talking about and went into a complete tailspin with the rest of his words.

"Fortunately, I have quite a bit of experience with the female mind." He walked around her, examining her from all angles. "Comfort, security, the ability to do what you wish without having to make hard decisions. Every need catered to," he whispered as he passed behind her, in a voice that sounded entirely too much like Sebastien's, but edged with words like Patrick's. "I think you can see the advantages of the situation."

She finally found her voice. "I'm appalled you would think so."

He lifted his brow again, in front of her once more. "Histrionics or bad acting, Mrs. Martin?"

She tilted her head, examining him further. She could see it from his perspective. This offer would benefit her immeasurably. She'd have plenty of money and perhaps even a step into society. Most women of her acquaintance would jump at the offer.

His hand moved along the head of his walking

stick. "I could give you just about anything you desire. Gowns, jewels, your own servants. You'd never want for anything."

There was something about the duke—a spark, a curling desire to play with the edged jaws, snapping and deadly. A man still considered in his prime, and one who looked twenty years younger. She could see exactly how he affected others.

"No."

"No? You would instead try and keep the attention of a man who even now intends to win this competition and forget about you entirely?"

"No."

"Well, which is it?" He touched her jaw, and she forced herself to breathe in regulated breaths. "Will you take that which I have so generously offered, an offer I don't have to make at all, mind you, or will you go on faith that your dear Sebastien will pick you?"

His allure reached out to her, tried to wrap around her, but his spark didn't resonate. She was instead repelled by the manner in which he treated his son. Sons, really, but her true care lay with the one.

"I go with neither. I'm not the ninny you think me, Your Grace. And furthermore, I find it interesting how scared you must be to approach me in this way. With your talks of dynasty and pride. A scared little boy afraid of someone disturbing his schoolboy game."

His fingers paused and then removed themselves from her skin. "Scared? What a lark." He tightened the valleys of each gloved finger against his skin. "You are a foolish girl, Mrs. Martin. If ever you decide otherwise, perhaps I will hear you out. Or perhaps I will simply close the door in your face."

"Yes, because in addition to all of those lovely qualities you listed, you think that taking me to mistress will hurt your son. You will take one more thing from him and prove yourself the worthier. I think you are intimidated by Sebastien, for all that you say you want him to succeed. And frankly, I find you lacking in any good character, Your Grace. Do not worry yourself that you will find me penniless at your doorstep. I would rather starve in the streets." She walked toward the door.

"Perhaps I will let Cheevers know that." His voice was silky, deadly.

She didn't stop, though she almost stumbled. "You do that, Your Grace." She opened the door and walked through.

It had taken most of the evening, a run-in with nearly every illegitimate child born to England, another with the duke and a scorcher with Everly, before he had finally run away to the only safe haven he knew.

He slammed down into a chair, flopping across it. His fingers played over the fabric, hell-bent on destroying it. She stilled his hand.

"What ails you?"

"Today ails me. Everyone who has spoken with me today. They can't get past my *regrettable* action, my moment of stupidity."

"I—I thought it was wonderful of you."

"Wonderful to lose?"

"No, to save the little girl." Caroline touched his shoulder but he pulled away.

"It was weakness."

"What?"

"Weakness. Can you see the duke doing something like that?"

"No." There was something dark in her tone. "That's precisely my point."

"I nearly gave up the win."

She leaned back, fingers playing with the muslin of her dress. "Would that be so bad?"

"Yes."

"Why?" He could hear the plaintive note in her cry.

"I'd lose Roseford."

"You have money. Buy a different property."

"It's not home." The feeling had always been off with any other property.

"But you haven't lived there in twelve years."

"It doesn't matter. What would you say if someone took your cottage from you?"

She stayed silent.

He laughed humorlessly. "Roseford Grange is the only true home I have ever had." He rose and began to pace restlessly. "All I need to do is win the contest and it will be mine again."

"Can you not convince the duke to release it to you?"

"If in twelve years I could not, I do not believe that anything I have done will convince him. Besides, the documents are sealed. I checked them myself to make sure the duke couldn't remove the property once I won."

"The King could undo them."

"The King loves this tournament. Your banners were divine, by the way. Just the key to his heart."

She chewed her lip. "You could find a different property. One like Roseford."

He shook his head. "You don't understand."

"What don't I understand? That you want to win? That you wish to prove to everyone you are worthy?"

"As if I care if they think me worthy."

"You do!" She rose from her seat. "Otherwise you would have told everyone to travel to Hades long ago."

He pulled her against him, bending her back, grinding into her in a purposeful motion that made her eyes darken. "I don't care what those bastards think. But I will show them what a true bastard can do with that kind of power at his hands."

"Because you want revenge."

"Of course I want revenge!"

"And you think getting that revenge will prove you worthy."

"What? That doesn't make any sense. You don't understand." He pushed away from her.

"I don't understand? I don't understand?" Her voice increased to a frenzied tone.

"Of course you don't. You don't walk in society and you don't have the black mark of an illegitimate birth."

"I don't understand?" She said it in a somewhat maddened tone. "You think I don't understand."

"I know you don't understand."

"Oh, wise one." She laughed a bit hysterically. "I don't understand?" She pointed at him, finger shaking. "Who do you think my father is?"

He paused in his scathing retort, taking in her angry and embittered expression, her features crisp and patrician, her blonde hair free about her face, her blue-gray eyes the exact shade of—

"My God. You're Cheevers's daughter."

She strode away from him, shoulder bumping against his as she took a pot on the drying rack and slammed it into its position.

Why hadn't he seen it before? All kinds of odd things clicked into place, except . . . "How can this be?" He thought of her heavy gold locket. The man inside posed with her mother, a man who looked nothing like Caroline except as a very distant relation.

"My mother was pregnant when she married Papa." She slammed another pot into place. "He was a distant cousin of the earl's, living in this cottage. That part has always been true. He married my mother, the earl's mistress, in order to cover things up."

"Why didn't the earl—"

"Oh, please. My mother was a nobody. The earl was already betrothed to Sarah's mother. He was hardly going to break the lucrative contract they had." Another pot slammed.

"Lady Sarah doesn't know, does she?"

"Nor will she." She walked up to him and

pulled his head down. "If she finds out, I will hunt you down and destroy you."

"I thought you two were close."

She closed her eyes, but not before he saw the deep pain reflected. "We are. I discovered the truth when I overheard the earl speaking with my mother when I was ten. I've had to keep myself from thinking of Sarah as my sister, even as I feel that exact way about her regardless of blood. I've never told anyone. Cheevers would kill me. Sarah would be beyond hurt."

"Cheevers doesn't acknowledge you."

"No, and if you say a word to Cheevers, I don't know what I would do to you. He'd likely turn me out with nothing. I have nothing he wants. I never have. And I've used up all of my chances by consorting with you." She gave a mirthless chuckle and wrapped her arms around her middle. "Do you know what a woman in my position would have to resort to with nothing to her name? The villagers would turn their backs on me should Cheevers tell them to. You think that being a bastard has made your life hard? Try being a woman who has to rely on someone else to survive."

"You own this cottage."

"Do I?" She laughed unpleasantly. "Cheevers could argue that the property be turned over to him. He would likely win. And even if he didn't, he could turn everyone against me. I wouldn't even be able to buy a loaf of bread." She looked at him from beneath her lashes, through narrowed eyes. "Isn't it what you are always saying, that a title and power will beat those without them every time?"

"Be my mistress," he said quietly, the words shocking him as they spilled from his lips, but then forming into a resolve as they echoed in the still cottage. "Leave Meadowbrook behind. I'll take care of you. Tell me you do not see Roseford in this cottage? You will have Roseford. We will have it."

She looked down, quickly enough so that he couldn't catch the emotions flickering through her eyes, then glanced back up, all sultry knowledge and carnal innocence. The sudden switch made him nervous. She walked toward him, a definite swing to her hips and fullness to her slightly parted lips, a knowledge in her suddenly heavy eyes.

He wet his lips as she insinuated herself in the vee in his legs and slowly slid her hands up his chest and around his neck. "A tempting offer. And if you don't win? What then will become of Roseford? Of me?"

He wound his hands down her sides and clasped her backside, hiking her up and into his heat. "I may have damaged my standing, but I will still win. Roseford will still be mine."

She worked her fingers into his hair, the feeling sending pure shocks straight down his cock. Her lips brushed against his. "Quit the tournament. Find another Roseford."

He brushed his lips back. "No," he said quietly. "I will have my revenge. I will grab the power. I will have Roseford back."

"Then you won't have me," she said just as quietly.

Something elemental surged within him. "I *will* have you."

He pulled her against him, grinding her back into the wall, dropping his lips to her neck, pulling the skin, marking it, traveling farther until he had one firm breast in his hand, pushing the rosy peak up, the perfect cherry sucked between his lips.

She arched and pleaded. "You won't. I'd never do that to Sarah."

He sucked harder, pulling his tongue across her nipple, causing her to push against him, one leg curling around his, bringing them closer.

He lifted her skirts and ran a hand along the heat of her, already wet. "I'll have all of you." He dipped two fingers into the liquid gold and pressed his mouth against hers, swallowing her cry.

Her breast, pushed above her bodice, rubbed against his chest, and she shuddered as he pressed into her in a riding rhythm. A rocking canter.

"Be here in the morning when I wake," she said between pants as his fingers stroked and begged, one of her legs wrapping around his thighs.

"No." That would mean he'd be there every morning thereafter. Something fierce and wild surged inside him, and he pulled his fingers to her hips. "But I'll be here right now." He lifted her in one motion and thrust into her, pushing up as deep as he could go.

The back of her head hit the wall, and a low

moan wrapped around him, emerging from her and disappearing into him as she clenched him inside.

His control broke, and he pushed into her again and again as she rocked against the wall, mewling sounds and his name on her lips, hands curled into his neck as she simply held on, drugged and wanting.

He was going to brand her his. He was going to—

A picture fell from the wall, and he froze as it hit the floor. A vision of the gaming hell filtered through his mind.

"Sebastien?"

He slowly pulled out of her.

"Sebastien?" Her voice was a little higher and completely unsteady as she gained her feet on the ground. Her chest rose and fell in great waves.

He looked at her for a moment, his breathing equally heavy and his thoughts terrifying.

He lifted her, and her arms automatically wove around his neck. Trusting. The terror dulled into a constant thump in his chest.

He laid her on the bed and quickly stripped first her clothing, then his, trying to keep his thoughts from spinning out of control.

She looked up at him, naked and beautiful, her trust entirely misplaced. What he would do to trust like that . . . What he had always done to trust like that . . .

He stroked her skin, smooth and perfect to his touch. He felt every shiver and shudder, every sigh and gasp as he put all his considerable knowledge to use, hating himself as he did so, and wanting so badly to make this the most enjoyable experience of her life that she'd never, *never*, forget him.

And they'd said he wasn't selfish.

He watched himself slide inside her, too scared to see her expression, so open and wanting. Wanting to see her expression so badly that he was nearly tormented by it. He shuddered as she closed around him, once again, as he pushed in farther, sweet, slick wetness encasing him in a velvet grip.

She tightened around him, squeezing in a welcoming embrace or final farewell. He pulled back out and watched between their bodies as he slid in again, disappearing into her heat. Little shudders gripped him, inside her, flowing out, over her stomach and up. He pulled back so that the only thing still inside was the very tip of him. He shifted his hips in small circles, trying to figure out how not to look at her, and at the same time how to make the entire act last forever.

Caroline seemed to have other plans as she arched up into him, seeking, pushing, wrapping her ankles around his thighs to pull him back inside.

He thought to teach her a lesson and thrust all the way in, all the way up in a movement that had her producing strangled sounds beneath him, her hands grasping his hips. What he hadn't relied on was being left gasping for breath himself.

They fit together so perfectly, like her body was a hand-tailored glove just for his fingers, his palm. Each finger covered and cared for.

It was too much. *Too* much.

He started to pull away. He couldn't do it. He needed to leave. Leave and board it all back up, swallow it all back in, find his identity again, and clasp the cold, comforting blackness to him.

She caught him just as he was almost out of her body.

"Sebastien?"

The whispered entreaty caused him to look at her. A fatal mistake. Eyes turned deep blue with passion questioned him, asking for answers. And beneath was a well of feeling, some sort of redemption that he could nearly touch. Nearly taste.

"Please. Please."

He wasn't sure what it was. The look in her eyes, her pleading words, the touch of her skin that felt so right, but his removal changed into the setup of a deep, soul-touching thrust that pushed her up the sheets of the bed and pushed the bed an inch across the floor. Her head arched back, but she kept her eyes open and connected with his. Staring out from under golden lashes.

"Please."

He slid into her again and again, pushing deeper and farther, softer and harder. Trying to reach something, to grab her heart, or her soul. She gripped the pillow above her head, and he didn't think he had seen anything quite so erotic as her complete surrender, her fine breasts up and stretched. Her back arched, her legs clasped around him.

Her head arched back on a particularly fantastic thrust, and he could feel the erratic build of an earth-shaking orgasm. She tipped her head to catch his eyes once more, and blue eyes were almost black with pure desire and complete want. A desire that transcended mere physical feeling.

This was what people said was love. There reflected in her eyes like shining beacons in the storm. Not mere desire that was so tangible you could taste it, but something behind the desire that lingered long past the sensations.

The moment hung, suspended. A precipice rife with feelings and illusions on the verge of irrevocable shatter. He laid his face bare to her for once. The vulnerability and uncertainty combined with the need he had for her that he'd never known for another.

His name stuttered from her lips as she burst beneath and around him, bucking and gripping. And as the last syllable still hung on her lips, he joined her, lost, lost, lost to himself.

She opened her eyes to the morning, the lightening shadows creeping up the walls. A quick glance and a clench of her eyes told her she was alone.

She touched the empty pillow next to her, fingers curving around the paper lying there. She tipped it to see a full sketch of her face, her eyes open and gazing back for the first time, all manners of things reflected. It was a magnificent sketch. She had never looked so seductive and sated and *in love*, except in her imagination.

A single rose brushed her fingers, lying next to

the sketch. She picked up the flower and brought it to her nose. Freshly picked.

A farewell. She knew it in every fiber of her heart.

She felt a sob building and tried to hold it in, her shoulders shaking as the dawn fully rose, as she clutched the bloodred flower and precious drawing to her chest.

Chapter 22

The glory! The pain! Pure entertainment for us all and pure heaven or hell for those involved.

Sebastien entered the arena for the final game. He sought the coldness, but it didn't come. He sought the heat, but it wasn't there.

Hands reached out to touch him and he barely felt the pats, barely heard the good wishes. The field spread out before him. The bright targets gleamed in the sun, as his fingers curved around the handle of his weapon. Gold rimmed circles promising all manner of prizes and glory should he extend his fingers and grasp the apple. Gold, that wretched color he had always hated, which still whispered of things he could never have, but in quite a different manner than before.

"Line up."

He took his place and extended his arm toward the gleaming gold. He had reached the apogee.

Shots rang throughout the arena as the men fired at targets located across from the stands. The gleaming banners shifted in the warm summer breeze, at odds with the stagnant cold feeling in her heart. Spectators shouted and cheered as one match after another was fought and then concluded. Rakish brown hair and aquamarine eyes held steady as the only competitor Caroline watched advanced from one round to the next.

Sarah gripped her hand more firmly as each round was completed and the men in the lower ranks of the competition bowed out. Only those at the top still had a chance and the factions were clearly delineated as natural sons stood to one side and legitimate sons gathered on the other to watch Everly, Sloane, Benedict, and Sebastien, the final four.

Sebastien was going to win. She knew it. Everything in her screamed the verdict.

Caroline squeezed Sarah's hand. "Pardon me, Sarah. I remembered something I must do for the earl."

"But Caro, don't you want to see—"

"No."

Sarah bit her lip and nodded, tears forming in her eyes. Caroline smiled as comfortingly as she could and made her way through the row of seats. She barely apologized to the disgruntled spectators she blocked or jostled as she shimmied through. She cared little about propriety at the moment.

She walked as nonchalantly as she could—with her heart racing and her knees buckling—to the box a few seats down from the king. A roar went up from the crowd as the final retorts from the weapons of the remaining four contestants blasted through the arena.

"Capital shot. Deville can't miss," a man boomed from a group watching from the space between the main stands and the private boxes.

She closed her eyes and touched the heavy draping cloth that hid the back of the stands from view. The weight of the fabric hung in her grasp. All she had to do was slide it up and slip inside. All eyes were firmly focused on the spectacle on the field.

The shaking in her arm combined with the feel of the cloth made the task Sisyphean with the weight of a thousand pounds. She closed her eyes and ducked inside.

Rows of feet clomped on the wood above her as people shouted and stomped their encouragement to the final competitors. She could see through the slats and feet as the championship match was called to order by a man in a frilly costume and repeated by the unwelcome tones of a triumphant trumpet.

She crouched on the ground and picked up the cord she had placed there. Just one pull of the rope when Sebastien was shooting . . . that was all it would take. No one would notice a target dropping a few inches, putting his shot off just far enough to lose. And if someone did, what had she to lose?

She watched through the jumbled feet and hems as he inspected his weapon and took aim. She gripped the twisted fibers in her hand, prepared to pull. If he failed to win . . .

Her heart raced. If he failed to win, he would probably lose the tournament. Sarah wouldn't have to marry him, but she'd have to marry someone else. Everly or Benedict. Maybe Sloane. She didn't know how the points would fall. If Sebastien failed to win this game . . .

He wouldn't gain all that he wished. Her grip tightened as he brought the weapon up. If he failed to win this game . . .

He would lose Roseford. He would lose his home, his heart.

He took aim, and there was a split second in which she could feel the rope burning against her fingers, the exact moment that he wouldn't be able to correct his aim and would shoot high.

The retort stung her ears. The rope felt heavy in her hands. She looked down and let the fibers fall. Let the last tear drop as the crowd roared above and around her and she stared at her perfectly fine gloves, not a mark or a tear in evidence. No rope burns from pulling the cord.

She wiped her eyes, brushed her skirt, and ducked back into the crowd, putting her hands mechanically together to celebrate Sebastien Deville's perfect shot and final victory.

The quill shook, droplets of ink plopped onto the parchment like little black tears. Sebastien stared at his fingers, at the foreign movement as they twitched.

Two months ago he would have signed with a flourish and not thought twice. He'd have signed the unholy agreement and sprinted off to collect the deed to Roseford, the letters-patent—proof of his new viscountcy—and all the rewards associated therein. Two months ago he would have collected Lady Sarah and dropped her off in his house in Town, leaving her there until she was needed—or at least, no longer forgotten. Two months ago he wouldn't have known what he would lose by accepting the bride price before him.

Another black tear of ink joined the others, staining the page.

It had come to this. Everything he had wanted, hoped for, dreamed of in life, lay before him, awaiting a simple scritch of the quill in the shadowed chamber. He'd have power—unimaginable power. He'd have revenge. And justice and all those other things that had tempted him and taunted him in the dark corridors of night. All those things that had seemed so vitally important no more than two months ago were his for the signing.

The gold of the mirrors, the gilt-edged ceilings, the honeyed metal of the clock as it tick-tick-ticked his fate, here in front of him, in mere words on a page.

Every slur, every taunt, every sneer wiped away with one press of the quill. A sweep of letters after the words, "I hereby stand by this troth," and he'd be beyond the grip of the law. He'd be above the law, never to have to pander to it again.

A lock of hair fell into his eyes, and he pushed it back. *I think you get by purely on the way you flip your hair back sometimes, Mr. Deville.* The teasing laughter, the gentle caress of fingers carding through the strands, of heated eyes and hands buried in his nape as she arched against him. Forever lost to him as soon as he formed the letters on the page.

The quill broke between his pressed fingers. The nib half clinging desperately, the ink spilling onto his fingers and spreading like blood from an open wound.

He stared at it for a second before taking a breath and setting the fractured piece down. He wiped his hand on a handkerchief, picked up another quill, and dipped it into the inkpot. The ink shook off on its own, through no extra motion from him.

All he had to do was give up Caroline. All he had to do was sign.

Who would have thought Sebastien Deville, ambitious, ruthless gambler and bastard in all ways, would be standing before the damn contract that would give him everything he had always wanted—through twenty-eight years of bitterness and need—and ten minutes later still not have signed it? Because of a woman? Because of an emotion he had never acknowledged.

He laughed without humor and set the tip of the quill to the parchment.

Chapter 23

And so we end our competition correspondence, Dear Reader, with a kind of nostalgic gaze. Oh the sights that we have seen and the hearts that we watched break.

Caroline watched the butterflies alight upon the blossoms, wave their wings, then lift off again to flutter to another bloom on the edge of the back gardens. She idly picked blades of grass and pulled them through her fingers. Her solitude and silence went unnoticed by the massive crowd on the edges of the back grounds as she was mostly hidden from view by the entrance hedges of the maze. The distant haunting cry of a peacock stalking the corridors behind her broke through the chatter on the other side of the green wall.

It was August the twenty-fifth and she was alone, even in a crowd of hundreds. Again. The starlings swirled above her, forming into a tight wave, breaking off, then forming again. Circling and playing.

She pulled another blade through her fingers, the malleable green shaft adapting to the movement, a formidable piece of nature, withstanding stomping children and mighty winds. Giving up only when cruelly plucked.

She let the blade fall to her lap. Cheevers wanted to see her as soon as the last of the guests left for the day. There would still be stragglers hoping to capitalize on the last of the gossip and the hospitality of Meadowbrook, but the bulk of the guests would thankfully be long gone. She didn't know why she had remained at the manor to see Sebastien claim his prize. To see Sarah given away. But running away had seemed cowardly somehow.

She watched as the guests continued to gather upon the lavishly adorned patio grounds, pushing closer to her partially hidden spot. Eager to gossip, to congratulate the soon-to-be viscount, and to make new inroads. The contestants had been escorted off to the library to commence the final tally of the points. But everyone knew the identity of the winner. Too many people had been keeping separate track of the points, and bets had been flying before the last game as bet makers had tallied the odds for each man.

She mechanically moved her locket back and forth along its long chain. Sarah and William were arguing heatedly at the other edge of the garden, so heatedly that they were drawing stares. Lady Tevon was hovering near trying to interfere.

She should go over to help, to mediate, but she couldn't quite work up the energy. Someone sat on the bench near her and she moved her eyes just enough to see Lord Benedict.

"Mrs. Martin."

"Good afternoon, Lord Benedict." The rest of the contestants had obviously been turned out from the library in order to let the winner sign. She didn't know whether to extend her condolences or to keep quiet. "You shot wonderfully today."

"Yes." He leaned back with his heels extended in front of him and watched the chattering crowd. "Thank you."

She turned fully toward him. "Forgive me, but you seem quite contemplative."

He fiddled with a watch at his pocket. "It is far less of a surprise to me that Deville won. He wins far more often than I."

A wave of whispers swept the crowd as the Tipping Seven stepped through the ornate back doors, followed by the King and his entourage.

The crowd pushed back to allow more room for an announcement. The Duke of Grandien looked beyond arrogant and smug. Caroline gripped her skirt and caught Benedict shifting from the corner of her eye.

Cheevers held up his hands and the crowd quieted. "Ladies and gentlemen, this has been an outstanding two months. Gentlemen of extreme quality have competed in this tournament—but only one man can be named the winner. I give you our winner, Mr. Sebastien Deville!"

The crowd roared and clapped as Sebastien appeared on the threshold. The ornate columns framed his body in a picture-like embrace and the gold accents glittered around him, marking him like some sort of demigod who had come down to see his worshippers.

"Thank you," he said smoothly. "It has been quite a remarkable experience."

The crowd cheered again.

"From the first day I was approached about this tournament it seemed like an answer to the prayer of every man who had ever stood under the auspices of the titled and wondered what it would be like to switch his place."

The crowd nodded, several men looking thoughtful or wistful.

"To pit oneself against others of equal standing and see who would come out on top. Brother against brother, in some cases."

Benedict shifted next to her.

"And all for the benefit of these fine men in front of us." He swept a hand in front of him to encompass all of the Tipping Seven. The duke's brows creased before he smoothed them out again.

"It is an honor to win a title from the King." Sebastien bowed to George. "And the accompanying spoils are also quite grand, but I find that the terms of the agreement no longer suit me."

A starling shrieked in the sudden silence.

"So I respectfully withdraw from this competition and bid you adieu. Perhaps another time, gentlemen?" Sebastien tipped his head and walked past the Tipping Seven and the King. He disappeared out of Caroline's view and into the crowd.

She swallowed, but there was no moisture in her mouth. The world had gone hazy around her.

Sebastien had just *turned down* the largest prize in England. And he had turned down the bride price.

"Unbelievable," Benedict whispered next to her as she reeled.

The duke looked as if he'd bitten into something rotten as the crowd erupted. His eyes followed Sebastien's retreat. His cane clicked against the pavers. The look on his face bode ill for anyone who would dare to approach him. Stunned, she continued to watch the older men as they fielded queries and shouts from the crowd. Cheevers sent a servant scrambling after Deville, but he was forced to swim upstream of the rowdy crowd.

Suddenly the duke's features smoothed and he held up a hand to quiet the onlookers. "Well, with Deville out, I believe that puts Lord Benedict Alvarest in first place."

"I demand a recount with Deville's scores removed," Bateman shouted from the side. Murmurs from the crowd grew once more.

The duke's fingers gripped the top of his cane. "I believe that to be unnecessary. The calculations were done, just in case of this instance and Lord Benedict is in second."

Caroline turned wide eyes to Benedict. Benedict's mouth parted, but nothing emerged. He swallowed, looked down at his hands, then resolutely stood and stepped forward so that he could be seen. "No. I withdraw from the competition as well."

"Pardon me?" the duke asked, in a silver-tongued viper's voice.

"I said that I withdraw," Benedict said in a louder tone. "I—I plan to travel to the Continent. Or to the colonies. To see some of the world."

He looked directly at the duke, a stare that she had never seen him give the older man. "To make my way in this world myself."

The expression on the Duke of Grandien's face could only be described as thin ice covering a deep, scorching flame.

Benedict brushed off his trousers. "So I too bid you adieu. Perhaps another time, gentlemen?" He repeated Sebastien's salvo and strode forward, the shocked crowd parting around him as he passed the duke and disappeared inside.

Caroline caught a swish of red and turned her gaze to see Harriet Noke step forward as well. Harriet gave the crowd an appraising look, smiled a secretive smile, then followed Benedict inside.

The King looked as shocked as everyone else, but there was something in his eyes. A sparkle. "Well then, who's next?"

"No."

Caroline craned her head, once again alone, to see Sarah step forward. Oh, Sarah. Her heart leapt. She didn't know if she could take any more shocks.

"I wish to remove myself from this competition as well."

"The competition is over, Lady Sarah," Cheevers said, looking as apoplectic as the rest of his compatriots. "You agreed to the terms. And when I am—"

"No." She folded her hands in front of her. "I will not marry anyone entered into this tournament. I plan to marry someone else, and the church frowns on double marriages, you see."

Oh, Sarah. Joy and fear mixed together. Joy that her sister would find happiness. Fear of what her father's reaction would be.

"And just who do you plan to wed?"

Sarah smiled, a secretive, but joyous smile. "My true love, father. My true love."

The crowd erupted, people pushing toward the Tipping Seven, yelling and demanding answers. Caroline covered her mouth, a beyond merry laugh threatening to escape. She wanted to stand and cheer. To run forward and embrace her sister.

Only tremors in the grass behind her held her still. The footsteps took sound. She tensed, wondering if it was a servant or guest who had wandered through the back of the maze, but the languid lope of the steps indicated someone else entirely.

A wild beat started in her heart as the footsteps stopped and a lazy body dropped next to her, long legs stretched out in front.

She turned her head slowly. Aquamarine eyes held hers, eyes lovelier than she'd seen them, full of emotion—a warmth and peace they had previously lacked.

"How—"

"Useful things, mazes, when they have multiple entrances and exits," he said, smiling.

She swallowed and attempted a nonchalance she didn't feel. "Clever of you."

"Supremely." He motioned toward the hedge which blocked his view of the crowd. "It appears as if we are missing the party."

"Yes." She wanted to touch him, to hug him to her. "I must congratulate you. Who else would drive the Tipping Seven to murder?"

His head tilted back and he grinned. "Listen to the challenges." The voices of the crowd shouted on the other side of their hedge. "It's like the finest music. They just might be in court for years over the results. The old men may have finally bitten off more than they can chew."

She drew a hand along the edge of the bench. "Did you really not sign the documents?"

"I really did not." He picked up a blade of grass and let it fall from his hand.

"But Roseford . . ."

The first show of tightening appeared in his shoulders. "I gave up Roseford by refusing to sign."

She stared at him as he let a clump of blades slip from his fingers in a cloud of green. "Why?"

"I'd have to scrub the house to make it habitable once more and it would simply be work, work, work." He shook his hand and the few blades still stuck blew away.

"How can you be so blasé?"

He stilled and turned fully toward her, drawing his hand over his knee. "Do you think I'm blasé about this, Caro, despite my words?" He reached forward and touched her cheek. "Do you think I did this on a whim?"

"I don't know," she whispered. "I don't understand."

"Yes, I know you don't," he whispered back, thumb stroking her skin. "It's because I didn't understand myself. I stood before that contract knowing the power I could hold, knowing I could have Roseford back, the only home I've known. And the one thing that kept appearing before and after each thought was a picture of you. You are where I could make my home, Caroline. The feeling of Roseford, that is what I wanted, needed, to have again. Where I know there is someone out there who is mine, and that I could be that person's in return."

She bit her lip. "Oh." It was an inane response, but she didn't know what to say that wouldn't include tears and blubbering.

He rose, brushed off his perfectly tailored trousers, and held out a hand. The voices in the background faded to insignificance. "Besides, you have that perfectly tidy cottage just waiting for me to soil with my debris."

She looked up at him, hair falling over her eye, her last defense. "Be there in the morning when I wake."

He crouched in front of her, smoothed back the fallen lock, his hand holding her cheek as aquamarine eyes held hers.

"Always."

Epilogue

A figure holding two scrolls rounded the hill. One appointing a new knight of the realm for true service rendered to the crown—for saving a child born on the wrong side of the royal blanket.

The other scroll was possibly even sweeter. He smiled. He had convinced his father to let him marry Sarah. And when it came down to it, the King's word was law. Sarah was no longer the contest's prize. He thought that fact might just change the mind of the man inside the cottage regarding the other document, which had been modified, but still included a daughter of the Cheevers's line.

Of course, if Sebastien Deville told them all to go to hell, he would applaud the decision.

It would be interesting to see what he decided. William smiled and knocked on the door.

Avon Romances

the best in
exceptional authors and unforgettable novels!

At Avon Books, we know your passion for romance—once you finish one of our novels, you find yourself wanting more.

May we tempt you with . . .

- **Excerpts** from our upcoming releases.
- Entertaining **extras**, including authors' personal photo albums and book lists.
- Behind-the-scenes **scoop** on your favorite characters and series.
- **Sweepstakes** for the chance to win free books, romantic getaways, and other fun prizes.
- Writing **tips** from our authors and editors.
- **Blog** with our authors and find out why they love to write romance.
- **Exclusive content** that's not contained within the pages of our novels.

Join us at
www.avonbooks.com

AVON

An Imprint of HarperCollinsPublishers
www.avonromance.com

Available wherever books are sold or please call 1-800-331-3761 to order.

Other **AVON ROMANCES**

Coming Soon

And Don't Miss These
ROMANTIC TREASURES
from Avon Books

"This conquest will truly be worth the cost."

"Conquest? You call charging someone to kiss you, a conquest?"

"A kiss is merely the toll. The real conquest happens when you beg for more." A finger idly moved over his full lower lip. "Passion unleashed."

She knew firsthand that unleashed desire could easily revert right back into caged aggression. "Passion burns brightly, then fizzles away."

Expressions, mercurial and rapid, charged across his face.

He reached over so quickly that she was too late to move away. He swiped a thumb across the top of the drawn roof on her lap, depressing the papers into her thighs.

"But if you capture desire, if you hold it . . ." He pulled his expensively gloved thumb across the bottom of the pillar and leaned toward her, a hairbreadth from her lips. " . . . then that moment will burn indelibly."

His eyes held hers, his face so close that if they blinked in tandem, their eyelashes might brush together. Desire like none she had felt in years pulsed through her, fear following on its heels with stomping strides.

A dark satisfied smile curved his lips. A hand reached into her hair, curling around her nape, a thumb touched her cheek, the silk sliding. She felt his inexorable pull as he drew her slowly forward. . . .